sweet
bliss

ALSO BY JENNIFER BARDSLEY

Genesis Girl

Damaged Goods

Writing as Louise Cypress

Shifter's Wish

Shifter's Kiss

Shifter's Desire

Bite Me

Hunt Me

Slay Me

Slayer Academy: Secret Shifter

Mermaid Aboard

The Gift of Goodbye

Books, Boys, and Revenge

Narcosis Room

sweet bliss

A Harper Landing Novel

JENNIFER BARDSLEY

Text copyright © 2021 by Jennifer Bardsley
All rights reserved.

Published by Montlake, Seattle

www.apub.com

Amazon, the Amazon logo, and Montlake are trademarks of Amazon.com, Inc., or its affiliates.

ISBN-13: 9781542028219
ISBN-10: 1542028213

Cover design by Letitia Hasser

Printed in the United States of America

To my friend Muffie Humphrey, for reminding me of my worth

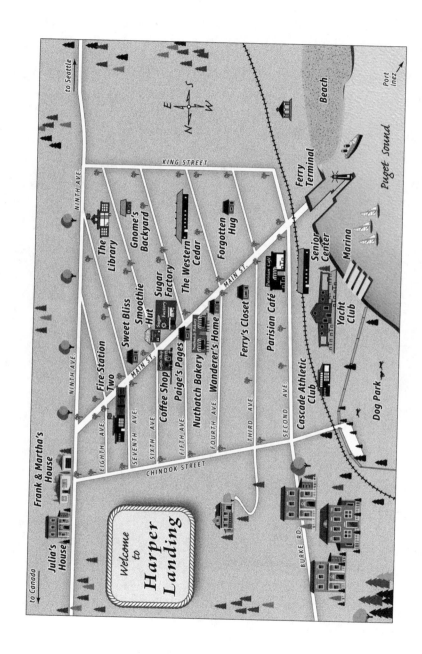

CHAPTER ONE

When Toby spotted the harbor seal, Julia knew that meant trouble. Her chocolate Labrador was a lot of things—loyal, affectionate, devilishly handsome—but clever wasn't one of them. Over the past six months of their relationship, Julia had cursed his pedigree on more than one occasion. If there were just a smidgen of shelter mutt in him, maybe he'd be smarter. Now, her adorably clueless puppy was swimming into open waters, and all Julia could do was scream at the top of her lungs.

"Toby, come back!" Julia cupped her hands around her mouth and shouted so loud her throat hurt. Harper Landing's dog park was triangular, with two fences and one fully exposed entrance to Puget Sound. The Olympic Mountains glistened in the background, still capped with snow in the middle of June. Julia jogged to the edge of the icy cold water and called to her dog again. "Toby! Come, boy!"

The Labrador didn't respond. He paddled furiously toward the harbor seal, which dipped below the surface again and again, only to reappear a few seconds later like a tantalizing prize.

"What the heck is Toby doing?" asked a gruff voice. "He's gotta be a hundred yards away by now." George Fiege, Julia's longtime friend and accountant, stood next to her with his Jack Russell terrier, Midas, at his feet.

"Toby'll come back. He's got to." Julia bit her lip and shielded her eyes with her hand. "Toby!" she called again.

"Dumb dog," George muttered. But he added his vocal power and hollered Toby's name.

Soon there was a small crowd of people standing on the rocky beach, shouting and praying for Toby's return. Julia and Toby were dog park regulars, and this was Harper Landing, a small town north of Seattle where everyone might not know everyone, but they certainly knew Julia Harper, the great-great-great-granddaughter of the town's founder. Julia was also the twenty-eight-year-old owner of Sweet Bliss Frozen Yogurt, as well as half of Main Street. She was proud of Sweet Bliss, but the rest of her inheritance made her uncomfortable.

"He's not turning back." Julia tugged at her long blonde hair. "Toby looks awfully tired. If he swims any farther, he might not have the strength to return." She reached down and unlaced her hiking boots.

"What are you doing?" George asked.

"I'm going after him." Julia yanked a shoelace out of its eyelet.

"But you'll freeze to death." George grabbed the back of her fleece jacket. "That water's so cold it'll knock you senseless."

"I don't have any other choice." Julia jerked out of George's grasp and stepped forward across the rocks in her wool socks.

"You can do it, Julia," said Paige Lu, who owned Paige's Pages, the local bookstore. "I've seen you at the gym. You've got stamina."

Julia wasn't so sure. She'd never been a strong swimmer. Back in elementary school, when she'd been on the summer swim team at the Harper Landing pool, her mother had told her she looked more like a beached whale than a contender. But if anything happened to her puppy, Julia would be devastated. "Toby!" she called desperately. "Come back!"

"There's a blanket in my van." George snapped his fingers, and Midas's ears perked. "We'll go get it for when you come back."

The other people in the crowd continued shouting Toby's name. The harbor seal was gone now, and Toby paddled in circles, trying to find him.

Julia knew her best friend was disoriented and that every second mattered, but stepping into the icy water made her gasp. It felt like all the blood in her body stopped pumping, and her feet, ankles, knees, and now thighs were numb. Could she do this? Brave the elements to save her dog's life? Julia took a deep breath and prepared to surface dive, just like during her days on the swim team.

"Stop!" commanded a firm voice. When Julia didn't respond, an ear-piercing whistle made her spin around. A tall stranger with broad shoulders and emerald-green eyes that matched his shirt kicked off his shoes and charged into the water. His shirt's high-tech fabric clung to his pectorals, and his running shorts billowed up like floats before sticking to muscled quadriceps. The stranger slipped his fingers into his mouth and whistled again. "Toby!" he shouted. "Here, boy."

Julia's eyes drifted from the man's dark-brown hair, damp with sweat, out to the horizon, where her dog paddled for his life. Toby whipped his head backward and gazed at the shore. He yelped and changed course, swimming back to the beach.

"You can do it, Toby!" Julia cried before her teeth chattered so hard that she could no longer talk. Her whole body shook, the cold water sending shock waves through her nervous system that her circulation couldn't abate. Her soggy fleece jacket couldn't protect her either.

"Go back to the beach and warm up," said the stranger.

"Not without my dog." Julia rubbed her arms to tamp down the goose bumps.

"He's swimming in the right direction now," said the man. "He'll be okay."

Julia shook her head. "But Toby's struggling. What if he doesn't have the energy left to make it to shore?"

"Damn, I think you're right." The man tilted his head to the side and rubbed his square jawline. "And I hate triathlons." But a second later, he dived into the water and swam out to Toby before Julia could stop him.

"Better get warm," said George, wrapping a musty-smelling blanket around Julia's shoulders. "Mr. Muscle out there will rescue Toby in no time."

"Thanks," Julia said, her teeth still chattering. She stumbled back onto shore and stamped her feet, trying to regain circulation.

Two minutes later, the stranger delivered an exhausted but not necessarily wiser Toby into Julia's arms. The puppy swiped his tongue across her face, and the crowd burst into cheers.

"Now that's what I call a happy ending," said Paige, waving her hands excitedly.

Toby shook himself, and droplets flew everywhere. Julia was grateful for the blanket. Even her soggy wool socks offered warmth. But Toby's savior shivered in his clingy running shorts. "I'm so sorry," said Julia, offering him the blanket. "Here, take this. I'm all dried off now." She wasn't close to being dry but felt that he deserved the blanket more than she did.

"Keep it." The man sat on a driftwood log and began to tie on his running shoes. "I don't live far away."

"No, really." Julia sat next to him on the log and threw half of the blanket around his shoulders. "If it weren't for you, Toby would be halfway to Whidbey Island by now. How can I ever repay you?"

"No need to repay me. I've got a soft spot for Labradors. And pretty blondes."

George chuckled behind them. "Good thing Toby's not a blond Labrador," he said, "or you'd be a goner."

The man laughed as he double knotted his shoelaces.

Julia looked over her shoulder and shot her accountant an annoyed look. "Thanks for the blanket, George. I'll drop it off at your house after

I wash it." She was glad when Paige grabbed George by the elbow and pulled him away. Heat radiated off the stranger next to her as the side of her arm pressed against his wet shirt. She was tempted to snuggle closer. Instead, she leaned down and yanked on her hiking boots.

"George is right," said the stranger, standing up suddenly. "The last thing I need is a dog in my life."

"At least let me give you some ice cream." Julia clutched the blanket around her shoulders. "And tell me your name so I can properly thank you."

"Ice cream?"

Julia rose to her feet. "Frozen yogurt, if you want to be technical about it." She pulled a strand of hair behind her ear. "My name's Julia, and I own Sweet Bliss on Main Street." She held out her hand.

"Aaron Baxter. Nice to meet you." He gripped her hand in a firm handshake. "But no thanks on the Froyo. I'm paleo."

"Like a caveman?"

The corners of Aaron's eyes crinkled as he smiled. "Something like that." He reached down and rumpled Toby's fur. "Good luck keeping this one out of trouble."

"Yeah. Thanks," said Julia, feeling deflated. "Toby loves trouble." A cruel wind wafted over her damp skin as she watched Aaron jog away. Julia shivered in June's early-morning gloom. She shouldn't have gotten her hopes up when he'd said she was pretty. He was probably just being polite.

Julia had learned a long time ago that she was as ordinary as they came. Her mother had told her that every single day for twenty-seven years until the day she'd died, gasping for breath, from lung cancer last fall. "You're plain," Waverley Harper used to tell her when she'd braid Julia's hair before swim team practice. "Homely and fat like your father."

Waverley was the one who was a great beauty. She'd been homecoming queen in high school, Miss Washington State, and a waitress at the Space Needle's exclusive restaurant before marrying Julia's father.

There was a fifteen-year age difference between Harrison Harper and his beautiful young bride, but his money and connections were enough to entice Waverley away from Seattle—and her high school sweetheart. Harrison and Waverley maintained a happy home for ten years before they had Julia and another ten after that before Harrison died of a heart attack in the middle of a Harper Landing City Council meeting.

Harrison was a kind and doting father when he was alive, but Waverley made it her mission to belittle Julia every chance she got. She blamed Julia for how pregnancy had ruined her figure, changing her from a size two into a size six who needed high-waisted jeans with elastic technology. One of Julia's earliest memories was visiting her mother in the hospital after her latest plastic surgery. She'd never forget the sight of gauze bandages wrapping Waverley's puffy red face, distorted beyond all recognition, or the citrus scent of the antiseptic the hospital used to sanitize the room. Julia had learned at a young age that beauty meant pain, and she'd decided long ago that it was a price she wasn't willing to pay, especially when she was so far from being able to meet her mother's lofty standards.

Most days, Julia threw on jeans and a T-shirt, bundled up in a fleece jacket, and pulled her hair back in a ponytail. She never bothered with makeup except for tinted sunscreen. Her footwear had sturdy treads to take her from her house on Ninth Avenue to Sweet Bliss. Her purse, if you could call it that, was an old leather bag she'd picked up at Goodwill. The only time Julia dressed up was when she served as a bridesmaid in her friends' weddings. That and when she captained a table at the Harper Landing Chamber of Commerce fundraiser at the yacht club every September.

She was the only one she knew from high school who wasn't married, engaged, dating, or even divorced by now. Julia felt deep down in her soul that what her mother had said all along was true. She was nothing special. Despite Toby's daring rescue, today was exactly like any other day: another chance for Julia—Harper Landing's proverbial girl next door—to be ignored.

"Paleo," she murmured to herself. "Aaron doesn't eat ice cream." She could only imagine what her mother would say about that if Waverley were still alive. Probably something sarcastic about fad diets, which was ironic because Waverley had loved diets. She was always on one or putting Julia on one too. When Julia was in the third grade, she was also the only kid she knew who had cottage cheese and half a grapefruit in her lunchbox. But that was a long time ago. Julia was proud of her curves and worked hard to eat healthfully so that her daily life could include frozen yogurt whenever she wanted.

"Come on, Toby." Julia leaned down and attached the retractable leash to the Labrador's collar. "Time to go home." Her feet dragged as she headed up the beach to the sidewalk. She saw families bundled up in coats enjoying chilly picnics and kids with kites fighting against the wind. There were teenagers vaping near the parking lot and retirees strolling hand in hand toward the marina. Julia nodded her head as she passed people. Usually they nodded back, but sometimes they didn't, making her feel invisible. Locals called it the Seattle Freeze, and it wasn't supposed to creep this far north into a small town like Harper Landing. But it did, and Julia felt the frosty bite.

CHAPTER TWO

Aaron's feet hit the pavement on his run home, and he thought about what Sara would have said about his heroics on the beach just now. Probably his sister wouldn't have used the word *heroics*. She would have said *antics*, more likely. She also would have called him a coward for not taking Julia up on her offer for Froyo or, at the very least, getting her phone number.

It's just ice cream, he could hear Sara saying. *You deserve to have fun.*

Sara knew everything. Was everything. She had been his friend and mentor. His protector from bullies when he'd entered middle school. His champion when he'd told their parents that instead of going to Princeton like them, he was headed to Stanford. Two years later, when Aaron had dropped out of college to form a business with his best friend, Sara had been the one who'd sent Aaron and Jared the seed money to get Big Foot Paleo started, even though she'd made a pittance on her teacher's salary.

Jared would have given him a hard time about Julia too. *You know what's better than paleo?* he might have asked. *Beautiful women.* Jared would have been right, because Aaron couldn't get Julia out of his mind. Her fresh face and pulled-back hair had looked so outdoorsy and casual that it was like she'd stepped out of the pages of an REI catalog. Even the old flannel blanket she'd been shrouded in had added to the effect of a Pacific Northwest beauty ready for an adventure. *Scoop her up,* Jared would have said. *Pull her into a tent with a campfire crackling outside.*

Aaron gritted his teeth and pushed Sara's and Jared's nagging out of his mind. One of the worst things was that even now that they were no longer here, the two most influential people in his life were still telling him what to do. He blinked back tears threatening to form and focused on the road ahead. The beach was five miles away from his house, and he still had three miles to go. The quiet residential streets bloomed with color, and eighty-foot cedars and fir trees towered over him. Sunshine peeked through the clouds, burning away the morning's dense marine layer. So far, during the month he'd lived here, it had rained every single day. But at least it didn't rain all day. Usually, the weather improved in the afternoon, when the sun came out. Aaron took one last look at the waterfront view and began a steep ascent toward home, his hamstrings working on overdrive to propel him forward.

It was weird thinking about having a house to call home. Aaron had spent the last ten years living in tiny apartments, the soaring Silicon Valley real estate market making living anywhere else tricky. Even last winter, when Big Foot Paleo had been purchased by General Mills, Aaron hadn't felt comfortable plunking down his hard-earned IPO money into something tangible like a property deed. His ex-girlfriend, Leah, had been irate. She'd planned a million ways to spend his money, and they had all started with her moving in with him rent-free.

Palo Alto had been the best—and worst—place to start a snack food company. The best because there were lots of urban, hipster wanna-be foodies with money to burn willing to spend twelve dollars on a six-ounce bag of grain-free granola. The worst because the real estate market was so tight that none of the Big Foot Paleo employees could afford to live there. Aaron and Jared found suppliers in Modesto, where the almonds were sourced and harvested, and ended up moving the factory there once orders picked up but kept the business offices in Silicon Valley. Jared tried to convince Aaron that spending two hours driving back and forth from the factory to the office each day was no way to live. He'd thought they should move the entire operation to someplace sustainable, like his hometown of Harper Landing, Washington, where there was cheaper real estate as well as a ready source of other ingredients, like dried berries.

Aaron pumped his arms back and forth as he ran uphill, keeping an eye out for traffic since there was no sidewalk. How had his mind wandered from Julia's face and her rascal of a puppy to his greatest regret of all time? His lungs felt like they would burst from the intense cardio, but even the blood pounding through his veins wasn't enough to keep his mind clear of darkness.

It was Aaron's fault that Sara and Jared were dead. It was Aaron's fault that instead of telling his best friend and future brother-in-law, *Yes, let's move to Washington,* he'd said, "No way. The business stays in California." Aaron had wanted everything his way. He'd wanted the convenience of Big Foot Paleo being close to the California distributors. He'd wanted the security of all his Silicon Valley friends. Hell, he'd even wanted to stay near Leah, even though she had only been using him for his money. Now, all of it was gone, destroyed by Aaron's selfishness. Sure, technically, a drunk driver had killed Jared and Sara on their evening commute home from Modesto, but Aaron knew the truth. He was the one to blame. If they'd been living in Harper Landing, they would have spent less time on the road. Jared would be alive right now, training for his next triathlon, and Sara wouldn't have spent five weeks in the hospital on life support as the doctors struggled to keep her alive long enough for—shoot. Aaron blinked back tears. Running used to be his escape. But no matter how hard he ran, his pain always caught up with him.

Aaron slowed down his pace when he reached the end of his street, cooling down to give his heart rate the chance to return to normal. "Hey," he said, waving in response to greetings from neighbors weeding flower beds in their front yards or packing up camping trailers. A roving pack of children on bicycles almost ran him over. Aaron sidestepped out of the way, just in time, biting back the urge to tell those kids to watch where they were going. He wondered for the millionth time if he would have been better off living in a high-rise condo in Seattle instead of Harper Landing, which was no place for a twenty-nine-year-old bachelor. But maybe *bachelor* wasn't the best way to describe himself anymore, even though Leah had given him the boot the moment he'd told her he was moving.

Aaron walked up the driveway to his "four-bedroom house with a midlevel entry and cedar siding," as the broker had gushed. He climbed the front steps up to the door, which was positioned in the middle of the two stories, and stretched on the landing before fishing out the key he'd stashed in a hidden pocket. Sure, Martha was inside, but Aaron didn't want to risk ringing the doorbell. Maybe if he hurried, he could jump in the shower really quickly before Martha needed to go home. Aaron hated imposing on her any more than he was already. His clothes were dry now, but he knew he stank.

As soon as he opened the door, the smells from the house greeted him. There was the clove-and-cinnamon fragrance that the house cleaners had used when they had come the day before. The juices from the grass-fed chuck roast Aaron had dumped in the Crock-Pot before he'd left for his run bubbled enticingly. But wafting over everything, like a swirling aromatic reminder of his new life, was the sweet heady scent of baby.

"You're home," whispered Martha, standing at the top of the stairs in a velvet tracksuit. "Jack went down an hour ago, almost right after you left." She pointed down the hallway. "He's sleeping in his crib right now."

"In his crib? How'd you manage that?" Aaron unlaced his soggy running shoes and dumped them next to the front door. He peeled off his wet socks and abandoned them. "Jack never sleeps in his crib. He usually sleeps in bed with me or in his bassinet."

Martha raised her eyebrows. "You know how I feel about cosleeping. You'll never get any rest if you keep that up." She shook her head disapprovingly. "Besides, babies need to learn to self-soothe."

Aaron rubbed the back of his neck and swallowed the words he wanted to say. He couldn't risk an argument with Martha. Jack's grandparents were his only support system here in Harper Landing. It was natural that Martha felt protective of her grandson, especially considering he was her living link to Jared. "Jack's three months old," Aaron said in his calmest tone. "He has plenty of time to learn to self-soothe. Right now, I'm focused on helping him sleep in four-hour increments so that he can be well rested, and yes, sometimes that means cosleeping."

"When Jared was three months old, he slept through the night from ten p.m. to five a.m. like clockwork." Martha lifted her chin. "Mix a little rice cereal in his bottle, and Jack can do that too."

Aaron tensed, his shoulders rigid with frustration. "You didn't do that with Jack, did you? His pediatrician said not to."

Martha patted the tight gray curls around her head into place. "Of course not. You didn't have any cereal in the cupboard. But pediatricians don't know everything. I'll bring some next time."

"No," said Aaron. "Please don't." He was still standing by the front door, looking up at her. Aaron took the steps two by two, brushing past her in his rush to check on Jack. He didn't bother explaining himself as he hurried down the hallway, his bare feet falling soundlessly on the new carpet. When he reached the back bedroom, he pushed the door open a crack, not wanting to wake Jack up but desperate to see him. The feeling of terror and love mixed together—a desire to protect his nephew with every power at his command—was something that had flowed through Aaron since the moment the doctor had laid the baby in his arms and the nurse had turned off Sara's life support.

There, visible through the slats of the crib, slept Jack, much tinier than a three-month-old baby should be. Sara's injury had made it necessary for him to be born three and a half weeks early, and he had yet to develop out of his preemie status. The mattress was bare, covered only by a fitted sheet, just like the book said. There wasn't a quilt or bumper pad in sight. But instead of lying on his back like he was supposed to, Jack was curled up on his stomach, his head tilted to the side and his tiny fists clenched next to him.

"Crap," Aaron muttered under his breath. He sprang across the room and stopped abruptly at the side of the crib. Then, as carefully as he could, he ever so gently rolled Jack onto his back. Aaron held his breath, hoping that Jack would continue sleeping, and sighed with relief when he saw the rise and fall of the baby's tiny chest.

As soon as he'd backed out of the room and shut the door, Aaron whirled around and strode down the hallway to the kitchen. Every fiber in his body was taut with anger. He'd been clear with Martha that Jack wasn't allowed to sleep on his stomach. The pediatrician and the books said it was dangerous. But he knew that blowing his top wouldn't do any good. Martha meant well, and she loved her grandson dearly.

"How was your run?" Martha asked. She'd taken the stove grates off and was cleaning underneath the range.

"It was fine." Aaron pinched the bridge of his nose, trying to find the words for the conversation he knew had to happen. "Thanks for watching Jack while I was out. I really appreciate it."

"No problem." Martha smiled, the lines of her face lifting upward as she beamed. "I love spending time with him. It's my pleasure." She looked around the tidy kitchen. "And since he took such a good nap, I was able to clean up the kitchen. What are you making? The slow cooker smells good."

"Beef stew." Aaron cleared his throat. "The kitchen looks great. I appreciate your help. I left in kind of a rush this morning. But listen, Martha, about Jack sleeping in his crib—the doctor said that he needs to sleep on his back, not his stomach."

"Oh, pishposh." Martha swatted her hand in the air. "Both my babies slept on their tummies and did just fine."

"I know, but I want what's best for Jack, and given his delicate medical history, I believe that means following the doctor's orders." Aaron opened the fridge and grabbed a can of coconut water. "That makes sense, right?"

Martha frowned and put down her cleaning rag. "I guess you're right. He *is* exceptionally tiny. That's why I think adding a little rice cereal—"

"The pediatrician said not to," Aaron said in a firm voice. "I'm following her recommendations."

"*Her*, is it?" Martha lifted her eyebrows. "Is she pretty?"

Aaron almost choked on his coconut water. "What's that got to do with anything?"

Martha put the grates back in place. "I worry about you here on your own. Jared wouldn't want you home alone every night with a baby." She wrung out the rag and hung it on the faucet. "Anytime you want me to babysit so you can go out on the town, just let me know."

"Dating is the last thing I need right now." Aaron drained the can and tossed it into the recycling bin. "And if I were going to ask a woman out, it certainly wouldn't be Dr. Agarwal. She's in her sixties and has two kids in college."

"Well, that's a shame," Martha said with a pout. "But I know some wonderful women at church I could set you up with. Or my daughter, Jessica, might have friends that—"

"No thanks."

"But—"

"No," Aaron said, sharper than he'd intended. When he saw Martha's hurt expression, he tried to backpedal in a way that might end the dating push. "I appreciate the offer, but I don't need help meeting women. I even met someone today at the beach."

"You did?" Martha leaned closer. "Who?"

"The owner of the frozen yogurt shop on Main Street. I think she said her name was Julia."

"Julia Harper?" Martha clapped her hands together. "My next-door neighbor? She's absolutely lovely. When are you going out?"

"Oh, we're not going out."

"Why not? Haven't you asked her yet?"

"No, Martha, it doesn't feel like the right time for that. I'm not going to." Aaron looked at the baby monitor. "Look, thanks for watching Jack this morning. I'd love to chat more, but I should jump in the shower before he wakes up."

"I don't mind staying a bit longer. I could start a load of laundry."

"Thanks, but no thanks," said Aaron. "I don't want to keep you from Frank."

Martha's face froze for a few seconds before she answered. "Don't worry about Frank. He won't notice that I've gone."

"I'm sure that's not true. It's Saturday." Aaron swept his hand to the side like he could usher her out of the kitchen. "I bet you have things to do. When I ran by the farmer's market just now, it was packed."

"Frank does love fresh doughnuts. Maybe I'll pick up a bag on my way home." Martha scooped up her purse from the kitchen table. "See you next week?"

"Yeah. Thanks." Aaron walked down the steps to the front door.

"Or I could come earlier if you wanted a break."

"I'm sure that won't be necessary, but thanks for the offer," Aaron said as he opened the door. All he wanted to do was take a quick shower before Jack woke up, but he'd never get the chance if Martha lingered.

"Give Jack a kiss for me." Martha looked up toward the nursery. "Oh, I could just eat him up. I love him so."

"Me too." Aaron shut the door as quickly as possible and hustled up the steps. He raced to his room across the hall from Jack's and stripped off his shirt. It had dried since his dip in the sound but smelled like sweat and seaweed. He was just about to pull off his shorts when the baby monitor crackled. Aaron stared at it, the red light flickering like it might explode. Jack cooed in the background but then drifted to silence. Hurrying in earnest now, Aaron stripped off his last article of clothing and hopped in the shower, not waiting for the temperature to warm up. He was just dousing his head with shampoo when the baby monitor began to wail.

Aaron squeezed his eyes shut and practiced the breathing exercise the grief counselor had taught him back at the hospital. But even though the technique was supposed to help him calm down, it left him feeling more agitated. No way could he handle a date with Julia, he realized, thinking about her offer of ice cream. He couldn't even manage a shower.

CHAPTER THREE

The cotton blazer Julia wore over her T-shirt and jeans was roomy and comfortable. It wasn't exactly business wear, but it was the most professional-looking thing she owned. Julia always wore her blazer when attending the Harper Landing Chamber of Commerce meetings. She'd shined her shoes too—one of the only bits of life advice from her mother that Julia followed. Waverley had said that freshly shined shoes expressed to the world that the person had their act together. Julia wasn't sure if she had her act together or not, but at least with her blazer and shiny boots, she could pretend she did.

"I hope this meeting ends quickly," whispered Paige, who was sitting next to Julia. "A sales rep from Emerald City Books is stopping by the store this afternoon."

"Send him up the street for some free yogurt when he's done," Julia offered. She knew that operating a small business was tough, and she would do anything within her power to make Paige's Pages a success, even if it meant bribing someone with ice cream. The bookshop owner was twenty years older than Julia but had become one of her closest friends ever since she'd agreed to mentor her as a new business owner when Julia had opened Sweet Bliss.

"Thanks," said Paige. They both turned their attention back to the meeting, where George was delivering the longest treasurer's report in the history of board meetings.

"In conclusion," said George as he pushed his glasses up the bridge of his nose, "since not everyone is contributing their fair share to the business district improvement fund, we don't have the resources to purchase replacement umbrellas." He gripped the edge of the podium and glared at a man sitting in the front row with fluffy white hair and a pinched expression. "And yes, I mean you, Walter," George said, pointing his finger at the candy shop owner.

"I'm barely breaking even," Walt Lancaster protested. "How can I pay my rent, and my taxes, and your stupid business district improvement fund, when candy sticks sell for fifteen cents apiece?" He took out a few sticks of candy from his apron pocket and waved them around.

Julia sighed because she'd heard Walt's arguments before—every month, in fact, since last September, when her mother had passed away and Julia had gained possession of the second half of her father's estate. Julia knew for sure that the rent she charged Walt was well below market rate, because a real estate developer had told her so, yet Walt complained bitterly that her greed was putting him out of business. But every time she walked past the Sugar Factory, it was packed with customers. Julia didn't know whether Walt was a poor money manager or a liar.

Unfortunately, Julia's problems with Walt ran deeper than that. Walt was her mother's high school sweetheart and ex-fiancé. Ten years before Julia was born, Waverley had jilted Walt at the altar and run off with Harrison. Walt had long blamed Harrison for stealing his woman. Now Walt unloaded his bad temper on Julia every chance he got. It didn't help that Julia looked so much like her father.

Even though she'd had nothing to do with the sordid debacle, Julia felt guilty on her parents' behalf.

"Figure it out," said George. "The Harper Landing Chamber of Commerce isn't a charity organization—unless, of course, we're discussing charity." He smiled at Julia. "Which brings us to our next presenter."

Julia hopped to her feet, her heart beating so hard she was sure the whole room could hear it pound. She hated speaking in front of a group.

She felt a nudge from behind. Paige handed Julia a file folder. "Don't forget your notes."

"Oh." Julia blushed. "Right. Thanks." She grabbed her materials and walked up to the podium. She leaned in too close to the microphone, and it bumped her chin, making a loud thump. Walt snickered, and Julia lurched back before regaining her composure. "Every year the Harper Landing Chamber of Commerce sponsors the Fourth of July celebration," Julia began, launching into the speech she'd practiced dozens of times in front of her bathroom mirror. "This summer, we've allocated forty-six thousand dollars for the parade, fun run, and fireworks show." She looked down at her notes. "From that total, four thousand dollars is to pay for emergency service personnel overtime, and—"

"The whole thing is a waste of money if you ask me," Walt blurted out, his wrinkled cheeks the color of purple beets. "Why are we spending money to entertain the whole town when the entitled millennials are going to set out chairs along the sidewalks the day before and block access to our shops?"

"Setting up chairs ahead of time to watch the parade is a cherished Harper Landing tradition," said Paige. "And some of the people stop by my shop to buy books."

"And frozen yogurt," Julia added. "Candy, too, right?" She looked at Walt hopefully.

The old man harrumphed. "Shows you what you know," he said with a scowl. "Nobody buys candy when they know they can get it for free once the parade starts. The floats literally throw candy at the crowd." Walt glared across the room at Dave Parson, who ran the Parisian Café. "Weren't you going to say something, Dave?"

Dave tugged at his collar. Around town, he was known for three things: baguettes, chicken cordon bleu, and his comb-over. "I'm not sure if the Fourth of July fits in with my business plan," he mumbled. "Being a French restaurant and all."

"What are you talking about?" George exclaimed. "Of course it fits with your business. The Fourth of July festivities are the heart and soul of Harper Landing. How can you not know that?"

"Plus, Bastille Day is right around the corner," said Julia.

"The Fourth is a money drain!" Walt bellowed. "Some of us are barely eking out a living because of greedy real estate moguls, and you want us to burn money to smithereens in the sky."

"Greedy real estate moguls?" Julia echoed in disbelief. "What's that supposed to mean?" She looked down at her notes, too flustered to continue with her presentation. All she could think about was getting out of there fast enough that nobody would see her cry. It had been easier when she'd been Julia Harper, owner of Sweet Bliss. But ever since the inheritance, her fellow business owners viewed her differently because she was so many people's landlords.

"Julia might be an inexperienced landlord," said Cheryl Lowrey, co-owner of the Nuthatch Bakery. "But she doesn't deserve snide comments like that."

"And she's definitely *not* a greedy real estate mogul." George had leaped to his feet and now pushed up the sleeves of his cardigan. "You take that back."

But Walt wouldn't back down. "She doesn't need the money," he said, his face the same color as the peppermint stripes on his apron. "She doesn't have a husband or family to take care of."

"That's got nothing to do with it," snapped Paige.

"It's dumb luck she owns the land to begin with," Walt continued.

"Dumb luck?" Julia felt the blood drain from her face. "I'm lucky that my father died when I was ten years old?" A lump the size of a barnacle formed in her throat.

"You're worthless," she heard Waverley say, deep in her memory bank. "You'll never be as smart as your father was or as beautiful as me."

"It's called the Fifth Amendment," said George. "Ever heard of it? Julia has the right to own property, and luck's got nothing to do with it."

"Don't preach the Declaration of Independence to me," said Walt.

"It's not the Declaration of Independence, numskull," said George. "It's the Bill of Rights." He and Walt had been spoiling for a fight ever since George had caught Walt parked in the space George needed for his wife's wheelchair-accessible van. Shelly had MS and looked forward to her outings on Main Street.

"Stop," said Julia in a weak voice. The lump in her throat threatened to choke her. She always had trouble speaking up for herself in an argument. Matt Guevara, the proprietor of the Gnome's Backyard and president of the association, pushed her aside and took the podium.

"Settle down," Matt called out, loud enough to get everyone's attention. "Since you boomers can't get your tempers under control, I'm moving the remaining agenda items to next week. This meeting is adjourned." He banged a wooden gavel down on the podium and slipped it back into his pocket.

"Let's get out of here," said Paige, walking up to Julia and tugging her sleeve.

Julia nodded and followed Paige out the door of the Harper Landing Yacht Club, where the chamber of commerce held their meetings, and out into the parking lot. The sun blinded her, and she lifted her hand to shield her eyes. "I had one job," Julia muttered. "And I couldn't even do that right."

"You were fine." Paige slipped on enormous sunglasses that were as black and shiny as her hair. "It's Walt who should be ashamed of himself. He shouldn't have accosted you like that in a public setting."

"But maybe he has a point." Julia reached into her bag for the sunglasses she'd purchased at the drugstore. "Is it really fair that I own a bunch of properties and he doesn't?"

Paige snorted. "You know my family left Korea to escape talk like that, right? What's yours is yours." She pointed to Harper Landing Beach, where Puget Sound glistened in the distance. "Your family built this town, and you have every right to their fortune."

"Their fortune, not mine." Julia shrugged out of her blazer. "All I've ever accomplished is a moderately successful frozen yogurt shop."

"Don't belittle your achievements. That property was a vacant building that your mother had let deteriorate. You're the one who came back from Italy with a business plan and the energy to put it into action."

"But that doesn't mean I know what I'm doing. I feel like an imposter every time I go to one of those meetings, like I don't belong in the room."

Paige rolled her eyes. "Of course you belong."

"I'm the youngest person there."

"And one of the smartest."

Julia folded her blazer. "I don't know about that. Maybe Walt's right about the Fourth of July parade hurting sales, and I'm too ignorant to see it."

"My sales are great on the Fourth." Paige grinned. "This year I'm offering preferred seating in front of my store to anyone who purchases one hundred and fifty dollars' worth of books. How's that for clever?"

"See?" Julia opened her eyes wide. "That's what I'm talking about. I'm not sure I have any business sense compared to you. You're making money on the chair situation, and I gave them away for free."

"What do you mean you gave chairs away?"

Julia sighed. "I donated my chair space to the Orca Street Preschool auction. Melanie Knowles was seeking donations, and I threw in the chairs along with free Froyo."

"Melanie Knowles, as in the volunteer admin of the Harper Landing Moms Facebook group?"

"That's right."

"Well, then that was a smart move." Paige nodded. "Buttering up the admin is a great idea, because one bad post on Harper Landing Moms, and you could have a mob of parents with too much time on their hands after you."

"Don't I know it." Julia shuddered. "Remember that storm we had last December? The power went out, and I had to cancel a birthday party in our event room. Apparently, the mom went onto the Facebook group and blasted me for being unprofessional."

"I think I saw that thread," said Paige. "So many people rushed to your defense that the birthday mom deleted her post." She patted Julia on the back. "Which is proof that you've got a solid reputation as a local business owner. Don't let jerks like Walt mess with your head." She clicked her key fob, and her Subaru Forester beeped. "I gotta run because that Emerald City Books rep is coming, but I'll text you later, okay?"

"Sure." Julia nodded. "Thanks." She fished in her pocket for her car keys before remembering that she'd walked. "Don't forget to send the rep up to Sweet Bliss for a free cup."

"It'll be okay, hon—you'll see," Paige said as she climbed into her car.

Julia watched her drive away and then spun on her heel in the direction of Main Street. Now that the marine layer had burned away, the temperature was climbing. She regretted her choice of footwear, even though her riding boots gleamed from the fresh polish. It was almost sixty-two degrees outside, practically short-sleeve weather by Pacific Northwest standards. Julia looked over her shoulder to make sure that Walt was nowhere to be seen. She didn't want to run into him on her way to work. But it seemed like most of the chamber members had already driven off in their cars.

Julia didn't mind the walk. It was less than a mile to Sweet Bliss and only a little farther to her house on Ninth Avenue. Sailboats rocked in the water, and seagulls squawked overhead. The marina smelled like sunshine and brine. Over on the pier, fishermen lined up with wire crab pots. Harrison had been a hobby fisherman, but he'd taught his daughter never to eat something caught off the pier, because food picked from the middle of Puget Sound was less likely to be polluted. It was ironic advice coming from a man who had smoked a pack of cigarettes a day.

Walking at a steady pace, Julia reached the Harper Landing Senior Center in a matter of minutes. There were clusters of people milling around, staring at their phones. Julia dodged people who weren't looking where they were going and took a sharp right when she reached the ferry dock. The Harper Landing–Port Inez ferry shuttled passengers back and forth from the greater Seattle metro area to the Olympic Peninsula. A long line of cars stretched out to the horizon as the Friday afternoon rush waited to board the ferry.

Julia pushed the button at the crosswalk for the light to change. But when the train whistle blew and the railroad crossing gates went down, she knew she was in for a long wait. When she was little, coal trains used to barrel through Harper Landing a few times a day. Now they came through every hour on their trips from the Midwestern United States to offload onto ships bound for China. It was a source of great irritation to the locals, as well as constant worry that one of the trains could derail and pollute Harper Landing's sensitive marine life.

"See the train?" asked a deep voice behind her.

"Yeah," said Julia. "It's kind of hard not to." She turned around to find out who would ask such a dumb question and instantly felt like an imbecile herself when she realized it was a dad bending over a jogging stroller. "Oh," she said, blushing. "Sorry. I thought you were talking to me." The man lifted his head, and Julia saw emerald-green eyes she immediately recognized. "Aaron," she gasped. "Hi." By now, her cheeks were the same color as her pink T-shirt. On the beach last Saturday, she'd assumed her Labrador's hero was single. It hadn't occurred to her to check for a wedding ring. Now here he was with a baby's ridiculously cute fist wrapped around his little finger. Julia put her blazer back on, even though it was too hot for a coat.

"Julia. Hey." Aaron stood up and adjusted the stroller's sunshade so that Julia couldn't peek inside. "How's Toby?"

"Probably in the backyard trying to dig his way to Australia right now." Julia shrugged. "He has a doggy door, so he can come and go, and on nice days like this, he likes to be outside." She felt proud of herself for stringing the words together into coherent sentences, especially since Aaron's sudden appearance had rattled her. But the very next thing out of her mouth came out in a squeak. "Is this your baby?"

"What?" Aaron jerked back as if she'd struck him. "No—I mean yes. I mean . . . kind of." He pulled the stroller in closer, and his biceps flexed.

Julia wasn't sure she had heard him right. Of course a handsome guy like Aaron would have a baby, but why be vague about it? "How do you 'kind of' have a baby?" she asked.

"Jack's my nephew. It's a long story, and I don't want to get into it," Aaron said defensively. "But yes, he's my baby now." He jogged in place and pressed two fingers against his wrist to check his heart rate.

"Um, great," said Julia, thoroughly confused. "Enjoy your work-out." She took a giant step forward, closer to the curb, and prayed that the train would hurry up. Fifty cars, fifty-one, fifty-two; it seemed like the coal train would go on forever. Maybe she should give up and board the ferry instead. There wasn't a line for walk-on passengers, and Julia was friendly with the creamery owner in Port Inez. He was always good for a complimentary waffle cone. She lifted her chin and stared at the passing train. She didn't have to stand here on the curb with a man who had said she was pretty a few days ago but was obviously unavailable. Besides, it was her fault for misunderstanding him in the first place. She shouldn't have let one word get her hopes up or allowed his toned physique and square jawline to captivate her.

"There's an infant-toddler group that meets at the library every Tuesday morning at nine," Julia said, glancing back over her shoulder. "I open Sweet Bliss an hour early at ten for them to come grab some Froyo. I even stock diapers in the bathroom for them, just in case." The train had passed now, and the gates lifted to the sky. "You might like it. The parenting group, I mean, not the frozen yogurt." The light turned green, and Julia charged onto the crosswalk before Aaron could reply.

CHAPTER FOUR

Seeing Julia had caught him by surprise, and he felt like a jerk as he watched her go. Aaron used to go months living in Silicon Valley without running into anyone he knew. Now there she was in tight jeans and black boots, with her hair pulled back in a sleek ponytail. She was the one woman who'd caught his attention since he'd moved here a month ago, and Aaron hadn't known what to say, especially when she had asked about Jack. How could he explain any of it? Was Jack his nephew or his son? He loved Jack with all his heart, but he wasn't proud of the fact that Jack was in his care. It was Aaron's fault Jack had been orphaned. No way could he push up the stroller's sunshade and show *his baby* off. Not without feeling more awful than he already felt every day.

So Aaron held back and stayed on the curb, looking longingly at the graceful curve of Julia's backside as she climbed up the street. His original plan had been to run home, but now the push and pull of parental guilt and responsibility paralyzed him, and he stood there for a full five minutes rocking the stroller back and forth. He felt waves of malaise wash over him, just like the waves of Puget Sound rolling up the beach. It had been a mistake to think he could do this. He couldn't be Jack's parent. Hell, he could never fully move on with his life after what had happened to Sara and Jared. Sure, he could buy a house and move to a new state, but guilt would always catch up with him in the end.

Aaron took a deep breath and let it out slowly, willing his nervous system to calm down. He opened the sunshade and peered at Jack to make sure he was okay. The baby was staring out peacefully at the world. Aaron adjusted the stroller's angle so that Jack could see better. "Hey, little guy," he said, bending down on one knee. "You decided to wake up, huh?" Jack wore a onesie with the words I PARTY ALL NIGHT LONG on it. He stuck out his tongue, like he was tasting the air, and drooled. "Dang it," Aaron muttered. "I forgot to put your bib on." Ever since he'd turned three months old, Jack had become a twenty-four-hour drool machine. Martha said that meant he might be cutting his first tooth, but so far, Aaron saw no sign of an eruption.

Aaron reached into the bottom of the stroller for the diaper bag, and that was when he realized the terrible truth—he'd forgotten it. No drool bib, no bottle, no diaper, no wipes; the only thing rolling around the bottom of the basket was his own water bottle. "Well, that's great," Aaron mumbled. "I guess you and I are going to run home at top speed before anything bad happens." Aaron leaned down and kissed Jack on the cheek. After he'd adjusted the sunshade one more time, he looked both ways and raced across the street, pushing the stroller in front of him on its rubber wheels.

Aaron ran so fast that he wished he could use the bike lane, but with all the traffic unloading from the Port Inez ferry, that didn't seem safe. Instead, he had to weave around pedestrians and jog in place when people didn't realize he was behind them. Charging up Main Street at full throttle wasn't the easiest way to run home, but it was the most direct. Aaron counted the hours back in his head and tried to remember the last time he'd given Jack a bottle. It had been at least two hours ago—before he'd loaded the baby in the stroller and set off for adventure.

Speaking of *loaded*, that was the other thing worrying Aaron. If he didn't get home soon, Jack might end up with a diaper blowout. He was running on borrowed time at this point, literally. Aaron and the jogging stroller blasted past the Parisian Café, zipped by the Ferry's Closet, plowed by Wanderer's Home, then crossed the street to avoid the crowds. They continued to chug up Main Street toward Ninth Avenue, where Aaron would hang a left for home. But when they reached the Smoothie Hut, Jack began to cry. By the time they were at Sweet Bliss, the babe was wailing. Aaron rolled to a stop and kicked on the parking brake so he could investigate. He'd barely lifted the sunshade before his nose told him all he needed to know. It was a full-on poop apocalypse, and poor Jack was squirming uncomfortably in his onesie and stained sweatpants.

"Oh man!" Aaron exclaimed as he stood there, rooted to the spot. His first instinct was to take off his shirt and wrap the baby up in something clean. But his exercise gear dripped with sweat. "It'll be okay, buddy," Aaron murmured. "I'll find a way to help."

An older man with puffy white hair and a striped apron walked by them and scowled disapprovingly. "You're blocking the sidewalk," he grunted.

"You can go around us," Aaron snapped. He looked left and right, trying to come up with a plan. There was a drugstore a couple of miles away, but without his wallet, that wouldn't be any help. Maybe his best bet was to keep running toward home and hope that Jack didn't get a rash in the hour it would take to get there. Aaron could normally run eight-minute miles, but the jogging stroller slowed him down.

Then, like music from heaven, the door to Sweet Bliss opened, and tiny bells on the door handle jingled, capturing Aaron's attention. As he watched a group of teenagers exit the shop, Aaron remembered that Julia had said something about keeping diapers on hand for the infant-toddler group she'd told him about. Maybe she had some stocked right now. It was worth a shot to ask, especially now that Jack was tomato red he was bawling so hard. "Hang on, little guy," Aaron said soothingly. He stopped the door before it could close and pushed his way into the Froyo shop.

Cherubic angels painted on the walls greeted him, floating on sponge-painted clouds. Chairs and tables made of twisted wire with heart motifs offered intimate seating, but there were also booths along the left-side wall. Self-service frozen yogurt dispensers lined the back of the shop, and to the right was a buffet of toppings. It was too far away for him to see what was offered, but Aaron smelled freshly baked brownies and what he thought might be waffle cones.

Of course, that wasn't all Aaron could smell. As soon as he entered Sweet Bliss, he and Jack brought the aroma of diaper explosion with them.

"Welcome to Sweet Bliss," chirped a middle-aged woman with ruby-red hair behind the counter. She worked the register as a family of four paid for the yogurt. Next to her, tying on her apron, was a woman with a blond ponytail Aaron recognized. Julia had lost the blazer she'd worn by the train, and the pink shade of her shirt made her skin look like porcelain. She either hadn't seen him enter the store or hadn't bothered to look up. Aaron wasn't sure which.

"Excuse me," Aaron said, clearing his throat. Jack's cries drowned him out. "I need some help here," he said again, a bit more desperately.

Julia jerked her head up to see what was going on. "Aaron," she said. "Are you okay?"

He shook his head and pushed the stroller forward. "No, actually. I left the house without a diaper bag like a total idiot. I don't suppose you—"

"Follow me," said Julia as she set down her knife. She hustled around the counter into the center of the shop and motioned for Aaron to walk to the corner of the store. "The changing table's in the restroom, and I have a basket of supplies in the storeroom. I'll go grab it."

Aaron felt relief pour all over him. "You're a lifesaver." He scooted the stroller into the unisex restroom and flipped down the changing table. Since he didn't have a changing pad with him, he lined the plastic shelf with paper towels. He was just unclipping Jack's safety harness when Julia knocked on the restroom door and pushed it open a second later.

"I hope one of these works." She looked down at the diapers in the basket. "I'm not sure what size you need."

"The smallest. Jack's only three months old." Aaron leaned down and scooped up the baby, then hugged him to his chest for a second before laying him down on the table.

"Yikes!" Julia stared at Aaron's chest. "Looks like you might need a change too."

"What?" Aaron kept his hands on Jack to keep him from rolling off the table and looked down at himself to see what Julia was talking about. There was gooey yellow-brown baby poop all over his shirt. "Yuck," he muttered, his humiliation complete.

"I'll change the baby while you clean up." Julia set down the basket and grabbed the wipes and diaper.

"I can't let you do—"

"I insist." Julia shooed him out of the way and leaned down to look at Jack. "It'll be okay," she cooed as she gently wrestled off his tiny sweatpants. "So many of my friends have little ones that I'm a professional auntie."

"Thank you for this." Aaron stepped up to the mirror and turned on the sink's faucet. He tried dabbing at the smears with a wet paper towel, but it was hopeless. His shirt was thoroughly soiled. "I think this is a lost cause," he said as he pulled it over his head. "Good thing it's not freezing cold outside." He felt calmer now that Jack had stopped crying. It was like all the anxiety in him had melted away once the baby was settled.

"There," said Julia in a bright tone. "All better." She picked up a freshly diapered Jack and gave him a gentle squeeze. Holding him against her torso with one arm, she bunched up the wipes and paper towels with her free hand and tossed them in the trash. When she turned around to face Aaron, she gasped.

CHAPTER FIVE

There she stood, her mouth gaping, acting like she was some innocent who'd never seen a man before. Julia felt like an idiot. But as her gaze passed over Aaron's well-defined pectoral muscles and chiseled abs, she wondered if she *had* ever seen a man before—a man like this, that was. Julia closed her mouth and desperately sought a way to iron over her own stupidity. "That's one way to handle a messy shirt. Just take it off." She grinned and handed Jack over to him. The sight of bare-chested Aaron snuggling the diapered baby was almost more than she could handle. Was it possible to feel your ovaries cry?

"I can't thank you enough for your help." Aaron glanced over at the trash can. "We've totally destroyed your restroom."

"It's not a big deal. I needed to take the trash out anyway." Julia opened the cabinet underneath the sink and took out a container of disinfecting wipes. She undid the lid and ripped one out. "I'll clean off the changing table before I close it."

"I should be the one doing that." Aaron took the cloth out of her hand and scrubbed away. He looked down at the stroller. "I might need one for the safety harness too. The blanket took most of the action, but it looks like other parts of the stroller got hit."

"Oh dear." Julia ripped out another wipe to handle the situation. "What should we do with the blanket?" she asked as she folded it up.

"I'll throw it in the bottom next to my shirt and torch it all when I get home." Aaron closed the changing table and clicked the lever shut. "We don't live too far away. Hopefully Jack won't get cold on the way home."

"I'd give you an apron to wrap him up in, but you don't want those straps tangling the baby." Julia tapped her chin and looked out the open doorway toward the Froyo shop. She couldn't stand the idea of the baby riding home in the chilly June air. Sure, the day had warmed up, but June in Harper Landing meant a high of sixty-four degrees. It certainly wasn't hang-out-in-your-diaper weather. "Stay here; I have an idea." She darted away before Aaron could say anything. She had hoped there would be someone in the Froyo shop who might have a blanket stuffed in their diaper bag. But there wasn't a baby or toddler in sight, and she had to think up another plan.

Her blazer had lived a good life, Julia decided. Plus, it was a soft cotton blend, like a T-shirt, only thicker. It would be the perfect thing to keep Jack warm on his way home. She ran into the back office and grabbed it off her desk chair underneath her bulletin board of mementos. Then she hightailed it back to the restroom. Aaron was adjusting the harness straps over Jack's minuscule shoulders. The whole room smelled like disinfectant. In the sixty seconds she'd been gone, he'd wiped off the sink and bagged up the trash.

"Here you go; this should keep him warm." Julia bent down over the stroller and wrapped the blazer around the baby, tucking the fabric around him like a blanket.

"He might destroy it," Aaron said in an uncertain tone. "You saw what happened to my shirt. And the blanket. And your restroom."

Julia shrugged. "The blazer's cheap and machine washable." She smiled and played peekaboo with the baby. "Besides, you saved my dog's life. I owe you."

There was a knock on the restroom door, and when Julia looked up, she saw a mom standing behind a four-year-old who was hopping from one foot to the other like he really had to go.

"Looks like we've hogged the facilities long enough. I better get out of here before the health inspector comes," said Aaron.

"No shirt. No shoes. No service." Julia stood up straight and held the door open.

"Thanks again." Aaron pushed the stroller past her. "You saved my bacon." He rolled the jogging stroller through the restaurant on the path to the front door.

Julia enjoyed watching him go, because his deltoids were equally as impressive as his pectorals. The wide expanse of his shoulders cut down to a narrow waist. Since she was standing behind him, she could ogle as much as she wanted without his noticing.

"Nice view," murmured the four-year-old's mother. "Go, Julia."

"What?" Julia snapped to attention and looked at the woman next to her. "Oh, hi, Melanie. I didn't realize that was you."

Melanie Knowles twisted a brown curl back behind her ear and grinned. "You obviously had more important things to capture your attention." She gave her son a pat on the back. "The bathroom's all yours now, Timmy."

Julia stepped out of the way so that Timmy could pass.

"Thanks for the donation you made to the Orca Street auction last spring," said Melanie. "If I remember correctly, that gift basket went for six hundred dollars."

"Six hundred dollars?" Julia raised her eyebrows. "That can't be right. The gift certificates were only worth three hundred dollars."

"It was the sidewalk space for the Fourth of July parade that drove up the bid price." Melanie removed the glasses that were resting on top of her head like a headband and put them in her purse. "People loved the idea of guaranteed seating."

"Really? But anyone can get a seat at the parade. All they have to do is put out chairs the night before."

"Some people are against that."

"You mean Walt?" Julia asked.

"Yup." Melanie held two chunks of hair up in imitation of Walt's white fluff. "I love having a local candy store in town, but at this point, I'd rather buy junk at the grocery store than take my kids to the Sugar Factory."

Walt was a jerk, as far as Julia was concerned. But she felt conflicted about disparaging a local business owner. Plus, the relationship between Walt and her mom had been complicated. Waverley had always spoken highly of her former sweetheart. That in itself had been unusual because Waverley had rarely praised anyone. Then, a couple of years after Harrison had died, Waverley had begun having lunch with Walt every Monday in Lynnwood. Julia didn't know what Walt had thought of those meetings, but Waverley had always polished her shoes before she'd left.

"The Sugar Factory has been around forever," she said. "Spending my allowance on candy sticks is how I learned to count change."

"It's not just Walt." Melanie frowned. "You're allowed to put chairs up on July third at six p.m. on the dot, but some people are putting out chairs on the second."

Julia nodded. "I've seen that happen. That's why I always put out extra tables along the sidewalk in front of Sweet Bliss on those days, to make sure my customers still have access to what's supposed to be my space. Then I swap the tables for the parade chairs at the last minute."

"People can be so rude." Melanie rolled her eyes. "Last year some people collected the chairs that were put out too early and trashed them."

"What? I hadn't heard about that."

"It was all over Harper Landing Moms. A woman posted pictures of folding chairs in the dumpster."

"Wow." Julia wrinkled her nose. "They could have at least brought the chairs to the Goodwill."

"I know, right? That's what I mean about it being a full-out chair war. People leaped at the chance to bid for your offer of guaranteed seats."

"I better deliver, then," said Julia, "and not forget to put chairs out in front of my own sidewalk." When she saw Melanie's alarmed expression, she quickly clarified what she meant. "I'm joking, of course. I never forget to put out chairs for the Fourth of July."

The toilet flushed, and a few seconds later, the restroom door opened. Timmy wandered out, zipping up his trousers. "Aren't you forgetting something?" Melanie asked him.

"No." Timmy rubbed his nose on his sleeve.

"Your hands." Melanie pointed at the sink. "Go back into the bathroom and wash your hands, Mister." She turned back to look at Julia. "So who was the man-chest in the bathroom with you?"

"What?" Julia asked.

"The shirtless Greek god." Melanie waggled her eyebrows. "I want details."

Julia's cheeks turned pink. "I don't know anything." She held her hands up to profess her innocence, even as her pulse raced at the memory of a half-naked Aaron snuggling with Jack. "I helped him with the baby's diaper explosion; that's all."

"You didn't get a name?" Melanie asked in a disappointed tone.

"Oh, no, I did get his name." Julia bit her bottom lip for a moment. "It's Aaron Baxter. You probably know more about his family than I do. His sister might be a member of Harper Landing Moms, or his sister-in-law or something."

Melanie whipped out her phone from her back pocket. "Lemme check."

The restroom door swung open again, and Timmy walked out, wiping wet hands on his shorts. "Can I get some ice cream now?"

"Sure," Melanie muttered, staring at her phone. "In a minute." Her thumbs tapped across her phone. "I don't see any member with the last name of Baxter," she said when she finally looked up.

Julia shrugged. "Maybe they just moved here. I'm not exactly sure." There was no point in her becoming invested in the mystery of it all, since Aaron was clearly not interested in her.

But Melanie was like a dog with a bone. "Wow. Look what I found." She held out her phone so that Julia could read the screen. "It's an article from the *Wall Street Journal* saying that Aaron Baxter and Jared Reynolds sold their company, Big Foot Paleo, to General Mills last year for an undisclosed amount."

"Jared Reynolds?" Julia felt the blood drain from her face. The name didn't mean anything to Melanie, since she'd only lived in Harper Landing for a few years, but to Julia, it cut straight to the heart. "Jared was my date for senior prom."

"No kidding. What a small world." Melanie walked forward a few steps toward where Timmy was evaluating his frozen yogurt choices. "Were you two serious?" she asked over her shoulder.

"No." Julia's voice cracked. She hadn't been in love with Jared, but she'd definitely nurtured a crush on him that he'd unintentionally fed with kindness. "We went as friends. He was the boy next door. Jared's parents are my neighbors." She stuffed her hands in her pockets, her mind swirling with memories of Jared.

When they were younger, they'd rode bikes down to the beach, and Jared would fix her chain if it got stuck. When she'd found an injured rabbit in her backyard, Jared had helped her feed it water with an eyedropper while Martha had called the local wildlife rescue. When Waverley had been too cheap to buy a Netflix subscription, Jared had told her his password so she could watch the popular shows.

"Where does Jared live now?" Melanie asked as she helped Timmy pull down the handle and dispense a few ounces of Pineapple Delight.

"That's just it," said Julia, staring down at the tips of her boots. "He passed away last January in a car crash in California."

"How awful!" Melanie gave Timmy his cup of ice cream and looked at Julia with concern. "Were you two still friends?"

"Yes, but we weren't close. I didn't make it to his wedding, because it was on the East Coast, but we used to chat every time he'd come home to visit his parents. I never did meet his wife, but I saw her picture. Sara was beautiful. It seemed like they were really in love." As much as it had stung at the time when Jared had gotten married, Julia was glad for it now. He'd deserved every bit of happiness his short life had offered him.

"What a tragedy." Melanie sighed. "Okay, okay," she said to Timmy, who was pulling her sleeve. "Yes, you can add some toppings, but you might want to think twice about putting brownie on pineapple." She looked back at Julia and waved. "See you around."

"Enjoy your Froyo." Julia smiled at Melanie, but as soon as she walked away, her happy expression faded. She went back behind the counter and checked on Tara at the register to make sure she had enough change in the till and then mindlessly sliced fresh strawberries for the buffet line. But after five minutes of chopping, Julia gave up. "Your break's in an hour, right?" she asked Tara.

"Yeah." Tara handed a compostable plastic spoon to a customer. She was a spunky divorcée with a good sense of humor who loved the flexible hours Sweet Bliss offered, because it gave her time to spend with her kids. "Jordan arrives for the second shift in ten minutes."

"Good." Julia set down the knife. "I'm going to check the tracking number on the vanilla extract. It should be here by now." She brought the dishes with her to the sink in the back room next to her office. Julia turned the faucet to hot and carefully washed and dried the knife. She loaded the cutting board into the dishwasher and wiped her hands on the towel. It was as if she worked on autopilot.

When she finally wandered into her office and turned on her computer, she avoided looking at the bulletin board. She kept her head down and sank into her office chair. USPS said that the box of vanilla should be delivered that evening, which was barely enough time to make tomorrow's batch of Tahitian Paradise, which she served every Saturday. The price of vanilla had gone through the roof, and she knew that if her mother were alive, Waverley would have balked at the expense, saying that imitation vanilla would work just as well. But Sweet Bliss was Julia's business, and she knew that real vanilla made the yogurt taste better. There was also an email from a property developer she'd been meeting with named Will Gladstone, confirming their appointment Monday morning. Julia had no interest in selling any of her buildings, but she did appreciate Will's insight. As her accountant liked to say, she was land rich and cash poor until she turned thirty and could access her trust fund. Julia responded to the email, then turned off her computer, and the monitor went black. Light from behind her transformed the screen into a mirror, reflecting the wall behind her. Finally, Julia couldn't take it anymore. She spun around in her chair and looked up at her bulletin board.

Normally the newspaper clippings, photographs, and old ticket stubs filled her with the warmth of twenty-eight years of memories. There were several pictures of her father: Harrison coaching her soccer team, the Mighty Ladybugs; Harrison holding a cigarette and standing in front of the original Sweet Bliss on its grand opening, way back before she was born; and Harrison holding Julia on his shoulders down at the beach. Julia had pinned up newspaper articles that featured Sweet Bliss throughout the years. She was especially proud of the one from the *Seattle Times* that said: "Generations agree, Sweet Bliss is the best ice cream shop north of Seattle." Next to it was a picture of Julia and her mom taken on the day Waverley had been honored by the Friends of Harper Landing Library for a sizable donation. Being generous with charities had ensured Waverley's position in town and helped sweeten her sour reputation. There were even five pictures of Julia dressed up as a bridesmaid, standing next to five different beaming brides. But today, it was the picture in the upper-right-hand corner that captured her attention. One glance at it, and her heart squeezed like it was being crushed. It was the picture of Jared and her at high school prom.

Jared hadn't just been the boy next door or the first boy whom she'd crushed on—he had been her hero that evening. When Julia's boyfriend dumped her three weeks before senior prom, Jared stepped in at the last moment, even though he went to a different school. Julia went to Harper Landing High School like most of their friends, but Jared went to Our Lady of Peace and Devotion, a private Catholic school in Seattle. He had a girlfriend at the time, who wasn't exactly pleased by Jared's chivalry on Julia's behalf, but it didn't dampen the evening one bit. Julia had made it to prom after all and had danced the night away next to Jared and all her friends.

"Oh, Jared," Julia murmured as she stood up and gazed at his picture. "Why does life have to be so cruel?" A stab of guilt cut through her when she remembered missing his memorial service. It had been a double ceremony back in New Jersey, where his wife was from. Martha and Frank had both flown out for it. But it was only five months after Waverley had passed away, and traveling wasn't a possibility for Julia. Not only was she grief stricken by her own loss, but the full extent of the family businesses and properties were finally in her control. Her days were packed with meetings with lawyers and property managers. So she had sent a huge wreath of flowers to New Jersey and had made sure to collect the Reynolds' mail and take out their trash cans while they were gone. Now, while staring at Jared's curly brown hair and boyish smile, she wished that she had done more. Julia dropped back into her chair, rested her elbows on the desk, and buried her face in her hands.

Everyone from her childhood was married or buried. But she was stuck in the same exact place she'd always been, alone.

Not quite alone. Julia remembered a faint bit of gladness that pierced through her gloom. At least there was Toby to keep her company. As soon as she could leave work, she was going to go home and walk her dog.

CHAPTER SIX

It was Friday night, and Aaron was googling nipples. Not the fun type of nipples, but the type that went on bottles. Jack had been gassy lately, and Aaron wondered if it might be nipple related. He still didn't feel 100 percent comfortable feeding Jack formula from a plastic bottle either. Sure, the companies said that the plastic was safe, but were they certain? Maybe he should switch to glass bottles while he was at it. Jack lay on a quilt next to him in the middle of the family room, kicking the squeaky toys hanging above him from his baby gym. The family room was downstairs, and the daylight basement was cool despite the warming temperature outside.

"How are you doing, Jack-Jack?" Aaron looked up from his computer on his lap. Jack giggled, and a bit of drool dribbled down his chin. Aaron wiped it off with the bib snapped around Jack's neck. "This is the third bib you've gone through today." Aaron contemplated getting out a fresh one but figured this bib was good for another hour. "Either Martha's right and you have teeth coming in, or you're just an overachiever like your daddy."

Aaron gritted his teeth almost as soon as he said it. He still wasn't sure what to tell Jack about his parents or what Jack would call him when he was old enough to talk. Was Jared Daddy or was Aaron? Maybe he should be Uncle Aaron. That would be the most legitimate title. But did Jack deserve to grow up without a father? Absolutely not! Aaron wasn't sure how he would manage it, but he knew that he would spend every moment of his present and future taking care of this child. Jack would know what it was like to grow up with a father; Aaron would make sure of it.

And he'd never be an absent parent like Darren Baxter had been. Growing up in Rumson, New Jersey, Sara and Aaron only saw their father in the late hours right before bedtime or on Sunday mornings when Darren dropped them off at church and then walked across the street to the pastry shop. Darren was a successful litigation lawyer who kept the family well heeled in a six-bedroom house with brand-new luxury cars purchased like clockwork every two years. Sara and Aaron both attended private school, which eventually meant being shipped off to Andover for high school. Their mother, Lorraine, was a public relations expert for a pharmaceutical company and equally prosperous in her own right. She traveled all over the world and was gone so frequently that when they were little, Sara and Aaron had a full-time nanny and a rotating army of au pairs.

Throughout it all, Sara and Aaron relied on each other. Even though they were two years apart, they were soul mates. One time, in second grade, when Aaron fell off the monkey bars and broke his arm on the blacktop at recess, Sara heard him cry all the way from the other side of the playground. She ran full throttle to help him and refused to leave his side. As Aaron was loaded into the ambulance, he watched the principal pry her back. Sara had wanted to go, too, so Aaron wouldn't be alone. Aaron blinked hard, remembering the moment, and rubbed his arm absentmindedly where it had broken in two.

The first thing Sara had told him when she'd announced she was pregnant was that she intended to be a stay-at-home mom. "I know that's not for everyone," she said, her curly brown hair twisted back into a coil, "but I don't want my baby to grow up like we did. And I realize that I'm incredibly privileged even to have this choice, and there is nothing wrong with paid childcare; I just want to be there for all her firsts. Her first bath, her first food, the first time she rolls over—all of it."

"Her?" Aaron asked. They were standing in the middle of the Big Foot Paleo office in Palo Alto on Sandhill Road. "You know it's a girl already?"

A guilty look crept across Sara's face. "Not exactly," she had said, scrunching up her nose. "It's more of a feeling."

Sitting on the carpet next to Jack, Aaron felt a pang as he remembered his sister's joy. He pushed the computer off his lap and lay down next to the baby. "Your mama was many things," he said. "But clairvoyant wasn't one of them."

Aaron rolled onto his back and looked up at the popcorn ceiling. The basement needed to be updated, but he didn't care. The only thing he'd replaced so far was the carpet, because the old rug had smelled like mildew. Now that the carpet was brand new, the wood paneling and brass light fixtures looked retro. It could be that the ceiling had asbestos, though. He sighed, thinking about what it might require to eliminate it. Money wasn't the problem. General Mills had paid them royally. But Aaron didn't want the hassle of needing to move out while an asbestos-abatement team moved in.

"Wow," Aaron muttered, ashamed of how banal his thought process had become. "It's Friday night, and I'm lying on the floor thinking about asbestos and talking to an infant." He rolled over onto his elbow and put his finger in Jack's fist. "Not that you're not a magnificent conversationalist." He yawned, and exhaustion made him ache. It had been months since Aaron had slept eight hours in one stretch. He yawned again and rested his head on the baby quilt, Jack's tiny fist still gripping his finger with kung fu strength. "I'm just going to close my eyes for a few seconds," Aaron whispered. "Don't go anywhere."

Ten minutes later, an incessant buzzing roused him from a dreamless sleep. The noise became louder and louder until his eyes fluttered open and he jerked awake. He scanned the room, trying to find the source of the commotion, his phone vibrating with an incoming call. "Where did I leave that thing?" Aaron lurched to his feet and stumbled across the room. The noise seemed to emanate from the laundry room. Sure enough, there it was, on top of the washer, centimeters away from falling off the edge and crashing to the linoleum floor.

Aaron answered the phone without bothering to read the caller ID. "Hello?" He brushed his free hand through his brown hair and then rubbed the tender spot on the back of his neck that had cramped up while he'd been lying on the floor.

"Aaron, it's me," said Martha, speaking faster than normal. "Have you seen Frank?"

"Frank?" Wandering out of the laundry room, Aaron did a visual check to make sure that Jack was okay. At three months old, he was still too young to crawl, but the pediatrician had said he'd be able to roll over any day now. "No, why?"

"He took the car keys!"

"Is that a bad thing?"

"Well . . ." Martha's voice wavered. "I don't think he should drive anymore, and he knows that."

"Why not? Is his eyesight bad?" Aaron thought back to his interactions with Frank, which had all been minimal. They'd met at the wedding and then later at the memorial service in Rumson. Frank hadn't spoken much, but Aaron had always attributed that to the man being uncomfortable in large crowds or overwhelmed by grief. Since moving to Harper Landing, Aaron had been over to Martha and Frank's house once for dinner, and Frank had mostly sat in his recliner reading the newspaper while Martha had fussed over the baby. Before he'd retired, Frank had been an engineer at Boeing, and pictures of planes he'd helped design lined the walls of his study, next to various service awards he'd won in the local rotary club.

"It's not his eyesight," said Martha. "It's his decision-making skills." She paused, and the line went dead for a few moments before she continued. "And his memory. That's why I haven't let him drive for months. I hid his keys in my sewing box, but he must have found my set. Now he's taken off in my Chevy, and I'm afraid he won't be able to find his way home."

"Oh, Martha, I'm so sorry." Aaron walked over to the front window of the daylight basement and stared out at the empty driveway. "I had no idea Frank was struggling with memory issues."

"He's not. At least according to him." There was a bitter edge to her tone. "Frank thinks everything is just fine. But he can't figure out how to use the television remote anymore, and the other day I found him brushing his teeth with his electric toothbrush without turning it on."

"Maybe it was out of batteries?" Aaron asked hopefully.

"It was perfectly fine. I checked it as soon as he was finished. When I asked him about it, he claimed that the electric part hurt his gums, but I think he didn't remember that he was supposed to turn it on."

"What can I do to help?"

"That's just it; I don't know." Martha sniffed and blew her nose. "I called Jessica to see if maybe Frank had driven down to Seattle to see her and the kids, but he's not there." Martha's daughter lived on Capitol Hill and worked for the local public radio station.

"How long does it take to drive to Seattle in work traffic?" Aaron asked. "Maybe he's not there yet."

"Sixty minutes, maybe seventy. And Frank's been gone for two hours. I'm tempted to dig Frank's keys out of my sewing box and take his car to drive around town and see if I can find him. But what if he comes home, and I'm not here? Or worse"—Martha gulped—"what if the police or a hospital calls, and I'm not here to answer the phone?"

"I thought you had a cell phone?"

"It was in my car!" Martha was weeping now, and her tears broke Aaron's heart.

"Here's what we're going to do," he said decisively. "I'm coming over right now, and you'll give me a list of all the places Frank might be. Then Jack and I will drive around until we find him."

"I can't ask you to do that," said Martha. "You don't want to drive all night with a baby in the car."

"I love driving around with a baby in the car. It's the best thing for settling Jack down to sleep." He scooped up Jack and headed upstairs, still talking with Martha on the phone. "Make that list, okay? I'll be over in ten minutes."

As soon as he hung up the phone, Aaron sprang into action. He'd learned his mistake from his morning run and would absolutely under no circumstances forget the diaper bag this time. He changed Jack, snapped on a clean drool bib, and grabbed a couple of bottles of pre-made formula. He'd fed Jack an hour ago, so it was highly possible the baby would drift off to sleep once they hit the road, but he brought along some car toys just in case. Jack loved his squishy orange octopus and crinkle blanket.

When Aaron had told Martha he'd be there in ten minutes, he'd been overly optimistic in his time frame. Sure, their houses were only ten minutes apart, but it took him a full eight minutes to be able to walk out the door and another five to get Jack properly secured in his car seat. Aaron plugged the baby's mouth with the pacifier, a special treat reserved only for car rides, and drove off for Ninth Avenue.

The sun hung high in the sky even though it was six o'clock and close to dinnertime. Aaron felt grateful for the lingering daylight, which he knew would be useful while searching for Frank. When he pulled into the Reynoldses' driveway, Martha was waiting for him, wearing gray slacks and a violet fleece. She waved a piece of paper in her hand and held a book in the other. Aaron rolled down the window of his Tesla so she could give them to him.

"I figured that with Jack in the car, it would be easier if you didn't have to come inside." Martha handed him the list and spiral-bound book. "Here're all the places I could think of to check for Frank, plus a *Thomas Guide* to help you find them. I never trust my phone when it comes to maps."

"Thanks." Aaron raised his eyebrows when he looked at the atlas of street maps. He hadn't seen one of these since he'd taken drivers ed at Andover. "I'll call you if I find anything." Aaron scanned the list, struggling at first to decipher Martha's spidery cursive. "You think he might have driven to Boeing?"

Martha raised her shoulders. "It's possible. Frank made that trip for thirty-five years before he retired."

Aaron set the list on the passenger seat and spoke the question that he'd ruminated on the whole drive over. "Should we call the police? Maybe we need a Silver Alert."

Martha grabbed her forehead, her fingers tugging at her gray curls. "He hasn't been officially diagnosed with Alzheimer's or dementia yet." She covered her face with her hands. "He refuses to see the doctor."

"Everything'll be okay." Aaron reached through the window and placed his hand gently on Martha's elbow. "We're going to find him."

She pulled down her hands and looked at him. "Thank you, Aaron." Big tears rolled down her wrinkled face. "I don't know what I'd do without you." In the back seat, Jack began to fuss. "Oh no," said Martha. "This isn't fair to Jack."

Aaron didn't want to add *care for a baby* to her list of things to deal with right now. "Don't worry about it." Aaron withdrew his hand and put it on the steering wheel. "I'll turn on *Baby Beluga*, and we'll be fine." He pushed a button on the dash, and Raffi's voice came to life. "Go inside, make yourself a cup of tea, and try not to worry." He put the Tesla in reverse and rolled down the driveway.

The first stops on Martha's list were the closest, and he decided to check there first: the grocery store, the post office, the doughnut shop, and the United Methodist church. All seemed to be likely places Frank might have driven to. Aaron didn't need to plug in the GPS coordinates, since he knew where all those locations were. After a couple of minutes of driving, Jack quieted. When Aaron looked back to check on him, he was sleeping soundly. Could he turn off Raffi now? Aaron sighed. Maybe, but it didn't seem worth the risk. He did lower the volume a few notches, though, to preserve his sanity.

It was approaching six thirty now, and there was still no sign of Frank. Aaron pulled over to the side of the road to check if there were messages on his phone, but there weren't. The next stop on Martha's list was the Boeing office in Everett, eighteen miles away. But before he drove north, Aaron figured it would be worthwhile checking a place that Martha had forgotten to put on her list: the spot where the rotary club met. The problem was, Aaron wasn't sure where that was. He typed the question into his phone, and the address for the Parisian Café popped up. Aaron called Martha to let her know his change of plans and also to keep her from worrying.

"Aaron? Have you found him?" she asked in a desperate voice.

"Not yet," he said in a calm tone. "I'm about to drive up to Boeing, but before I do, I thought I'd swing by the Parisian Café. Is that where the rotary club meets?"

"Yes. That's correct. Good thinking. My mind is so frazzled right now—I should have thought of that myself."

"It'll be okay. We're going to find him. I'll call as soon as I have news."

They said goodbye, and Aaron put his phone in the console. As he drove through Harper Landing, he scanned to the left and right, inspecting each parked car he passed. But there was no sign of Martha's green Chevy anywhere. Not until he reached the bottom of Main Street, where he finally found it parked around the corner from the Parisian Café, alongside a red curb. A police officer was standing in front of it writing a ticket.

Aaron double-parked his Tesla right next to the police car and turned on his hazard lights. He hurried out of the car, flung open the back door, and wrestled the infant seat out of its latch. "Officer!" Aaron called, jogging over to the woman. "Wait!"

The statuesque redhead eyeballed him over the electronic device she held in her hand—a piece of paper printed out of the bottom. "What's the matter?" she asked. Thick lashes rimmed her green eyes.

"The driver of this car has memory impairment, and I've been driving around town looking for him. Have you seen him?" Aaron rattled off a description of Frank: five feet, eleven inches, with balding brown hair and glasses. He couldn't remember what color Frank's eyes were, so he guessed and said the same color as Jared's—cobalt blue. "Here. I have a picture of him on my phone." Aaron set the car seat down on the sidewalk and scrolled through his pictures, finding a recent one of Frank holding Jack.

The officer looked at the picture and then over at the illegally parked Tesla. "Sir, you go park your vehicle, and then we'll work on this together. Okay? I'll go check in the restaurant right now and meet you back here."

"Thanks." Aaron picked up the infant carrier again. "Thank you so much." Jack was out cold now, and jostling him back into the car didn't bother him one bit. But finding a parking space on a Friday evening in downtown Harper Landing was difficult. The vibrant restaurant scene meant that every spot was full. They drove around in circles for five minutes before Aaron gave up and crossed the tracks for Harper Landing Beach, hoping he could find a place by the beach, which he did. He popped the hatch and took out the stroller.

Aaron was great with the jogging stroller. He used it every day. But this wasn't the jogging stroller; it was the one that had come with the car seat. He fumbled with the levers and felt his face growing hot as he inwardly cursed how difficult it was to assemble. Who designed these things? Sadists?

"Aaron?" a voice called.

When he turned around, he was overcome with relief. It was Julia, holding Toby's leash in one hand and Frank's hand in the other.

"Hi, Aaron." Julia spoke in a bright tone but wore a forced smile. "I'm walking Jared's father home, and I wondered if you might be able to give us a ride in your car. I'm not sure what's going on, but he seems a bit confused."

"Frank!" Aaron opened his arms up to hug the man.

Frank jerked back, looking at Aaron without any sign of recognition.

Aaron felt like he'd been struck. He immediately dropped his arms. "It's me, Aaron, with Jack." He pushed the stroller forward slightly.

Frank stared into the stroller. "Who's Jack?"

Aaron tried not to panic, but his already elevated heartbeat rose further. "Your grandson." Sweat beaded along the back of his neck. Martha hadn't been kidding when she'd said Frank was having memory problems. Damn, on top of them losing their only son—now this. "Remember, we had dinner at your house last week?" he prompted. "Martha made meat loaf."

"Martha?" Frank's eyes darted around. "Is she here?"

"No, she's at home waiting for you." Aaron pulled out his phone. "I'm going to call her right now to let her know we found you." His gaze drifted over to Julia for a moment, and they locked eyes. Her worried glance mirrored his own.

"That sounds like a good idea." Julia nodded.

Aaron dialed Martha's number and steadied his breathing. He had to remain calm. Jared's parents needed a rock right now, a rock of strength that could handle everything: the loss of their son, the birth of their grandchild, and now Frank's confusion. When Martha answered the phone, Aaron became granite. "Martha," he said in a voice that took charge. "I'm here with Frank, and everything's okay."

CHAPTER SEVEN

Of course Aaron and Frank knew each other; that wasn't a shock to Julia. She figured they must have previously met, since Aaron had been Jared's business partner. But Jack being Frank and Martha's grandchild wasn't something Julia had expected, and it rattled her. Julia looked back at the beach, where ten minutes ago she'd found Frank wandering around in circles. Her evening walk with Toby had climbed a ladder of complications with no end in sight.

What was going on? Frank was one of the smartest people she knew—and one of the most reliable. Frank had looked out for Waverley and Julia ever since Harrison had died. He'd cleaned the gutters, figured out the circuit breaker when the power had gone off, and helped Julia jump-start her car when she was eighteen and late to her first final exam at the University of Washington. Julia felt ashamed at her surprise that Frank had aged so quickly. She should have paid better attention to what he and Martha were facing. It had been months since she'd had a real conversation with either of them—not since they'd given her instructions to watch their house before they left for Jared's memorial service. Martha had mentioned her new grandbaby, but she hadn't gone into specifics, because she'd been crying so hard. Since then, Julia hadn't spoken to the Reynoldses beyond a passing wave at the mailbox. No wonder she didn't know about Frank's confusion.

Julia peeked into the stroller. Jack was grinning, and he had Jared's smile. Jack was Jared's baby; he had to be. Instead of Jared and his wife holding that child in their arms, he was here, being raised by Jared's friend. Aaron wasn't just Jared's business partner anymore; he was Jack's "uncle." She blinked back tears.

Toby nudged at Aaron and licked his knees, eager for attention. Julia pulled the leash back. "Sit," she commanded. Toby ignored her. "Sit," she tried again, this time speaking more forcefully.

"Where?" Frank asked. "I want to sit down, but there isn't any bench."

Aaron brought out a key fob from his pocket and unlocked the doors to his Tesla. The lights blinked. "Say hi to Martha, and then get in the car, where it's warm," he said as he handed the phone to Frank.

"Martha? Is that you?" Frank held the phone to his ear. He smiled as soon as he heard his wife's voice. "Yes, I'm okay. Can't a man go for a walk if he wants to? Yes. I'm coming home now." He gave the phone back to Aaron.

"We'll be there soon. Okay, goodbye," said Aaron before hanging up.

"Come on, Frank." Julia squeezed his hand again. "We're going home." She guided him toward the sedan.

"Did you find him?" called a female voice.

Julia froze, unwilling to let go of Frank's hand to open the door and equally unwilling to turn around and meet the woman in Aaron's life who was helping him look for Frank.

"Yes, he's safe." Aaron's deep voice resonated behind her.

Julia put on her fake smile again and turned part of the way around, Toby's leash twisting next to her ankles. When she saw who Aaron was talking to, she was relieved. It was Officer Dillan, who'd worked in Harper Landing for over five years. She'd taken Julia's statement last month when someone had stolen fifty dollars from the Fourth of July fundraising jar next to the register at Sweet Bliss.

"Julia," said Officer Dillan. "Good to see you again." She was in her early thirties and a regular at the CrossFit gym in Lynnwood. Julia knew this because one of her friends from high school frequently shared photos of her CrossFit crew on Facebook, and Officer Dillan was usually in the picture in a sports bra and leggings.

"Officer Dillan, hi." Julia waved with the hand that held Toby's leash.

"Fancy meeting you here." Officer Dillan shifted her focus from Julia to Frank. "And you must be Frank—is that right?"

"Oh yes, that's me." Frank nodded. "Do I know you?"

Officer Dillan shook her head. "No, we just met. But I found your car parked where it shouldn't be parked a few blocks from here."

"Thank you so much for your help," said Aaron.

"That's what I'm here for," said Officer Dillan. "I'll do a wellness check tomorrow. Right now, we need to move that Impala because it's illegally parked."

"Can I please have the car keys?" Aaron asked, holding out his hand.

Frank scowled. "You can't have my car keys. Why would I give them to you?"

"Because it's me, Aaron."

Frank took a step back, closer to the Tesla.

"How about I take you home?" Julia stared at her neighbor with the sweetest expression possible. "Would you like to drive home with me?"

Frank's face creased with confusion. "I don't want to bother you."

"It's no bother." Julia patted his arm. He wore a lightweight windbreaker, and she thought she spotted the keys in one of the hand-warmer pockets. She opened up the front passenger door of the Tesla and motioned for Frank to get inside. "Why don't I take your jacket? The car's a bit stuffy."

"Oh, okay." He shrugged out of it and handed it to her.

Julia passed the coat to Aaron and made sure the part with the keys landed in his hand. Then she opened the back door so that Toby could climb inside. Hopefully Toby's dirty paws wouldn't destroy the interior, but she supposed that was the last thing that mattered now. But when she saw the car seat base, she realized her error. "I'll need to drive Jack, too, won't I? Or does Martha's Impala have a car seat?"

"It doesn't, as far as I know." Aaron unclicked the car seat from the stroller and settled him in the back. "I'll trade you. Jack for Toby."

"I didn't realize you two were married," said Officer Dillan.

"We're not." Aaron bumped his head on the roof of the car. "I only met Julia last week."

"My mistake." Officer Dillan ripped off the piece of paper attached to the electronic device she held and passed it to Julia. "Here's Mr. Reynolds's ticket. I'm sorry to be harsh, but it might be better in the long run for him to have this on his record."

"Thank you, Officer Dillan." Julia stashed the ticket in her pocket. "I'll see that his wife gets it."

Officer Dillan put her hand on her hip with a nod at Aaron. "You probably want to get home to *your* wife, too, I assume?"

He shook his head. "I'm not married."

"My mistake." Officer Dillan looked up at Aaron and fluttered her lashes. "Are you new in town? I haven't seen you around."

"Brand spanking new." Aaron grinned awkwardly and leaned against his car. "I'm still learning my way around."

Julia had heard enough. Sure, it was interesting settling the question once and for all about Aaron's marital status, but she didn't want to stand around and watch the two of them flirt. "I'm taking Frank home," she said, interrupting them. "Can I please have the key?"

"Oh, sorry." Aaron wiggled his hand in his pocket and pulled out the key fob a second later. "The Tesla will drive as long as this is in the vehicle. Step on the brake to start it. Reverse and drive are on the right wand. Push the silver button to put it in park. I'll make sure Toby gets home in one piece." He looked anxiously in the back seat. "Be careful driving home. It's getting dark."

Julia rolled her eyes. "I'm an excellent driver. We'll be home in two minutes." She marched around the car and climbed into the driver's seat.

"I didn't know you bought a new car," said Frank.

Julia stepped on the brake, and the headlights flickered on. She put the car into reverse. "This one's a loaner." She watched the huge backup-camera screen as she drove in reverse.

"Well, when you're ready to buy a new one, let me know, and I'll come to the dealership with you."

"Thank you, Frank. That's a kind offer."

"Don't mention it, Waverley. That's what neighbors are for."

Julia winced. She didn't know which hurt worse: Frank not remembering who she was, or being mistaken for her mother. She put the car into drive. "I'm not Waverley; I'm her daughter, Julia."

"That's right. That's what I said." Frank turned away and looked out the window.

They crossed the train tracks and drove up Main Street, past where Martha's green Impala was parked on the left-hand side of the road. Aaron wasn't there yet. At least Frank's parking job looked decent. He hadn't jumped the curb or hit anyone. Frank was gazing at Main Street whizzing by. "How are you feeling?" she asked.

"Fine. Just fine." He pointed through the glass. "Look, the Nuthatch Bakery. I love that place."

"Me too. It's a great spot to eat lunch."

Frank looked at her. "Have you had their chowder in that bread thingy?"

"The bread bowl? Yes, it's delicious." Julia turned on her blinker and prepared to turn left onto Ninth. Her shoulders relaxed. *Frank must not be too bad off if he can talk about chowder,* she hoped. Still, she didn't know enough about Alzheimer's disease to understand whether that was normal. Maybe she could stop by Paige's Pages tomorrow and purchase a book about it.

"I used to take the kids to the Nuthatch on Saturday mornings for doughnuts when they were little," said Frank. "It was an easy way to give Martha the morning off."

"That's sweet." Julia turned left. "My dad used to take me out for doughnuts too."

They pulled into the Reynoldses' driveway a minute later. Julia put the car in park. Martha rushed out the front door before Julia had even opened her door. Frank undid his seat belt and struggled to open the door until Martha opened it for him.

"Oh, Frank!" Martha threw her arms around him in an enormous hug. "You sure did give me a fright."

"What do you mean? All this fuss for nothing."

"What are you talking about, you old goofball? You worried me sick. Why'd you take my car keys? Where did you go?"

Julia, still in the driver's seat, caught Martha's eye and slipped her the parking ticket while her hands were still behind Frank's back.

"I was at the beach." Frank pointed at Julia with his thumb. "Down at Harper Landing Beach with Waverley's daughter."

"I'm taking you inside now and warming up your dinner. The chicken's cold, you've been gone so long." Martha grabbed Frank's elbow, helped him out of the car, and steered him up the driveway to the front porch. She looked over her shoulder at Julia, mouthed, "Thank you," and put the parking ticket in her pocket.

Julia waved and then turned around to check on Jack. He had fluttered his eyes open as soon as the car had stopped. The cutie-pie popped his pacifier up and down and stared at her intently. "Well, kiddo," she said. "You did great through all of that. No diaper explosions, no crying jags—you must have been as worried about your grandpa as I was." She wiggled his toes. "And now it's just you and me." There still wasn't any sign of Aaron. "Your uncle's too busy with Officer Dillan." Julia struck a pose, fluffing her hair and batting her eyelashes.

Jack spit his pacifier out and laughed. His tongue stuck out, and drool dribbled down his chin. He waved his tiny fists in the air and giggled.

"Oh, you like that, do you?" Julia reached back and wiped spit off his face with the bib. "You and your uncle are both suckers for flirts, it would seem." She covered her eyes with her hands and flipped them open. "Peekaboo!" Jack was in stitches now; he was chortling so hard. Julia had never made a baby laugh before, and it made her feel powerful—like she had superwoman abilities that until now she'd never unleashed. "Peekaboo," she said again and again, to Jack's delight. She might have gone on playing forever, except there was a rap on the driver's side window that interrupted the merriment. When she looked up, she saw Aaron staring at her, his emerald-green eyes full of mischief.

"That's quite the performance," he said as he opened her door.

"Jack seems to agree with you." Julia tried to exit the car, but Toby jumped into her lap and whacked her in the nose with his wagging tail. "Ahh! Toby, get down!" Julia shoved him back down to the pavement. "Sorry," she said when she finally stood up. "He's a dog school dropout. I need to hire him a personal tutor because he never listens."

"Toby was fine with me on the way home." Aaron snapped his fingers and pointed at the Labrador. "Toby, sit!" The dog immediately obeyed.

"Wow." Julia knit her eyebrows together. "It's like you speak canine."

Aaron shrugged. "We raised Portuguese water dogs growing up."

"Portuguese water dogs?" Julia handed Aaron the key and took back Toby's leash.

"They're like poodles, only less froufrou. But my parents never trained the dogs themselves. That was what the dog nanny was for."

"You're making that up. There's no such thing as a dog nanny."

Aaron grinned and rubbed the stubble of his chin with his right hand. "Okay, actually Greta was a dog trainer, but Sara and I called her the *dog nanny* behind her back because she worked the same hours as our real nannies did—at least when our dogs were puppies. Greta only stuck around until they were nine months or so. Then she was off to another job."

Something clicked in Julia's mind. "Sara . . . as in Jared's wife, Sara? She was your sister?"

Aaron nodded. "That's right. I thought Martha must have told you."

Julia shook her head. "No, when you said Jack was your nephew, I thought it was a term of endearment."

"Sorry for the confusion," said Aaron. "I'm still working out how to explain it to people."

"The dog nanny is hard to explain too. Where'd you grow up, Mercer Island?" asked Julia, referring to the exclusive island where Bill Gates lived. But then she remembered that Jared and Sara's memorial service had been on the East Coast and felt stupid.

"No, Rumson, New Jersey." Aaron leaned against his car. "Where did you grow up?"

Julia pointed to one house over. "Right there. The one with roses along the fence."

Aaron whistled. "A real picket fence. I thought those only existed in fairy tales."

"Fairy tales and small towns like this one." Julia wrapped the leash around her wrist. "I never had a dog growing up, but I watch every YouTube video on dog training I can find." Toby was already standing up again, sniffing the tires of Aaron's car. Julia yanked the leash and pulled him down.

"Dog training's not so hard. You just need to stick up for yourself. Try it now. Get him to sit."

Julia scrunched up her face. "Sometimes I can get him to sit, but not always. He does better when I have treats in my pocket." She stared into the Labrador's eyes. "Toby, sit."

The dog ignored her, sniffing a trail of ants on the driveway instead.

"Point at him this time, and lift up your finger. Speak it like you mean it."

Julia took a deep breath and tried again. "Toby, sit!" This time she did the hand motion too. Toby looked up at her and dropped his butt to the ground. "Good boy!" Julia patted his head, her fingers massaging his soft brown fur.

In the back seat of the car, Jack began to fuss. "Uh-oh." Aaron stood up straight again. "I better go. I'll call Martha when I get home to make sure everything's all right. She's probably busy settling Frank right now."

Julia zipped up the polar-white fleece she wore. "Jared was your business partner, right?"

"Yup." Aaron's broad shoulders sagged. "He was."

"I'm sorry."

"Yeah, me too." Aaron looked up at the front windows of the house, where a light shone through the curtain. "I better get Jack to bed. Thanks for your help tonight." He hopped in the car before she had the chance to reply. She stood there on the driveway and watched Aaron and the baby drive away.

When the Tesla crested the hill, Julia and Toby trotted down the driveway and up the sidewalk to the gate in her picket fence. Her front yard smelled like roses, and the evening shade colored everything in a golden glow. Her thoughts swirled around Aaron. He'd certainly made her surprise evening with Frank easier to handle, and she wished she knew more about him. He was Jared's trusted friend; that much was clear. Jared had chosen Aaron as guardian for a reason, and after seeing Aaron spring into action to help Frank tonight, Julia knew it had been a wise choice.

A shiver of hope raced across her body from her head to her toes when she thought about Aaron being single. But then she remembered how Aaron had acted around the might-have-been-a-model police officer. Julia wasn't anything special. She looked across her fence to the sun setting behind the Reynoldses' house and sighed. There was one thing she knew for sure. Nobody ever noticed the girl next door.

CHAPTER EIGHT

It was three o'clock in the morning, and Aaron was finishing a load of laundry. He sat on the washing machine, holding Jack in his arms and feeding him a bottle. Aaron tipped the bottle back to the perfect angle so that air wouldn't fill the nipple and give the baby gas. The steady whir of the spin cycle provided white noise and helped Jack fall asleep. The baby kept drifting off and then opening his eyes again to suck. Hopefully any second now he'd fall asleep completely. Aaron yawned, desperately wishing he was in his cozy bed instead of the utility room. But at least he'd dealt with Julia's blazer so it wasn't ruined. He'd applied a stain stick as soon as he'd gotten home from finding Frank but had forgotten to toss the garment into the wash until the middle of the night when he'd woken up to give Jack a bottle. If only every problem was as easy to fix.

Martha and Frank needed his help. He could see that clearly, and he was willing to step up, but the more he thought about it, the more annoyed he became with Martha's secrecy. It must have been tremendously painful for her to deal with Frank's memory loss on her own. Why hadn't she told him? Maybe because Aaron wasn't part of their family—not really. Jack was family, but not Aaron. He pulled the bottle away from Jack's lips and watched to see what the baby would do. At first Jack looked like he might drift completely to sleep, but then he roused. Jack's lips rooted back and forth in search of the bottle. Aaron plugged it back in.

Not being part of Martha's inner circle didn't surprise him. In his experience, people used family ties to manipulate and exclude each other. *Do what your family says, or you don't belong. Go to this school. Don't go to that school. Live up to your parents' expectations or else.* The only family member he had ever trusted was Sara. So if Martha wanted to keep secrets, that was her choice. It was none of Aaron's business. He had a baby to raise, after all.

Or was it his business? Aaron yawned as fatigue overwhelmed him. Did Jack make it his business? If Sara were here, she'd do everything in her power to help her in-laws, even if it meant butting in. Martha and Frank weren't Aaron's relations, but they *were* Jack's grandparents, and of course Martha was a much better grandma than his own mother, Lorraine. Frank too. Sure, he'd forgotten who Jack was tonight, but at least he had an excuse. Aaron's father, Darren, had only seen Jack once, and that was at the memorial service.

Thinking about Jack's grandparents frustrated him, but when his thoughts floated back to Julia, he smiled. He told himself it was because he was washing her blazer, but really it was because of how glad he'd been to see her standing there on the beach holding Frank's hand. Her fleece jacket had been the color of snow, and her hiking shorts had shown off well-toned legs. It was like she'd stepped off the page of yet another outdoor adventure catalog—Patagonia this time, or the North Face.

Why hadn't Jared ever mentioned his childhood neighbor? Aaron recalled meeting a few of Jared's friends at the wedding—only a handful of people had flown to Jersey. Julia hadn't been among them, or Aaron would have remembered. He was sure of that. She had a natural beauty that glowed from the inside out. Plus, she was kind. Maybe that was why she was so gorgeous. Julia had saved his butt twice in one day. Jack's butt, to be technical about it. Aaron looked down at the baby, who was finally nodding off for good. He set the bottle on the dryer and threw a burp cloth over one shoulder. There was a danger that burping the baby would wake him up but an even greater risk that Jack might puke after eating.

As gently as possible, Aaron shifted Jack into position over his shoulder and tapped him on the back. A minute later, he heard a pop of air that meant success. Aaron walked carefully back upstairs to the second floor and laid Jack down in the bassinet next to his bed. The baby was usually pretty good about sleeping two or three hours on his own. Probably around five o'clock, he'd wake up, then rest a while longer if he snuggled on Aaron's chest.

The problem was, once Jack was down, Aaron felt wide awake. He felt like he'd drunk three cups of coffee. His mind raced with a thousand plans and worries. Even idle thoughts such as *Did Mom secretly dislike Portuguese water dogs?* flipped through his mind. Insomnia was the cruelest part of parenting an infant. The baby book Aaron had read said it was because being a parent put your hormones on high alert for any type of danger. He was definitely wound up. There was no way he could fall asleep now. Instead, he reached for his computer.

His search history was still queued up with articles about nipples and gassy babies, but soon Aaron was searching for what he really wanted to know—more about Julia. He typed in her name—Julia Harper—along with *Sweet Bliss* and *Harper Landing* and eagerly scanned the results. Her Facebook profile picture was a shot of her and Toby. They sat in front of a Christmas tree glittering with lights. Julia wore a blue sweater the color of midnight, and Toby had on a bow tie around his collar. It said she was a University of Washington graduate and owner of Sweet Bliss.

Aaron scrolled through Julia's Facebook feed but couldn't see anything. All her content was set to private. He thought about turning the computer off and trying to fall asleep, but he was just exhausted enough to make a decision he probably wouldn't have made in daylight. Aaron clicked out of his own Facebook profile and typed in the info for Jared's. As the executor to Jared's estate, Aaron had access to all his passwords. The only thing he'd done with them was share Jared and Sara's joint obituary, linked together in one post. He supposed he should have included a picture of Jack, but he hadn't because it hurt too much.

Now that Aaron was viewing Jared's feed, he could see everything on Julia's profile because they were Facebook friends. She wasn't someone who posted frequently, but when she did post, it was usually a picture of her dog or the latest flavor creation at Sweet Bliss. He wondered if the dairy-free Pineapple Dream would bother his stomach, because it looked delicious. Aaron had spent eighteen years suffering from gastrointestinal issues before realizing that dairy and sugar bothered him.

Scrolling back through time, Aaron discovered the obituary for Julia's mother. Waverley had passed away from lung cancer last fall, only a few months before the accident. There was an outpouring of condolences from Julia's friends on the statement about losing her mother. "Losing a parent is hard," Julia had written. "Losing a second parent is crushing." Aaron leaned back on his pillows and squeezed his eyes shut. He assumed Julia and her mother must have been close, based on what he read. He looked at her Facebook history again. The first picture Julia had posted of Toby was a month after her mother had died. "That's one way to overcome grief," one of her friends had commented, and Aaron agreed. His eyes drifted over to the bassinet at the side of his bed, where the baby slept. He didn't know how he would have survived the past four months without Jack.

Feeling more relaxed now, Aaron thought about trying to fall asleep, but since he was already logged into Jared's account, he kept going, scrolling through Julia's Facebook feed, hungry for each new detail he gleaned. She'd been in numerous weddings and must have an entire closet in her house dedicated to bridesmaid dresses by now. Last year on the Fourth of July, she'd passed out free popsicles to all the Girl Scouts who had marched in the parade. Apparently, the Boy

Scouts had gotten squat. No, that wasn't true. Someone had posted a comment underneath the picture that showed her passing them out to boys as well.

The Christmas before last, Julia and her mom had gone to Victoria, British Columbia, for a holiday. They'd stayed at the Fairmont Empress and had high tea on Christmas Eve. Did that mean she didn't have any brothers or sisters? Aaron searched for Waverley's obituary again, skimmed the paragraphs about her winning multiple beauty pageants, and confirmed that she only had one child. It said that she had died of lung cancer from secondhand smoke. He wondered if Julia felt alone, now that she was the last Harper left in Harper Landing.

Aaron dived deeper and deeper into Julia's past until he found pictures of her from college. She'd gone to Italy for her junior year and interned at a gelato shop in Florence. "This is the most delicious way to earn money while studying abroad," she had written, captioning a picture of herself wearing an apron and holding a scoop of mint-green gelato. Her blonde hair was plaited into a long braid that fell almost to her waist. In several of the pictures, there was a dark-eyed Italian guy about her age, with his arm around her shoulders or embracing her in a courtyard. Aaron skimmed past those photos quickly and was glad when the Italian Romeo was gone.

After twenty minutes of diving into the deepest recesses of Julia's Facebook archive, he found a picture from her five-year high school reunion. It was a group shot of a bunch of people he didn't recognize, except for Jared. Sitting next to Julia, a massive smile on his face, was his best friend. It must have been right around the time that Big Foot Paleo had been getting off the ground. Jared wore a sweatshirt with the original Sasquatch logo on it. He held a lettuce-wrapped burger in two hands and was laughing at something. Julia was slightly sunburned and eating a hot dog. They sat at a picnic table at a park with tall green trees in the background. Aaron was too exhausted to think straight, and the photograph was more than he could handle. His eyelids felt too heavy to keep open. He tapped the touch pad, liked the picture, and closed the computer. Aaron didn't wake up again until five hours later.

It was nine o'clock, and Jack was screaming his head off. Normally the baby didn't wail the moment he woke, but this time he did. Aaron lurched up, his heart racing. "What's the matter?" He looked all around the room, trying to get his bearings. It took a second for him to remember that he was in his new place and not in his old apartment in Palo Alto. When he saw what time it was, Aaron couldn't believe his eyes. This was the longest stretch Jack had ever slept without waking up. That explained why the poor baby was crying so hard. His diaper was sopping wet. Aaron even needed to wash the bassinet sheet and wipe down the mattress protector.

"It's okay, little buddy." Aaron scooped him up and brought him across the hallway to the nursery, where the changing table was. "I'll get you cleaned up and ready for the day." He spent several frustrating minutes unsnapping snaps. That was it, he decided. From now on, Jack was only sleeping in pajamas with zippers. As soon as Jack was diaper-free, the baby reached for his feet and giggled. Then he peed directly into Aaron's pursed lips.

"Dang it!" Aaron slapped his own face, trying to protect himself from the spray. It was too late. He tried not to retch as he blindly patted around the changing table for the box of wipes. As soon as he found it, he stuffed his fingers into the opening, and the plastic sliced his knuckles. "Ouch!" Aaron pulled out the wipes and mopped off his face. There was urine everywhere, including on the white T-shirt he'd worn to bed. He stripped it off and tossed it into the clothing hamper next to the diaper pail.

He sighed and took a deep breath. He couldn't be mad at an infant, no matter how annoyed he felt. "Let's try this again," said Aaron. He put a fresh diaper on Jack as quickly as possible and fastened the side tape. Then he suited Jack up in a lounge outfit with baseball-playing teddy bears.

"You know," said Aaron as he picked up Jack in one arm, "before you hosed me down, I was about to tell you how proud I was of the amazing job you did sleeping last night. Five whole hours at a time!" He gave his nephew a tiny fist bump. "Stupendous job, buddy. Let's get you a bottle to celebrate."

Aaron made his way to the kitchen, where he mixed up some formula and assembled a bottle while a fresh pot of coffee brewed. Feeding Jack was the priority, but Aaron was also starving. Eggs, hash browns, and avocado would be the next step. They settled down in the armchair in front of the television. Twenty minutes later, he heard a car pull up in the driveway just as Aaron was burping the baby.

"Who could that be?" Aaron stood up and walked to the front window. He pulled back a curtain and saw Martha getting out of her green Impala. Frank wasn't with her. "What the hell?" he muttered before remembering it was Saturday. He hurried down the hallway to his bedroom, laid Jack in the middle of his bed, and put on the first shirt he could find from a pile of dirty laundry on the floor. Aaron couldn't believe Martha had left Frank home alone, especially after what had happened last night. Not that it was his place to judge, but still . . . Aaron picked up Jack and raced back down the hall to the stairs and to the front door.

"Martha," Aaron said as he threw the door open. "Sorry to keep you waiting."

"No problem." She smiled and reached for the baby, then cuddled him in her arms. Jack grabbed hold of one of her tight gray curls. "Naughty, naughty." Martha tugged her head to the side and disentangled herself.

"Is Frank okay?"

"Frank's fine." Martha hugged Jack closer and rocked side to side.

Fine? "Come on upstairs. There's coffee." Aaron led the way up the short landing to the second floor. "I'm surprised you're here. I would have totally understood if you'd canceled."

"Cancel Grandma Day?" Martha kissed Jack's cheek. "Never."

Aaron took two mugs from the cabinet. They both had the current Big Foot Paleo logo on them, a Sasquatch wearing sunglasses and running shoes. He poured coffee into each cup and offered one to Martha. "But seriously, where's Frank?"

"I drop Frank off at church every Saturday morning to meet with his men's Bible study group. They all go out to lunch afterward, and one of them drives Frank home. It's an outing Frank looks forward to all week." Martha took a sip of coffee and grimaced. "Got any milk?"

"Sorry. I drink mine black, so I forgot." Aaron opened the fridge. "I have Nutpods and coconut milk. Which would you rather?"

"What's a Nutpod?" Martha raised her eyebrows. "That sounds obscene." Aaron showed her the carton of paleo creamer. She sniffed it and shrugged. "Might as well try something new," she said as she added a couple of tablespoons to her java.

"What about the rest of the week?" Aaron asked. "Can Frank still be home alone?"

"Oh yes." She sat down at the kitchen table. "Well, at least I used to think so. But after last night, I'm not so sure anymore." She stared into her coffee mug. "Jessica says he needs to see an Alzheimer's specialist for an official diagnosis as soon as possible, and I agree." Martha squeezed Jack.

Aaron felt honored that Martha was finally confiding in him, but also wary. What did becoming part of Martha's inner circle mean? He couldn't replace Jared. Sure, he could assist with Frank, but not like their son. Frank already had moments where he didn't know Aaron. Still, he had to try. Aaron pulled up a chair next to her. "I think seeing a doctor is a great idea. It will be good to get clarity."

Martha frowned. "I suppose."

"What can I do to help? If this is your only day off from being with Frank, I don't want to steal it from you."

"Don't be ridiculous." Martha kissed the top of Jack's head. "My grandchildren mean everything to me. Jessica's kids are too old to want to hang out with me anymore unless I take them shopping at the mall. I have to get my snuggles in while they last."

Aaron sighed. "I just feel so selfish. I had no idea what you were dealing with at home. I've been so self-absorbed with my situation that I didn't notice."

"Why would you?" Martha shrugged. "You only saw Frank in his prime that one weekend at the wedding. It's hard for people who've known him all his life to see how far he's slipped, let alone someone new to the family."

New to the family? That was it, then; he was officially an honorary Reynolds. Pride tainted by grief washed over him.

Martha held Jack up so he could stand on her knees. Now that the baby was three months old, he loved to stand. "Frank does great in the mornings, which is why he has no problem at his Bible study group. It's in the evening that he fades. But what are you sitting around here for? This is your free time. Shouldn't you be running all the way to Canada by now?"

Aaron grinned. "Canada's a little out of my mileage zone." He finished the last drop of his coffee. "I would like to go for a run, though. Are you sure you don't mind?"

"Get out of here," Martha said with mock sternness. "Don't come back until this afternoon."

Aaron loaded his mug into the dishwasher so that Martha wouldn't be tempted to clean up after him. He grabbed a couple of protein bars and his refillable water bottle. Then he trotted back to his room to put on his newest running outfit. *After all,* he mused, *you never know who you might run into at the beach.*

CHAPTER NINE

Barre class at the gym, a visit to Paige's Pages right when it opened to buy some books about Alzheimer's disease—Julia's Saturday morning was going strong. Now she was preparing herself a kale-and-strawberry smoothie with greek yogurt and chia seeds. Toby nudged her knee as she stood in front of the blender, guilt-tripping her for not taking him on a walk beyond just a quick pee outside. He was constantly underfoot in the kitchen, hoping that she'd drop a morsel of food. It was one of the many bad behaviors they needed to work on together.

"Don't give me that look." She poured her leafy-green drink into a tall glass. "I can't take you to the dog park anymore because last time you almost swam out to sea." Julia walked over to the counter and pulled out a barstool to sit down. "And I just took you on a long walk last night." She looked across the kitchen to the clock on the oven. "Besides, I need to swing by Sweet Bliss and double-check that the vanilla showed up and that Tara was able to prepare a batch of Tahitian Paradise."

Toby whimpered and looked at her accusingly.

"Okay," Julia admitted. "You don't know how harried Saturdays are, because I've never allowed you in the store. But trust me; the weekends are packed, especially in summer. Sweet Bliss needs me more than you do." She poked a metal straw up and down in her drink to break up a piece of fruit the blades had missed. "When I get home tonight, we'll go out—I promise." As soon as she said it, she felt ridiculous. Not only was she talking to her dog, but her hot night out on the town involved a Labrador. Julia sighed and pulled out her phone. She'd scroll through Facebook for a few minutes while she finished her smoothie and then hop in the shower.

But when she saw her notifications, she inadvertently gasped, causing her to choke. Her airway burned from the accidental sludge going the wrong way down her throat. Toby whined and paced around in circles, sensing that something was wrong. "I'm okay, boy." She coughed and pounded her chest. "It went down the wrong tube, is all. Nothing to worry about." She looked at her phone one more time. There, in her notifications, was the alert telling her that Jared had liked her picture.

How was that possible? He'd died in January. How could he have liked her post now? Julia removed the elastic band holding her ponytail in place and massaged her scalp. Maybe it was a Facebook glitch, a delay from when Jared had clicked on a reaction option to when it registered in her feed. Yeah, that made the most sense. But still, it unnerved her. She clicked on the notification to see what the post was about in the first place.

It was a picture from their five-year reunion down at the park next to Harper Landing Beach. Julia had been on the planning committee, since she lived in town, and had arranged the picnic shelter rental. There was a barbecue, coolers of drinks, and potluck salads and desserts. "I've met the most amazing woman," she remembered Jared telling her. "You'll adore her. Sara loves to travel and also knows how to knit."

At the time, Julia was obsessed with knitting. She even brought fingerless gloves she was working on to the barbecue.

"That's awesome," Julia had said, when what she'd really wanted to say was, "*I* love to travel. *I* love to knit. Why don't you ever notice *me*?"

Now, Jared had noticed her—at least her Facebook post from five years ago. It was just weird that it had popped up in her feed now.

"Consider yourself lucky you don't have to deal with social media," Julia told Toby as she plugged her phone into the charger. "It can make life so much more complicated."

After she'd rinsed out her glass and deposited it in the dishwasher, Julia ran upstairs to shower and change before work. She put on a pair of skinny jeans and a yellow tank top that showed off all the tiny muscles she'd worked at barre class that morning. It took her a while to blow-dry her hair, and by the time she came back downstairs, there were only thirty minutes left before she needed to walk to the shop. That was the perfect amount of time to spend with Toby, working on his doggy manners.

Julia still couldn't believe that Toby had flat out ignored her commands last night in front of Aaron. Half an hour a day teaching him to do better was the rule from now on. She tried to fill her pockets with treats, but her jeans were too tight, so she held on to the bag instead. "Toby," Julia called, "come." She stood in front of the fireplace, right underneath the portrait of Waverley that Harrison had commissioned a local artist to paint for a wedding present. The picture showed Waverley crowned as Miss Washington State. Her hair was lighter than Julia's and looked like spun gold cascading down her bare shoulders. A rhinestone crown sparkled on her head. The strapless pink dress she wore was tight in all the right places and showed off her slim figure. Waverley's eyebrows had been plucked into an angle that was popular at the time and gave her the look of someone who was inwardly judging everyone who crossed her path. Julia knew what it felt like to bear the brunt of that judgment. She'd lived with it every day for twenty-seven and a half years.

When Toby didn't come after Julia called him, she could hear her mother's voice in the back of her head. *I told you a dog didn't belong in this house. How could you be so stupid?*

Julia squared her shoulders and jostled the bag of liver treats. She didn't know where Toby was, but he might still be upstairs since he'd followed her up to her room when she'd taken a shower. "Toby!" She slapped her thigh with the palm of her hand a few times to get his attention. Too bad she couldn't whistle on her fingers like Aaron. Pretty soon, she heard the jingle of a collar and the sound of Labrador claws scratching the wood floors. Toby barreled into the living room at top speed and plowed into her.

"Oof!" Julia hollered, knocked backward. The liver treats flew out of her hand as she threw her arms behind her to brace her fall. She landed hard on the hearth, her tailbone smacking against the brick. The fireplace tools wobbled and fell over to the side. Julia sat there, too stunned to move, as she tried to ascertain her injuries. It felt like she'd been kicked in the butt. Hopefully nothing was broken. She gingerly rose to her feet, crouched over, and grasped her backside. When she stood up all the way, her head whacked the mantel, and she saw stars. Her father's rotary award, a solid cube of glass, slid off the mantel and hit her head before smashing into smithereens. "Ouch," she cried, tears rolling down her face. Julia stumbled to the couch and lay on her side, trying to master the pain. It was then that she realized her mother's portrait had also careened off the mantel and landed dead center on the wrought iron fireplace tools. The stoker had pierced straight through Waverley's crown.

Toby whined and jumped up onto the couch and curled up into a ball at her feet. Julia tucked her toes underneath his warm fur and closed her eyes. It probably wasn't a good idea to fall asleep. What if she had a concussion? But Julia couldn't help it. Her eyelashes fluttered, and she drifted off.

The sound of the doorbell woke her up a while later. Julia didn't know how long she'd been napping. Toby morphed from snuggle pup to warrior pup. He leaped off the couch and barked viciously, which made Julia's throbbing headache even worse. She pressed her hand to the back of her skull and was surprised that her scalp was so tender. She wasn't sure if it was morning or night—or even what day it was. All she knew was that someone was at the door, and if she didn't get up to answer it, Toby would never stop barking.

"I'm coming," she called out in a weak voice. When Julia stood up, her bum hurt. She walked a few steps forward, and it felt like her backside was bruised. She plodded along, her bare feet on the cold wood floor, and didn't stop until her toes touched the wool rug that graced the entryway. "Who is it?" She stared through the peephole but didn't recognize the back of the head she was staring at. The person standing on her front porch was looking out at the street, not the door. "Who's there?" Julia tried again.

"Julia? It's me, Aaron." He turned around to face the house and smiled. A baby hung from a carrier on his chest, fast asleep. Aaron held a hanger with her gray blazer on it.

Still feeling confused, Julia opened the door. At least Toby had quieted down now. Instead of alerting the neighborhood to a dangerous invasion, he licked Aaron's knees. "Hi," said Julia. When she shifted her weight from one foot to another, her tailbone hurt so severely that she winced.

"Are you okay?" Aaron wrinkled his forehead and looked at her with concern.

"Yeah, um . . . I woke up from a nap, and I don't remember falling asleep. I have a wicked headache, though." She waved them inside. "Come on in."

"I don't want to bother you." Aaron held up the hanger. "I was in the neighborhood and thought I'd return this."

"Thanks." Julia took the blazer off the hanger and couldn't figure out where to put the garment, so she dropped it on the ground. "Why did you have my blazer?" Everything around her was becoming white and hazy, like the room was melting into a giant puddle of frozen yogurt. "Like Tahitian Paradise," she murmured.

"What?"

"I think I need to sit down." The words were barely out of her mouth before she collapsed on the rug.

First there was white, and then only darkness. But Julia felt better now that she was horizontal. "Jared liked my picture," she mumbled.

"I'm sorry." Aaron crouched down next to her. "That was me. It was an accident."

"Tahitian Paradise . . ." Julia's face scrunched up in distress. "Where's the Tahitian Paradise?"

"Julia?" Aaron shook her shoulders, but she barely noticed. "Have you been drinking?"

Drinking. She thought of the smoothie caught in her throat, the chunky bits of strawberry that the blender couldn't cut. The way the kale burned in her airways. And then she was retching, right there on her mother's Turkish carpet. The one she'd brought home from an estate sale on Mercer Island. The one that Waverley had bought with the money earmarked for Julia's senior portraits.

Aaron grabbed Julia by the shoulders and lifted her up, the baby's feet kicking into her backside. When he propped her to sitting, she yelped. Toby nosed into them, whacking her with his tail and generally being a nuisance.

"Oh, sweet girl," said Aaron, holding back her hair. "What happened to you?"

"Vanilla . . . the vanilla needs to come from Tahiti. And the liver treats. They're everywhere."

"Okay, that makes no sense whatsoever, but you stay here while I go get some paper towels." Aaron leaned her gently against the wall. "Toby," he said sharply, pointing at the dog, "lie down." Toby obeyed and provided a wedge against Julia's leg that helped prevent her from falling over.

She didn't understand what was happening. She couldn't fathom why she was sitting on the floor in the entryway of the house. She wondered what her mother would say when she saw puke splattered across the ugly Turkish rug.

"Oh wowzers," Aaron called from the other room. "What happened in here?" He and the baby rushed back to her a moment later. Aaron knelt and gently touched her shoulder. "Did you hit your head? It looks like you had an accident."

Julia stared at him blankly. Did she hit her head? She touched the crown of her head, which stung. But it didn't hurt as much as her tush, which felt like it was badly bruised.

"Is it okay if I touch your hair?" Aaron asked. After Julia nodded, he carefully inspected the top of her head. "I don't see anything bleeding, but that doesn't mean you aren't experiencing a concussion. Nausea, disorientation, headache . . . this is taking me back to the days when I played soccer. I think we should take you to urgent care to be certain."

"Okay," said Julia uncertainly. "But first, we need to get the vanilla."

"What?"

"The vanilla. Where's the vanilla?"

"That makes no sense at all. I'm going to find your wallet. We'll need your insurance card." He left her for a few moments and came back with her worn leather purse. "Looks like you'll need some shoes too." He put the purse next to her and took off again.

Julia wondered if Aaron knew about shoe polish and how freshly shined shoes told the world that you mattered. She wished she had socks on. Her feet were cold. But not as cold as Tahitian Paradise, the vanilla-based flavor Sweet Bliss only served on Saturdays. But only if there was vanilla. Where was the vanilla?

"Success!" Aaron hustled down the stairs from Julia's bedroom. "I found your shoes."

"When did you go upstairs?" Julia asked him.

"A moment ago." He unballed a pair of socks and gave them to her. "Can you put these on?"

Julia started to nod but then winced again. Keeping her eyes closed, she pushed a foot into each sock. Before she knew what was happening, Aaron shoved her sneakers on and tied the laces. He slung the purse over his shoulder and helped her rise to stand. Julia spaced out after that. The next time she was aware of anything, it was the scratchy surface of her chair in the waiting room of the urgent care clinic in Lynnwood.

CHAPTER TEN

There was no way Julia was a secret day drinker who'd consumed so many glasses of Tahitian Paradise—whatever that was—that she'd blacked out. Aaron figured that a concussion was the most logical explanation for her behavior. Or, worse, that she was the victim of a home invasion and could have been assaulted. But when he had searched the downstairs for her shoes, he hadn't seen any broken windows or unlocked doors. Upstairs, her bedroom had been as neat as a pin, and the other bedrooms had been locked. That had seemed odd to him at the time, but he had been in too much of a rush to think about it. Now, as Aaron paced around the waiting room in circles, humming "Baby Beluga" to keep Jack happy, he considered those locked doors again. *That was weird*, he thought. *Who locks doors in their own home?*

It had been forty minutes since the medical assistant had wheeled Julia away. Aaron had filled out the insurance paperwork the best he could using her wallet. Between her driver's license and her insurance card, he knew way more personal information about her than he'd been able to find searching her Facebook feed last night. Her age and weight, for example. Aaron felt like a heel for knowing those details, but the intake forms had requested them. She also had a library card, a Costco card, and a gym membership. At the bottom of her purse was a small stone with the word *Onward* etched into it.

Jack began to fuss, so Aaron walked over to the glass window, where the baby could see his reflection. "Who's the cute baby?" he asked, waving at the window. "Hi there, Jack." Aaron smiled, and Jack grinned in response before leaning forward and chewing on the front of the infant carrier. It was more of a gumming, really, since Jack didn't have teeth yet. The fabric was damp with drool. Aaron made a mental note to wash it when he got home—in the delicate cycle. He felt proud for thinking of it—and also pathetic that flexing his newly acquired laundry knowledge made him feel proud.

"Excuse me, sir?" the receptionist at the front desk called out to get his attention. She wore a thin sweater over a polyester blouse and a thick layer of makeup. "You're the one who accompanied Julia Harper?"

"Yeah, that's right." Aaron crossed the room in long strides. "How is she?"

The receptionist sat behind the counter. Her fake eyelashes made her look like Bambi. "I don't know, but the doctor asked me to call her emergency contact person."

"What?" Aaron gripped the edge of the counter and then quickly removed his hands, worried he might bring germs home to Jack. He pumped a dab of hand sanitizer into his palms and rubbed vigorously. "That sounds serious."

"This is a standard procedure when a casual acquaintance brings a patient in. The problem is the primary emergency contact number on Ms. Harper's list is disconnected."

Aaron thought fast. Who would Julia have written down? The answer came to him a second later. "Was it her mother, Waverley Harper? She passed away last fall."

The receptionist nodded. "That explains things. Perhaps Ms. Harper didn't update her form yet." She tapped a pencil against her desk and made a phone call, blocking the receiver with her hand so that Aaron couldn't hear. "Okay," she said when she hung up. "The good news is that her second emergency contact person is on her way right now. You are free to go home."

"You're sending me away? Without telling me what's wrong?"

A line of people had formed behind Aaron. The receptionist looked past him to the next person who needed help. "I'm sorry, sir, but I can't violate HIPAA."

"I'm not going anywhere until I know that Julia's okay," Aaron said in a firm but polite voice. "I'll wait here for Julia's emergency person to come."

"As you wish." She nodded curtly.

By now, it was dinnertime, and Aaron was starving. He knew Jack was probably getting hungry, too, so he should get out a bottle. Before he sat down, though, he checked out the vending machine to see if there was anything remotely wholesome to eat. His stomach growled, demanding real food, not a food-like substance packed with soy, high-fructose corn syrup, and "natural" flavors that would give him cramps an hour later. Luckily, there was trail mix available. It had chocolate candies in it, but Aaron could pick them out. He unfolded his billfold for the cash and purchased his snack, as well as a bottle of water.

Jack began to fuss as soon as Aaron sat down on a vinyl chair in the waiting room. He wasn't crying so much as groaning out his displeasure that his exciting tour of the waiting room was over. "Hang on, little guy," Aaron said in a soothing voice. He dug into the diaper bag for the bottle. "Dinner's coming." Removing Jack from the infant carrier was tricky, but Aaron had become pretty good at it. He palmed the baby's front with one hand and unclicked the snaps with the other. Once Jack was disentangled, Aaron shimmied him out of the harness one shoulder at a time. He set the contraption on the chair next to him, leaned back in his seat, and cradled Jack in an upright position to feed him. "Dinner is served." Aaron inserted the nipple into the baby's mouth. Jack latched on and began gulping. "You were hungrier than I realized," said Aaron.

Now that his hands were full, he couldn't eat the trail mix. He stretched his left arm around so he could hold Jack and steady the bottle at the same time. Then he used his teeth to rip open the bag of nuts and dumped them in his mouth. The chocolate candies crunched under his teeth and tasted so good that he forgot all about things like red dye or the glycemic index. His sensitive GI tract would make him pay later for eating them, but hopefully he'd be home by then and close to his own toilet.

Aaron had no idea who Julia's second emergency contact might be. For all he knew, it might be an old boyfriend. He remembered the picture of her and her Italian Romeo and wrinkled his nose. Hopefully that guy was still in the Mediterranean, where he belonged. Aaron dumped another cluster of trail mix in his mouth. In the Bay Area, he'd always listed Sara and Jared as his emergency contacts on forms like these. But since moving here to Harper Landing, he hadn't found a new doctor, so he'd never figured out how to answer that question on medical forms. Jack had a local pediatrician, of course, but Aaron had been too overwhelmed to find a physician for himself.

The outer door to the waiting room opened, and a short middle-aged woman with shiny black hair hurried into the room. She looked familiar, but Aaron couldn't quite place her. One thing he'd noticed about Harper Landing was that he kept seeing the same people over and over again. It was like knowing people without really knowing them. The woman got in line and waited for her turn. It wasn't until she spoke that Jack realized that she was the owner of Paige's Pages, the local bookshop where he'd recently bought a book about cosleeping.

"I'm Paige Lu, here for Julia Harper," Paige told the receptionist.

"I'll let the doctor know you're here."

Aaron kept a secure hold on Jack and stood up. "I brought Julia in," he said, waving to get Paige's attention.

"I remember you," she chirped. "You're the one who rescued Toby."

"Guilty as charged. Did they tell you anything about Julia's condition? They won't give me any information because of HIPAA."

Paige sat down on the chair next to where the infant carrier lay. "The doctor said she has a mild concussion and a bruised tailbone and needs someone to stay with her overnight. I packed a bag before I left and put a TV dinner in the microwave for my husband, Bob, so I'm all set. As soon as they release her, I'll take her back to her house and spend the night so I can keep an eye on her."

Aaron wished fleetingly that he could be the one staying overnight with Julia but pushed that thought aside since it was impossible. "That's good." Aaron sat down and zipped up the diaper bag.

"Do you know what happened?"

"I'm not exactly sure." He described the scene in the living room, with the speared portrait and the knocked-over fireplace tools. "There was also an empty bag of dog treats on the floor," Aaron recalled. "But I didn't see any signs of forced entry."

"A mystery!" Paige clapped her hands together. "If it weren't for Julia being hurt, I'd say this was exciting. I'll see what I can figure out when I bring her home tonight."

"Hopefully you brought a sleeping bag with you for the couch, because all the upstairs doors are locked," he said before he realized how creepy that made him sound. "I mean, since we're talking about mysteries," he added.

"I've never been upstairs at Julia's house." Paige tapped her chin. "But that's interesting that you have."

"I was getting her shoes and socks."

"Of course you were." The corners of Paige's mouth turned up. "I have a pretty good idea of what might be in those locked rooms upstairs, even though I'm not certain, and believe me—it explains a lot about Julia."

"What's that supposed to mean?" Aaron had been preparing to leave, but curiosity got the better of him. He left the diaper bag where it was on the floor.

"How she constantly devalues her worth. Why she never sticks up for herself. How she's one of the smartest, kindest, most beautiful people I know—on the inside and out—but lets everyone in this town walk all over her, including her dog."

Aaron was shocked at how harsh Paige sounded. "I thought you two were friends," he said.

Paige folded her arms across her chest. "I *am* her friend. That's why it pains me to see people take advantage of her. Giving out donations to school auctions is one thing—that's good for business, and I do it too—but she should have raised the rents on half the properties she owned a long time ago." Paige eyed him up and down. "So don't you start taking advantage of her too."

"I would never." Aaron brushed his fingers through his hair. "Why would you even suggest that?"

Paige held out her hand and counted off her fingers. "First, you buy *Precious Little Sleep: The Complete Baby Sleep Guide for Modern Parents.* Next, you purchase *The Single Dad's Survival Guide* and *It Takes a Village.* Then you come in for *Colic Solved.*"

"Jack does *not* have colic. That was just background research."

Paige grunted and kept counting. "Then, you interrupt her workday with a poop explosion."

"I was desperate," he explained. "It was an emergency."

"Yeah right, buddy. It looks to me like you're exhausted, in over your head, and could use some help."

"So?" Aaron asked. "What's wrong with that? I *am* in over my head. I *do* need help." He felt his blood pressure rise.

"There's nothing wrong with any of that except that Julia will always say yes, because she says yes to everyone, and you'll be getting her hopes up for nothing." Paige opened her purse and took out a magazine.

"I'm not trying to get anyone's hopes up," said Aaron. But what he felt on the inside was, *There is no hope.* Hope was gone. Everything hopeful in his life had ended the moment Sara had died in the hospital, hooked up to machines. He had no business hoping that a woman like Julia would be interested in him.

Paige flipped open her magazine and held it in front of him. She pointed to a glossy colored picture. "This is you, right? Silicon Valley's most eligible bachelor from last year?"

Aaron shuddered like he always did every time he saw that picture of himself. He wore a tight gray T-shirt that showed off his biceps, faded jeans, and suede sneakers. The photographer had positioned him at an awkward angle sitting on the sandstone steps in front of Stanford's quad. What had been a wickedly uncomfortable pose turned out to be perfect on camera. The way he'd perched on the sandstone and sprawled out his legs exuded confidence and a nonchalant attitude that Aaron wasn't sure he had ever possessed, even back then. Sure, maybe that first week after the General Mills deal had gone through, Aaron had walked on air, but not normally.

Paige pointed to a highlighted paragraph. "It says right here that you have no interest in getting married." She held up the print closer to her face so she could read. "Palo Alto's newest millionaire is a confirmed bachelor who would rather do a triathlon in Half Moon Bay than settle down with long-term girlfriend, Leah Noble."

"Lies," Aaron sputtered. "I hate triathlons." It still burned him that Leah had whined to the journalist about all his faults. He never should have agreed to that interview.

"And the part about your long-term girlfriend?" Paige looked at him over the edge of the magazine. "Is that 'fake news' too?"

Aaron wrinkled his nose. "No. I have no interest in marrying Leah—that's for sure. And she's not my girlfriend anymore. We broke up in January."

Paige rolled up the magazine and stuffed it in her purse. "Just as I suspected. You're a serial monogamist who never actually commits. Well, move along, buddy, because I won't let Julia be your next doormat."

"Not that it's any of your business, but I'm not dating right now, and even if I were, I would never treat Julia like a doormat."

"How would you treat her, then?" Paige arched one eyebrow. "I mean, if you were to ask her out."

"Well, first of all, I wouldn't be able to ask her out because I'm kind of occupied." He shifted Jack from one arm to the other.

"I could babysit," Paige said quickly. "For the sake of argument, let's say Bob and I were babysitting. Where would you take her? She loves hiking, you know."

"No, I didn't know."

Paige nodded. "And rock climbing. Normally she goes to the climbing gym for the auto belays, but she loves outdoor climbing too. She even climbed in the Dolomites when she spent a year in Italy."

"I didn't know there was a climbing gym nearby."

"Yup." Paige leaned back in her chair. "I've never been, but Julia goes once or twice a month. She's also a regular at the Cascade Athletic Club down by the water. Did you know they have childcare there? You might want to check it out."

Aaron shook his head. "I prefer running outside."

Paige raised her eyebrows. "That's hard to do with a baby when it's raining."

"I bought a rain cover for the stroller."

"A rain cover." Paige snorted. "Right. Like that's going to help. You've spent too much time in California. But back to the topic—where would you go?"

"With the stroller?"

Paige let out an exasperated sigh. "No, silly, with Julia."

"Oh." Aaron tilted his head to the left and rubbed a knot in his shoulder. Paige was confusing the hell out of him. He wasn't sure if she was trying to scare him off or set him up. "I guess I'd take her to this restaurant I've wanted to try in Seattle, called Pure Food and Wine. Then maybe we'd come back to town and see a movie at that old-fashioned theater on Main Street."

Paige nodded her approval. "That sounds perfect. Julia would love that." She flipped back her hair. "Too bad I can't let you date her."

"I don't want to date her," Aaron said, louder than he'd intended. "I mean, not when she has a concussion. Shouldn't she focus on getting better?"

"Absolutely."

"Paige Lu?" called the receptionist. "You can come back now."

"That's me." Paige rose to her feet. She looked down at Aaron, who was still seated. "Thanks for bringing Julia to urgent care." She stroked the silky soft hair on top of Jack's head. "Good luck finding your village."

Aaron watched the older woman walk away with the medical assistant, feeling relieved and yet disappointed that Paige wasn't part of his and Jack's village. She was fierce, that was for sure, and Aaron wished that he had someone like her on his side.

CHAPTER ELEVEN

Even the baggy sweatpants she usually threw on over her swimsuit when she went to the gym and her old University of Washington Huskies sweatshirt couldn't make Julia feel better. She lay on the couch with Toby curled up at her feet and tried to make sense of what Paige and Bob were talking about. It had been twenty-four hours since the accident, and she was still having trouble processing information. There was a box of pad thai on the coffee table in front of her as well as a stack of napkins, but Julia wasn't hungry. Her stomach felt queasy, though it didn't churn enough to actually make her puke.

"The store was packed with the after-church crowd today." Bob picked up noodles with wooden chopsticks. The red flannel shirt he wore was the same color as his rosy cheeks. "That new display in the window with the miniature kayak is bringing people in." Bob owned an outdoor outfitter shop called Wanderer's Home, two stores down from Paige's Pages. He was an introvert who preferred Mother Nature to humans, so he rarely attended social events. But on his home turf, or with a select group of people, Bob was quite chatty. Julia always checked with him before she went on hikes so that someone knowledgeable would know where she was headed, in case she didn't come home.

"That's great." Paige slurped up a bite of noodles and finished chewing before continuing. "I didn't get a chance to call the bookshop for today's tally, but hopefully it was high."

"Should I do that too?" Julia asked. "Call my store?"

"I'm sure it can wait until tomorrow," said Bob.

"The doctor said it would take at least five days for you to recover from your concussion and that you're supposed to take it easy. I'm sure Tara can handle Sweet Bliss until then," said Paige.

Julia adjusted her position on the inflatable doughnut they'd given her at the hospital and winced when her bruised tailbone brushed against the back of the couch. "My side hurts from laying in this position, but it's even worse if I try to sit up all the way." She squeezed her eyes shut and breathed through it.

"Can you go through the chain of events with me again?" Paige asked. "What's the last thing you remember?"

"You and I were at that business lunch at the yacht club, and Walt was a jerk to me." Julia rubbed her temple.

"Yes, and after that, you walked home," Paige prompted. "You told me all about it. Do you remember who you ran into?"

"No." Julia stretched out her arm so that it dangled off the couch. "Sorry."

"Aaron Baxter. Jared's friend and business partner." Paige looked at Julia expectantly.

"I feel like you want me to say something, but I'm not sure what," said Julia.

"His baby had a diaper explosion?" Paige said it like it was a question before exchanging a worried glance with her husband.

"Oh," said Julia. "Yikes." She squeezed her eyes shut again.

Bob crumpled up his napkin and put it in his dish. "I'm going to take Toby for a walk. He probably wants to get out of the house."

At the mention of the word *walk*, Toby's ears perked up. When he heard Bob gather the leash from its hook next to the back door, he leaped off the couch. They took off a couple of minutes later.

"Bring a poop bag!" Julia called after them. "No, wait—bring two."

"At least you remember that," said Paige. "I'll consider that a good sign."

Julia moaned and grabbed her head. "Why is this happening to me?"

"Not being able to remember the twenty-four hours before a concussion is normal." Paige stood up and picked up the takeout trash. "Lucky for you, I know everything that happened to you after that Harper Landing Chamber of Commerce meeting, because you told me all about it when you stopped by my store to buy this book about Alzheimer's." Paige walked to the edge of the couch and picked up a book on the end table called *The 36-Hour Day*.

"Alzheimer's?" Julia panicked. "Oh no! Is that why I'm losing my memory?"

Paige sighed and collapsed in the easy chair. "No, sweetie, I just explained that to you. Your concussion is messing with your brain; that's all. The doctors said you'd get better." She spent the next ten minutes filling Julia in on the past forty-eight hours, beginning with the diaper explosion and going all the way to hanging out on the couch all day together and watching *Rick Steves' Europe* on PBS. Julia loved travel shows. The two semesters she'd spent in Italy had given her a taste of adventure, and she wanted more.

"Maybe if I look at Facebook, it'll jog my memory," said Julia. "Where's my computer?"

"I think I saw it in the kitchen. I'll go grab it." Paige came back a few moments later and waited until Julia had propped herself up before handing it to her.

The first thing Julia noticed when she opened Facebook was her notifications. "I got a friend request," she said, her heart skipping a beat. "From Aaron." She turned her computer around so that Paige could see. Aaron's profile picture was a picture of him with a marathon medal around his neck, standing in front of a giant cardboard cutout of a Sasquatch. The words **Big Foot Paleo** loomed behind him in giant letters. Aaron dripped with sweat, and it looked like every fiber of muscle in his body was taut with exertion. "Should I accept?" she asked Paige.

"Why are you asking me?" Paige responded. "You're an accomplished twenty-eight-year-old woman who can make her own decisions."

Julia sighed. "You're right," she said after a pause. "I'm just so confused right now."

"So don't make any decisions until your brain's up to snuff." Paige stood up and walked over to the empty mantel. "Maybe you can pick out something you love for this spot. Go down to one of the art galleries and choose a painting that speaks to your soul."

Julia's gazed drifted up to where her mother's portrait used to reside. *You stupid idiot,* she heard Waverley scold her. *That painting was priceless. Have you no respect?* The part of her brain that contained Waverley's lectures seemed untouched by her recent trauma.

"I wouldn't know what to pick." Julia looked back at her screen and scrolled through her notifications, most of which were people tagging her in pictures of Sweet Bliss creations they'd concocted themselves. "Looks delish," she wrote on their photographs. "Yum, yum." Her brain was at least up to that task. But when she got to a notification saying Jared had liked her picture, she clammed up again, completely unable to function.

"What's wrong?" Paige asked.

Julia shook her head. "Nothing," she said as she closed her computer.

Paige adjusted the headband she wore. "I think I should stay another night." She pointed at Julia. "You're not one hundred percent."

"I know, and that's okay. I probably won't be one hundred percent for at least a few more days." Julia tucked her feet underneath her knees. "But I don't need you to babysit me. I've bothered you enough as it is."

Paige swatted her hand in the air like she was brushing off the comment. "It's no bother at all. It's good for Bob to have to make his own breakfast occasionally. It reminds him how much he loves me."

"But I don't need you here anymore." Julia sat up straighter and tried to look convincing. "I'm on the mend now, and I won't do anything stupid. I'll lay around on the couch, and order takeout, and take lots of naps." She leaned back a bit more and tweaked her injured tailbone in the process. Her smile turned to a grimace as she quickly shifted positions. "If I need anything, I can call Martha and Frank."

"We just learned that Frank has Alzheimer's now, remember?" Paige prompted.

"Oh, that's right. I mean, I don't remember him being lost, but I remember you telling me about that." Julia picked up the book on the end table. "I'll read up on it."

"Tomorrow," said Paige. "Tonight, you rest." She clicked on the remote, and Rick Steves blared to life again, describing a trip to Munich.

They watched for twenty more minutes, and Julia began to feel better. Her mind felt clearer and less fuzzy. "I always wanted to go to Munich," she said. "But the Eurail trip from Italy was twelve hours. It seemed too far to go."

"You've got your whole life ahead of you to do fun trips like that. Maybe you could sign up for a tour when you feel better."

"Maybe I will." Julia pulled an afghan over her knees. "I'm still grateful you talked my mother into letting me go to Italy junior year. I'll thank you for that forever."

Paige chuckled and pointed to the beer garden that was flashing across the screen. "Alcohol helped that conversation, as I recall."

"Beer?" Julia asked in a shocked tone. Her mother never drank beer, at least not in Julia's presence.

"Not beer—champagne." Paige grinned. "We were at the yacht club for the chamber of commerce fundraiser in September. Bob and I hosted the table, and it was a bunch of people, including Walt, your mom, and Cheryl and Nick from the Nuthatch Bakery. Well, you know Nick—he hardly ever says two words. I could put him in a room with Bob, and they'd be happy not talking the whole evening. But Cheryl told us about their daughter, Grace, backpacking across Europe that summer."

"I know Grace. She was a year ahead of me in school. Now she rents the apartment above the Nuthatch."

"That's right." Paige nodded. "Anyhow, Walt made a big deal about how he thought they wasted their money, and your mom said that sending daughters off to Europe alone wasn't safe."

Julia sighed. "That sounds like them, all right."

"Yup." Paige nodded. "I never could figure out what was going on between your mom and Walt. I realize they used to date in high school, but as adults were they friends, or was there something more?"

"I'm not sure." Waverley had been free with her criticisms but tight lipped about sharing details of a personal nature. "I know my mother looked forward to her weekly lunches with Walt," said Julia, "but she never invited him over for dinner."

"Interesting, and I'm not surprised, really. Walt has a nasty temper, and your mom was used to your father treating her like a queen."

"You were telling me what happened at the yacht club," Julia prompted.

"Oh yes. That's right. Walt claimed sending a daughter to Europe was a waste of money, and he shouldn't have said that, not in front of Cheryl—or Bob, as it turns out. Cheryl lectured Walt about feminism for at least five minutes. Then Bob jumped in, and you know how strongly Bob feels about backpacking." Paige squared her shoulders, a proud smile on her face. "It turns out, he was the one who sold Grace her kit: sleeping bag . . . backpack . . . energy bars . . . everything. Apparently, Grace did the whole summer on the cheap. Staying in youth hostels and out of restaurants."

Julia could see where this was going. Outside of being crowned Miss Washington State, Waverley's brief career as a waitress at the top of the Space Needle had been her proudest accomplishment. "Let me guess," she said. "My mom made rude comments about Grace eating power bars instead of enjoying authentic cuisine."

"That's right." Paige snapped her fingers. "It annoyed me because I knew how hard Cheryl and Nick worked over the years to build up their business. They would have sent Grace to Europe with a fat wad of cash if they could have afforded it. Who was your mom to judge them?" Paige frowned. "Especially since she was always so stingy with you."

"How'd you know about that?" Julia asked. She hadn't become friends with Paige until the chamber of commerce mentoring program had matched them together.

"Waverley never bought you one book at my shop, even though you clearly loved to read."

Julia nodded. "That's true. She said that's what libraries were for, which I guess is true. But it meant that I couldn't read what my friends were reading in high school because the hold lines were so long for the young adult bestsellers."

"Your father bought you books," said Paige in a soft voice. "Huge stacks of them."

Julia swallowed back the lump in her throat. "I remember."

"So do I. Anyhow, that night at the yacht club, Waverley bugged me so much that I decided to needle her. I flagged the waitress over and made sure she refilled your mom's flute of champagne. It didn't take much to get Waverley going after her second glass. *Her* daughter would never sleep in a youth hostel in Europe. *Her* daughter would have more than enough money to eat in European restaurants like a 'normal person.'" Paige lifted her fingers to make air quotes. "*Her* daughter would travel in a properly supervised group so she wouldn't need to travel alone."

"You primed the pump." Julia smiled and appreciated Paige more than ever.

"It's what I do best." Paige buffed her fingernails on her sleeve. "But what I didn't expect was Walt's unintentional help."

"What?"

"He told your mother that she was too poor to send you to Europe. I believe his exact words were 'Women who use coupons at the Olive Garden can't afford to be extravagant.'"

"Uh-oh," said Julia.

"Yup. Waverley turned eggplant purple and told Walt to mind his own business. That's when I dived in and suggested the University of Washington study-abroad program. By the time dessert arrived, she was ready to sign you up. Walt stormed off in a huff, and your mom made excuses for his sudden departure. She blamed it on his blood pressure medicine."

"How did my mother know what prescriptions he was on?"

Paige raised her eyebrows. "I don't know, but that's an interesting question."

Julia felt unsettled but wasn't ready to explore those thoughts further at the moment. "Going to Italy was the best thing that ever happened to me," she said instead. "Thank you."

"My pleasure."

Neither of them said anything for a while. PBS switched over to an episode of Rick Steves visiting Croatia, and they both watched as warm Mediterranean scenery filled the screen. But when they got to Dubrovnik, Julia burst out with a question that was nagging her. "Why do you think she agreed to it?" she asked.

"Who?" Paige was still looking at the TV. "The tour guide in Dubrovnik? Being featured on a television show is probably good for business."

"Not Rick Steves—my mother. How did you know that you could talk her into sending me to Europe?"

Paige settled back in her chair. "I didn't, but I had a hunch. See, you and Waverley share one thing in common, besides your last name."

"What's that?" Julia couldn't think of anything about herself that was similar to her mother.

"You've both got low self-esteem."

"I don't have low self-esteem." Julia wiggled into a new position on the couch so that her tailbone wouldn't hurt. Normally she thought Paige was astute in her judgments about other people, but in this case she was flat-out wrong. Julia had an excellent understanding of her own character. Who knew you better than yourself, right?

"You do too," said Paige. "That's why I worry about people like Walt taking advantage of you."

Julia blew a puff of hair out of her eyes and frowned.

"I blame your mother," Paige continued. "Anyone who knew Waverley could tell she hated children. That woman didn't have a maternal bone in her body."

"I won't argue with you there. My father told me he wanted me to have a brother or sister, and my mother said no." Julia wasn't sure if being an only child had made it better or worse. A sibling would have at least offered company. "But what does my mother having low self-esteem have to do with her paying thousands of dollars for me to go to Europe when she was so frugal?"

"Because she couldn't stand to look less when compared to Cheryl and Nick. They helped Grace go to Europe. Once I pointed that out in the right way, Waverley had to make sure everyone knew that her daughter would go to Europe, too, in a bigger and better way."

There was a knock at the door, and Paige got up to open it. Bob and Toby had returned from their walk. Toby barreled to his water bowl and lapped from the dish while Paige and Bob whispered in the front room. When Paige came back, she relented about staying a second night. "Okay," she said. "It does seem like you're feeling better. If you want me to stay, I'd be happy to. But—"

"I'm fine," Julia interrupted. "I've taken up enough of your weekend already."

Paige gave her a sharp look. "Promise you'll call me if you need anything?"

Julia nodded slowly so her head wouldn't throb. "It's a deal," she agreed.

But later that night, after Paige and Bob left, Julia had regrets. Her pride at not wanting to impose on her friend any longer seemed foolish. The century-old house creaked wickedly, and since the curtains were still wide open, everyone who drove down Ninth Avenue could stare inside, as if Julia was living in a zoo exhibit. She hobbled from window to window the best she could and drew the curtains one at a time. It took all her effort, and when it was time to go upstairs and brush her teeth for bed, Julia wobbled unsteadily at the base of the stairs. Toby made things worse, always underfoot, and at one point, she almost tripped over him. When she made it up to the landing that was halfway up the stairs, Julia sank to her knees to rest. She couldn't sit down all the way because of her tailbone, so she curled up in the fetal position until the dizziness went away.

Julia slept on the landing all night. When she woke up, it was morning, and sunshine poured through sidelight windows that framed the front door. Julia felt like she was a million years old. There was a crick in her neck, and her shoulders throbbed from the funny way she had slept. Her breath reeked. But the good news was, her mind was clearer. She couldn't picture the accident that had caused her concussion, but she remembered yesterday morning. Julia relived her excitement as she'd walked briskly down Main Street to the bookshop and told Paige what she'd learned about Aaron—that he was single and that Jack was Jared's baby. She recalled that yesterday was supposed to be Tahitian Paradise day at Sweet Bliss but that they had been waiting for the vanilla order to come through. With great sadness, she also remembered her walk Friday night and how she'd come across Frank, wandering and confused.

Julia pushed herself up to her knees and used the railing to stand. She climbed the steps to her bedroom and brought out her favorite pair of leggings, the ones that were so soft they would pill if she didn't take care of them. She filled the claw-foot tub in the hallway bathroom with warm soapy water and added half a cup of Epsom salts she'd purchased in the Gnome's Backyard's homeware section. When she submerged herself in the water, she had to be careful, resting more on her hip than her back, but the water felt good, like everything awful from the weekend was washing away. It was Monday, Julia realized. The horrible weekend was over, and she could begin again.

Julia knew exactly what she wanted to do. As soon as she got out of the bathtub, she'd dry off and put on her comfiest outfit. She'd brew herself a latte and pour a bowl of cereal for breakfast. Then, when she was cozy on the couch in her living room, Julia was going to accept Aaron's friend request. She leaned back into the water, a huge smile on her face, thinking about what that would be like, and was surprised to hear an involuntary giggle escape. Toby whimpered from his place on the bath mat and looked at her with concern. He was terrified of bathing but put one paw on the tile, willing to rescue her if she was in trouble.

"I'm fine," she told her loyal companion. "Nothing's wrong. I'm just silly—that's all."

Reassured that she was safe, Toby curled back up on the mat and rested his head on his paws. Then the doorbell rang, and he royally freaked out. Toby leaped to his feet so fast that he pushed the bath mat out from under him. He jumped up on the door and scratched the paint. The doorbell rang again, and he howled.

"Toby!" Julia sloshed out of the bathtub and grabbed a towel. "Hush." She toweled off as fast as possible and yanked on her leggings. Not bothering with her bra, she threw on her sweatshirt and walked gingerly downstairs to open the door. Julia assumed it must be Paige, because who else would be bothering her on a Monday morning? If she'd stopped for one second to ask who it was first, she might have reconsidered her appearance.

There, on her doorstep, standing next to the white pillars, was Will Gladstone, the real estate developer from Mercer Island who was interested in her properties. Forty years old with salt-and-pepper hair, Will wore khaki slacks, an orange polo shirt, and aviator sunglasses. Toby stepped between them and growled.

"Toby, no!" Julia grabbed the Labrador by his collar and pulled him off.

"Julia," Will said, removing the glasses and looking at the towel wrapped around her head. "Forgive me. Did I get the day wrong?" He took a step backward and held up his hands. "I'm sorry. I didn't mean to intrude."

"No, you're not intruding," said Julia, desperately wishing she had put on a bra. The way she was holding Toby right now, Will could probably see straight down her shirt. "Hold on a sec while I put Toby in his crate." She shut the door and brought Toby upstairs to her bedroom, where the crate was, and gave him a rawhide bone to quiet him. Julia unwrapped the towel from her head, gently rubbed her hair with it, then tossed it on her bed. She removed her sweatshirt and put on a bra before throwing the sweatshirt back on again. Julia couldn't find her hairbrush, so she finger-combed her tresses instead. Somewhere in the back of her mind, she vaguely remembered having an appointment with Will. She pictured herself sitting underneath the bulletin board in her office at Sweet Bliss and replying to his email. Julia scrambled back downstairs and opened the front door wide. "Come inside so I can explain."

Will crossed the threshold. "I went to Sweet Bliss first, but the shop wasn't open yet."

"That's right. The shop doesn't open until eleven a.m. during the summer." The hallway clock told her it was 9:22, which helped jog her memory. "I was going to meet you there before the customers came. But that was before I got a concussion. I'm so sorry." Julia frowned. "At least come into the kitchen so I can offer you some coffee."

"A concussion?" Will tilted his head to the side. "Julia, I had no idea. You have nothing to apologize for." He put his hand on the doorknob. "I should go and let you rest. We can reschedule."

Julia sighed. "That would probably be best. I'm so mixed up I haven't even had breakfast yet."

Will let go of the doorknob. "Now *that* I can fix. Why don't I take you out for brunch?"

"Thanks for the offer." Julia stared down at her bare feet. "But I don't feel like going out yet."

"No problem. I used to be a short-order cook at the first restaurant I ever owned. You rest, and I'll whip you up something delicious."

"Really? That's so nice of you." Under normal circumstances, Julia wouldn't have allowed it, because she would have felt like she was taking advantage of him, but she hadn't eaten anything since last night's pad thai. She was starving. "Maybe we can discuss business over breakfast, and that way you won't have to drive up from Mercer Island again."

"Oh, I don't mind the drive," said Will. He grinned, and Julia was impressed by his perfectly straight teeth. His parents must have spent a fortune on braces. "The living room is this way—am I right?" he asked. Will put his hand on her back and led her through the hallway without waiting for an answer.

CHAPTER TWELVE

The first thing Aaron smelled when he rolled the stroller to a stop on Julia's front porch was the rich scent of fried bacon. He smiled, taking that as a sign that she must be feeling better. Aaron kicked on the parking brake and bent down to check on Jack, who was thankfully still enjoying his midmorning nap. They'd left home forty-five minutes ago and walked the whole route. Aaron rationalized that it was a recovery day and he didn't need to run, but really it was because he didn't want to get sweaty. He also told himself that stopping by to see how Julia was doing was perfectly normal, especially since he was the one who'd taken her to the doctor in the first place. Sure, she hadn't accepted his Facebook friend request yet, and maybe that was a bad sign. But perhaps she hadn't been using screens since the accident. Aaron hadn't gotten where he was in life without taking risks, and going for a walk and casually stopping by to say hello was a risk he was willing to take. Even though all he was looking for was friendship. Obviously.

At least that was what he kept telling himself.

Aaron patted his dark-brown hair back into place and took a deep breath before knocking on the door. He didn't use the doorbell in case Julia still had a headache. She opened the door a minute later wearing tight gray leggings and a pink sweatshirt that hung off one shoulder. Her blonde hair hung in ripples down her back, as if she'd just climbed out of bed. She clasped a giant mug of coffee in front of her and smiled.

"I was just in the neighborhood," Aaron said, his voice squeaking with nerves. He coughed and tried again. "I was just in the neighborhood," he repeated, this time a full octave lower, "and I decided to stop by to see how your recovery was going."

"That's so kind of you." Julia peeked over his shoulder toward the stroller. "Is Jack sleeping?"

Aaron looked behind him before turning back to Julia. "Yup. He's out cold. What about you? Have you been getting lots of rest?"

Julia nodded. "I haven't spent as much time in bed as I would have liked, though." She pointed to the landing in the middle of the stairs. "Last night I—"

"Julia?" a man's voice called from the kitchen. "Would you like some more french toast?" A tall guy with tanned skin and slicked-back hair sauntered into the room wearing an apron from Sweet Bliss. He walked right up to the doorway and stood behind Julia, nodding his head to greet Aaron. "Hey," the man said.

"Hey," Aaron answered. A tiny muscle at the back of his neck twitched. "Sorry. I didn't realize you had company." He turned to go, feeling as stupid as he'd felt that time Jared had convinced him to go line dancing at a country-western bar. How could he have misjudged Julia's situation so completely? Sure, he'd never directly asked her if she had a boyfriend, but when he talked with Paige at the urgent care clinic, Paige hadn't mentioned that Julia was serious with anyone.

"Wait," said Julia. She twisted a strand of hair around her finger. "Thank you for stopping by. And for all your help getting me to the doctor. I don't remember any of it, but Paige told me that you were wonderful."

"It was nothing." Aaron shrugged.

"Will Gladstone," said the man, holding out his hand for Aaron to shake. Will's tanned skin was browner than his orange polo shirt, so Aaron suspected the tan was real, but he wasn't positive. "Of Gladstone Enterprises."

"Aaron Baxter, Big Foot Paleo." He made sure to keep full eye contact while shaking Will's hand. Just because the man was half a foot taller than him didn't mean he'd let the guy assert dominance over the situation. The guy looked like he spent more time on his yacht than he did lifting weights. Not that Aaron was a gym rat, but he did do circuits three times a week with the free weights in his basement. Aaron looked at the powdered sugar sprinkled across the front of Will's apron. "Looks like you're baking. I should leave now."

Will squared his shoulders. "A man should know his way around the kitchen, don't you think?" He turned toward Julia and flashed a smile. "Speaking of which, would you like a second helping? There's still three more slices of french bread."

"You had me at *bread*," she said. "Yes please."

Did this Will dude know nothing about Omega-3s? Poached eggs and salmon—that was what Aaron would have made Julia for breakfast, along with a side of sautéed kale to nourish her brain. How was he supposed to compete with french toast?

He wasn't, Aaron reminded himself. This wasn't a competition. "Glad you're okay." He grabbed the stroller and unlocked the parking brakes. "I'll see you around, Julia."

"The infant-toddler group meets at the library tomorrow," she said. "If you go, be sure to stop by Sweet Bliss afterward. The moms tell me it's the best part."

"The moms?" Aaron raised his eyebrows. "You didn't tell me it was a moms group."

"Dads can come too." Julia bit her lower lip.

"Have you ever seen a dad in the group?"

"Yes," she declared. "Once."

Will threw his head back and laughed. "Julia, Julia, Julia," he said. "I'm sure the last thing Aaron wants to do is join a mommy-and-me group at the library."

Will was right. That was the last thing Aaron wanted to do with his time. But he also felt the unexplainable urge to prove Will wrong. "Actually," said Aaron, "I love the idea of meeting local parents, and I don't mind one bit if I'm the only man." He was careful not to say *dad*, and the avoidance filled him with sadness. Aaron gripped the handle of the stroller so tightly that his biceps flexed. "What time did you say the group meets?"

"Nine o'clock. I open Sweet Bliss for them at ten."

Aaron looked straight into Julia's brown eyes. "I'll see you tomorrow, then." He nodded at Will again. "Nice to meet you," he said before strolling away. Aaron took off in the first direction the stroller rolled, which happened to be in the direction of Main Street. He charged down Ninth Avenue with no particular plan other than to tamp down the irritation that bubbled up inside him. How come some guy in a polo shirt was cooking Julia breakfast? He was wearing her apron, no less!

Aaron arrived at the intersection with Main Street and hung a right. Maybe he'd stop by the Smoothie Hut and gulp down a glass of carrot juice. Aaron normally disapproved of consuming juice since it wasn't the fruit's or vegetable's pure form, but he was feeling dangerous. Heck, he might even stop by the Parisian Café later and get a croissant. So what if it made him cramp up an hour later? Mr. Polo Shirt wasn't the only one who could eat gluten.

He took a deep breath and counted to four before letting it out and counting to five, just like the grief counselor at the hospital had taught him. He took another deep breath and counted to four, but this time he counted to six on the exhale. Aaron kept going until his lungs couldn't take it anymore. His pulse was slower, but his pride still stung. Before he realized where he was or what he was doing, he was standing at the entrance to Paige's Pages, which was perfect, because Aaron wanted to give Paige a piece of his mind.

The tricky part was entering the store. The door opened outward, which would have been no problem with the regular stroller, but the jogger was extralong. He had to open the door with one hand and spin the stroller around backward with the other.

"Thanks," said a ten-year-old who assumed Aaron was holding the door open for her. She barged ahead and entered the shop with her little brother behind her. The kids were quickly followed by an elderly couple and a family of tourists complaining about how long the ferry wait was. Aaron stood there, an impromptu doorman, until he finally had the opportunity to enter.

The bookstore smelled like cinnamon and paper. Most of the stock was new. Hardbacks and *New York Times* bestsellers lined the front wall. There was also an extensive collection of hiking books, trail guides, and nonfiction books specific to the Pacific Northwest. A giant rack of coloring books and brightly colored pencils sat by the register, where people might make impulse purchases on their way to the ferry. But the back wall housed Aaron's two favorite sections: used books and parenting guides. It was difficult to imagine a time when he'd have the opportunity to read the mystery suspense thrillers he used to read on a weekly basis, but it was nice knowing there was a thick stack of well-loved paperbacks waiting for him when life became less complicated. The parenting aisle was also a source of comfort, although he was a bit disturbed knowing that Paige had profiled every book he'd bought. Good thing he'd left *Baby Poop: What Your Pediatrician Might Not Tell You* on the shelf. He wouldn't want Paige to assume he was a weirdo.

Thinking about Paige and what she'd neglected to tell him about Julia's dating life made Aaron's blood pressure spike all over again. He saw her standing next to the cookbook section, speaking with a customer who was trying to decide between two books. Paige wore charcoal slacks and a flowing green tank top. Her chin-length bob was the same shiny black color as her sensible shoes. "Ah, Aaron," she said as soon as she saw him. "What perfect timing." She waved him over.

"Hi, Paige," he said in a grim tone. It was hard to be friendly with the woman who'd gotten his hopes up about a hypothetical date with Julia without telling him about Will.

"I'd like you to meet Lawrence Knowles, owner of Emerald City Books." Paige stepped back so there would be room for the stroller in the tiny aisle. "Lawrence, this is the man I was telling you about— Aaron Baxter, superstar of the paleo world."

"Huh?" Aaron had never heard himself described that way, although he supposed it was partially true. As the owner—or former owner—of Big Foot Paleo, he'd represented the movement for years. "I wouldn't call myself a superstar," he said with a grunt. "More like an ordinary person whose health problems were solved by realizing I had food intolerances."

"And you have a baby," the book publisher said in a bright tone of voice. He leaned down to peer in the stroller. "Hello, little buddy!" Lawrence said in a voice loud enough to wake Jack up.

Aaron's temper was officially shot at this point. If Lawrence woke up the baby, words would be said—words that he couldn't take back and that would probably get him banned from Paige's Pages for eternity. "It's Jack's nap time," he growled. "I'd better go."

"Wait," said Paige, stepping closer. "Lawrence is looking for an author to write a book for parents about packing paleo lunches for kids. You'd be perfect for that."

"But I'm not a parent," said Aaron.

"You're not?" asked Lawrence.

Aaron couldn't take it anymore. His nebulously defined role as Jack's guardian was none of this man's concern, and what business did Paige have talking about him behind his back? Aaron would make damn sure to stay away from her web from now on. But first, he was going to get what he'd come for: information.

"Why didn't you tell me Julia was dating someone already?" Aaron demanded.

"What?" Paige lifted her eyebrows in shock.

"Some guy named Will with a tan so dark it looks like he just flew home from Maui."

"I don't know what you're talking about." Paige shook her head apologetically at Lawrence. "Would you excuse me for a moment?"

"Of course," he said.

Paige grabbed Aaron's elbow and led him away to the back of the store, and he dragged the stroller behind him. "Are you nuts?" she asked. "I was introducing you to the biggest publisher in the Pacific Northwest. That was a golden opportunity for you."

"I don't want to write a cookbook for parents. I'm not a parent." Aaron crossed his arms over his chest.

"You *are* a parent, you moron. How many uncles do you think come into my shop to load up on parenting guides?"

"Don't change the subject. You led me to believe that Julia was single."

"She *is* single."

"Not seeing anyone exclusively." Aaron uncrossed his arms and dangled them at his side. "You know what I mean."

"She's not, at least as far as I know."

"Then who's Will, and why was he wearing her apron?"

"What?" Paige put her hands on her hips. "That doesn't sound like Julia at all. Did you catch Will's last name?"

"Glad something. Gladstone. Gladiolus. I don't know."

"Will Gladstone? The real estate agent?"

"He didn't say anything about being a real estate agent."

"Property developer. Whatever. Will Gladstone is a property developer who wants to buy up Harper Landing and turn it into mixed-use housing. He offered me a fat price for my bookshop, but I turned him down." She lifted her chin. "This building is over a hundred years old and on the historic register. I won't let it be torn down for condos."

"Property developer?" Aaron stood there, not knowing what to say at first. "What I witnessed didn't look like it was a business meeting."

"Not that it would be any of your concern." Paige tapped him on the chest. "You said you weren't interested in dating Julia."

"I don't have any interest in dating," Aaron clarified. "That's different than not having any interest in dating Julia. Two separate things."

Paige nodded, a pleased expression on her face. "Then let's pick a time. I'm available Friday night. You can drop Jack off at the bookstore with me and come get him later that evening after you take Julia home."

"I can't leave my baby with someone I've only known for a few days." *Martha isn't an option either,* he thought to himself. Not when she had her hands full with Frank.

"Ha!" Paige waved her index finger in the air. "You said *my baby.* Only a parent would say that."

"You know what I mean."

"For your information, Mister, I know plenty. I raised two kids, and they're both college grads. It would be a treat to watch Jack for a few hours, because grandkids are hopefully a long way away for me at this point."

"I never said I was going to ask Julia out on a date," Aaron protested.

"You never said you *weren't* going to ask her out."

Aaron sighed. "What if she says no? Things looked pretty cozy with Will."

"Then at least you tried." Paige pushed in a paperback that stuck out at an odd angle. "The alternative is to not ask her and wait for Will to take her out this weekend. Is that what you want?"

Aaron clenched his jaw. "No."

"Then be brave, soldier." Paige slapped him on the back. "I have another great idea. You should go to the infant-and-toddler group at the library tomorrow. They always go to Sweet Bliss afterward. That would be the perfect opportunity to ask her out."

"That's what Julia said too."

Paige arched an eyebrow and looked up at him.

"I mean, she didn't say I should ask her out," Aaron clarified. "She said I should go to the library group."

"Then that's exactly what you should do." Paige beamed. "Join the group and ask her out."

"Why don't you plan out the rest of my life while you're at it?" Aaron looked up at the ceiling and counted to ten. Life in Palo Alto had never been this complicated. Back in Silicon Valley, nobody had monitored what books he'd read, encouraged him to join new clubs, or even bothered to learn his name. Small-town living was either heaven or hell. Aaron wasn't sure which.

CHAPTER THIRTEEN

Mylar balloons drifted overhead from a birthday party a couple of days ago, occasionally tickling Julia's and George's faces with ribbon. They sat in the birthday room in Sweet Bliss with spreadsheets papering the table. There was a golden throne in the corner and a brightly colored bin for presents next to it. The whole room was cheery and festive, which made Julia's meeting with her accountant more depressing by contrast. Julia stared at the display on her calculator one more time. "One million dollars? There's no way I'll be able to come up with this amount by August."

"I know it's a staggering figure, but this is what comes from your mother's penny-pinching ways." George pushed his glasses farther up the bridge of his nose. "I told her that patching roofs instead of replacing them would be a bad idea in the long run. Now you have eighteen properties that all need to be reroofed at once and not enough money in your maintenance fund to cover it."

"What about my trust fund? Isn't that where all the rent income has been going all these years?"

"Yes, most of it," said George. "But the terms of your father's will stipulate that you can't access that money until you're thirty years old."

"That's still two years away." Julia rested her head in her hands. It was Tuesday morning, only three days after her concussion. The doctor had told her to take it easy, but this meeting with George couldn't wait, especially not after what she'd learned yesterday at breakfast with Will. He had offered to buy one of her parcels for a sum that would solve all her problems. But Julia was reluctant to sell. "Why do I need the money by August? If I raised rents, I could save money to replace the roofs next summer."

George pushed pictures in front of her of the roofs of various buildings she owned. "It's too late for more patching. The situation is serious. Dave is already complaining about leaks dripping into his kitchen at the Parisian Café."

"Dave is complaining about me?" The chef had never struck her as a gossip.

George scrunched up his face. "Well, no, actually. Walt is complaining on Dave's behalf. He tells anyone who'll listen that you're not only charging too much rent but that you're letting your buildings fall to pieces. Shelly was at the Smoothie Hut one day and overheard Walt tell the new owners to be careful or your poor maintenance could cause the health department to shut them down."

It felt horrible knowing that Shelly Fiege, Julia's former fifth-grade teacher, had heard such awful things about her. "But the Smoothie Hut is one of my newest buildings," she protested.

"I know." George nodded. "Shelly stuck up for you and said Walt was a liar. That's when he called you a glorified slumlord."

"I might as well be." Julia pointed at one of the worst pictures, which showed a gaping hole where shake shingles should have been. "This roof is horrible." She lifted the lid of her computer. "I don't have the cash on hand to replace the roofs right away."

"You're land rich and cash poor—that's what you are."

Julia nodded. "But there's a solution to that. What if I sold one building and used the income to pay for the rest?" She rifled through the paperwork until she found the file folder that Will had given her. "If I sold the land on Second and Main, I'd bring in four million dollars.

That would be enough to pay for all the roofs plus begin upgrading the electrical and plumbing. Will said that the way some of the old buildings are wired is a liability risk at this point."

George looked at the comp sheet and whistled. "That's a ton of cash, all right, but we're talking about two rental houses and the Parisian Café. Could you bear to sacrifice assets like that? That land has been in your family for over a century."

"I know." Julia's shoulders sagged. "It feels awful even broaching the idea of selling land. But think how horrible I'd feel if one of the buildings burned down from an electrical fire and people were injured."

"Injured or worse," confirmed George. "Well, this is your decision to make. I'm only your accountant." He stared at the paperwork some more. "What does Will want to do with the land?"

"He calls it *mixed-use properties*, which means stores on the bottom and condos on top."

"And on Second, they'll have killer views. Ka-ching. Ka-ching. I bet he'll sell each condo for three million apiece. We're talking about an opportunity that will quadruple Will's money."

She sighed. "And tear up Harper Landing history in the process." Julia raked her fingers through her hair and lifted it up at the roots. "What would my great-great-great-grandparents say?"

"That you owe it to Harper Landing to make Main Street proud. If that means making hard choices to ensure that the buildings you own are safe, then so be it." George shuffled some papers together. "But there are other ways you could gather that money. What about a mortgage to access your home equity? Your house on Ninth is worth a million, easy. Mortgage it, like your father did."

"You know how my mother felt about debt." Julia could hear her mother's warnings now. "Only stupid people pay interest," Waverley used to say with an intense look in her eye. "She made difficult sacrifices to pay off that loan."

"Your mother was a beauty queen, not a financial analyst." George rapped his knuckles on the table. "I'm sorry to speak ill of the dead, but it's the truth. I dealt with your mother's mismanagement for seventeen and a half years. You wouldn't be in this mess if she didn't have such warped views about money. She squirreled every single penny away into that trust fund of yours that only she had access to. You're completely locked out of your own cash."

Julia's cheeks turned pink. "My mother grew up in a bad part of Seattle. She didn't have a lot of money growing up, so she learned the value of frugality. If it weren't for pageants, she probably would have ended up like her friends in high school."

Julia could picture her mother ranting now. "Pageants or death," Waverley used to say. "Those were my options. Only Walt and I got away."

Julia swallowed hard before continuing. "Did you know that the year my mother won Miss Washington, her best friend died of an overdose?"

George shook his head. "No, Waverley never mentioned her childhood. She was always the epitome of class, as far as I was concerned."

Julia nodded. *Poised, rich, beautiful, thin*—those were all words that described her mother. But also *cheap*. Waverley had never wanted to spend a dime on anything except herself. When Harrison was alive, she complained nonstop about his smoking—not because cigarettes might kill him, but because they cost so much. Frugality made her furnish their home with estate sale finds. To pay for her plastic surgeries, Waverley served peanut-butter-and-jelly sandwiches for months. When college came around, she made Julia live at home and commute to the University of Washington in a beat-up car rather than take on the added expense of dorm fees. Even in Florence Julia had needed to work part time at a gelato shop.

"Maybe my mother did mismanage our assets over the years, but have you ever stopped to consider that the reason she didn't raise rents to the market level was because she didn't want to be a greedy landlord?"

"Did she not want to be a greedy landlord, or did she not want to be *called* a greedy landlord?" asked George.

Julia didn't answer, because she knew he had a point. Reputation had been everything to her mother.

"Waverley couldn't stand people saying bad things about her—that's true," said George. "But asking to be paid what you're worth isn't greed; it's good sense."

"But Walt says he's barely getting by."

"Walt Lancaster's full of it. He makes a killing with his candy-of-the-month subscription program. You know he lives on Burke Road, right?" George asked, naming the mansion-lined street in the north of town. "His garage is bigger than your whole house."

"If I take out a loan on my house and can't pay it back, I could be ruined." Julia's forehead knit together with worry.

"Ruined? You wouldn't be ruined. Worst-case scenario would be bankruptcy. And you'd likely sell the house before that."

Julia patted the tender spot on top of her head from the accident and squeezed her eyes shut before opening them again. "How is any of that different from financial ruin?"

George let out an exasperated sigh. "Forget I mentioned bankruptcy, because that's not going to happen. For one thing, you run a profitable business. For another, all you would need to do to pay off a loan would be to sell another property." He lifted the file folder from Will and let it flutter to the table. "Like the parcel on Second."

Julia chewed on her bottom lip and considered it. Why was she being so crazy? When George explained it to her that way, it made perfect sense. But sitting here at the birthday table, she felt like she was ten years old again and her mother was wearing all black. "Banks take away houses," Waverley had told her when she'd come back from seeing a lawyer. "It's your father's fault I have to sell Sweet Bliss." That was what Waverley had done, too, in a manner of speaking. In order to pay off the entire loan on their house, she'd leased the business to an outsider from Seattle, who'd promptly run it into the ground. The building had sat vacant for ten years until Julia had come back from Europe and reenvisioned the brand as a Froyo shop.

"I have a lot to think about," Julia admitted, her head aching.

"Thinking is good, but ticktock." George pointed up at the ceiling. "Or should I say drip drop?"

Julia gathered up the paperwork. "Schedule the roofers for August. I'll come up with the money somehow. But let's wait until after the Fourth of July." She stuffed the materials into her briefcase.

"What about raising rents to market levels?"

Julia shook her head. "I'm not ready to consider that at this time."

"At least let us keep up with inflation. Otherwise you're losing money."

"But it will look bad." Julia's stomach twisted in knots. "My renters will think that I'm off-loading the costs of the new roofs directly to them."

"Because that's what needs to happen. They're not paying their fair share, and they haven't been for eighteen years."

"Okay, okay." Julia's shoulders slumped. "You're right. Send a notice that we're adjusting rent for inflation." She stood up carefully, her tailbone still sore.

"You're not running a charity, Julia," said George. "It's perfectly fine to demand what your properties are worth. What *you* are worth."

"I know." Julia pushed in her chair.

"Do you?" George gave her a concerned look. "Every time I head out the door to meet with you, Shelly reminds me that you were one of her favorite students."

"She probably says that about all her students."

"She does, actually." George chuckled. "But it's the truth. Just like you're one of my favorite clients. You've got heart and creativity, and you understand what this town needs. When your mom was my client, I had to do what she said, but now you're in charge, and I won't let anyone take advantage of you. In many ways your life is easier now without her. Financially, at least."

"That's a horrible thing to say!" Julia was shocked. She'd never heard her accountant bad-mouth anyone. That it was about her own mother made it even more out of character. Usually George was as steady as they came.

George's face turned red. "I am sorry—I overstepped. Shelly would have my head if she knew I spoke ill of your mother." He cleared his throat.

"It's okay. I understand what you mean about the finances. It sounds like my mother wasn't making good decisions."

"No." George shook his head. "She wasn't. Promise me you won't sign anything with Will Gladstone or a mortgage broker unless I've looked at the contract too. Got it?"

"Yes sir." Julia saluted. She hated being lectured, but she knew George was right. Julia was great at running her own business, but landlording made her squirm. She checked her watch. "It's ten forty already. The library group's probably in the front room." Julia fluffed up her hair. "How do I look?" she blurted out before thinking.

"What?"

"Never mind." Julia blushed. "Forget I asked."

"Hang on there a second." George removed his glasses and wiped them on the hem of his shirt. He put them back on and inspected her closely. "There's something wrong with your collar."

"There is?" Julia patted her neckline and realized that one part of her blouse stuck up at an odd angle. She smoothed it down with her fingers.

"Much better." George nodded with approval. "There wouldn't be a certain dog hero out there waiting for you, would there?"

Julia dropped her hands. "What do you know about that?"

George chuckled. "I might have wandered into the bookshop yesterday when Paige was telling him about the baby group that stops by every Tuesday."

"George." Julia covered her face with her hands. "Please don't tease me."

"I would never." George picked up his computer. "He'd be an idiot not to notice you."

"Thanks," she said, pulling her hands down. Julia opened the door to the main part of the store and found the tables and chairs arranged in a circle. At least half a dozen strollers were pushed to the side of the room, against the booths, and the atmosphere was filled with laughter. Women of various ages bounced babies on their laps or nursed them under blankets. Cups of half-eaten frozen yogurt sat abandoned on tables. A toddler with his tummy hanging out over his corduroy pants danced around in the circle, stuffing cereal puffs in his mouth. It was the normal chaos that accompanied the parent group every week, with one exception. All eyes were on Aaron, who stood near the front windows, holding a baby girl out in front of him and gently swaying her up and down.

"Twenty-six pounds and six ounces," he announced with a grin. A lock of his brown hair flopped across his forehead, which would have given him a boyish look except for the way his biceps bulged as he held the child. Instead of the workout clothes Julia was accustomed to seeing him in, he wore well-fitting jeans and a green shirt that matched his eyes. Aaron was cleanly shaven, and although Julia missed the stubble, his clean-shaven appearance was equally appealing.

"That's right!" called out the mother standing to Julia's left. She wore jogger pants and a stained T-shirt. "Evelyn weighed exactly that at the doctor's office last week." She took her daughter back in her arms.

"Do me next," said a woman wearing shorts and a wrinkled blouse. Her brown hair was tied back in a messy ponytail. "I mean Ethan. Do Ethan." She walked over and handed Aaron a chubby baby who was so bald he resembled Winston Churchill—but in a cute way.

"Whoa," said Aaron as he stared into the baby's eyes. "What a hunk of love."

"I'll say," said the woman standing next to Julia. When Julia realized who it was, she had to say something.

"Melanie?" she asked. "What are you doing here? I thought Timmy was in preschool."

"He is." Melanie dug her spoon into a spiral of orange-cream swirl. "I happened to be at the library and . . ." Her eyes drifted over to Aaron. "I developed a sudden yearning for Froyo."

"Mm-hmm." Julia rolled her eyes and looked back at Aaron.

"Thirty-six pounds even," he declared.

"You did it again," said Winston Churchill's mother in a high-pitched girly tone.

"How did baby weighing become your secret talent?" asked a woman Julia recognized from the gym.

Aaron shrugged. "I spent a lot of time in my early twenties weighing granola."

"Granola?" Melanie repeated.

Aaron's eyes crossed the room to her and Julia. As soon as he saw Julia, he grinned. "Jared Reynolds and I . . ." Aaron paused and looked around the group. "Did anyone know Jared?"

I did, thought Julia, but she didn't say anything.

The woman from the gym nodded. "I'm friends with his sister, Jessica."

"Yes, well . . . Jared and I started a company called Big Foot Paleo, and when it was just getting off the ground, we did most of the labor ourselves. That meant weighing bags of almonds, dried fruit, and other good stuff." He handed Winston Churchill back to the baby's mother and sat down.

"Where's Jack?" Julia asked.

Aaron pointed over to the row of parked strollers. "Sleeping off his big day at the library."

The woman in the jogger pants cradled her daughter in her arms and swayed side to side. "Do you work from home now? We don't get many stay-at-home dads in our group."

"Many? Try any," added a woman by the topping buffet.

Aaron's face froze. "Jared and I sold our business before he passed. So now, I can focus on Jack." He crossed the room to Julia and whispered in her ear. "Can I bother you for a sec?"

Julia's heart fluttered, and it wasn't because of the death stares the women in the room shot at her now that she was taking their hunk away. "Sure—what's up?" Julia asked.

Aaron led her over to the self-serve dispensers. "Which flavor has the least amount of added sugar?"

"Oh." Julia squared her shoulders and shifted herself into business mode. "Well, while none of our flavors qualify as truly paleo, we do have two dairy-free offerings right now—Cocoa-Lama and Limeade. The Cocoa-Lama has coconut milk–based yogurt, but the Limeade is more of a sherbet, really." She took a sample cup from the rack. "Do you want to try one? The Limeade has the least amount of sugar, but the Cocoa-Lama tastes the most like ice cream."

"I haven't had ice cream since Jared and Sara's wedding, and that was only because my mom insisted," Aaron said in a somber tone.

Julia crumpled the cup and threw it in the recycling bin. "Of course. Sorry."

"No." Aaron touched her arm, sending a shiver of delight across her bare skin. "Wait. What I was trying to say is, I would love some ice cream, or frozen yogurt, or sherbet, or whatever you're selling."

"Really?" Julia lifted her chin and looked at him. "Are you serious?"

"Absolutely. Life is too short to go one more day without something sweet." Aaron slid his fingers down her arm and took her hand in his. "How are you feeling? Postconcussion, I mean?"

Julia was feeling so many things at once—nervous, exhilarated, flattered, hopeful—she wasn't sure if she could speak. Surely her heart was beating so loudly that the whole room could hear it. "I'm getting better," she managed. "It still hurts to sit down for too long, and I can't remember Saturday at all."

Aaron squeezed her hand. "What a scary thing to happen to you when you were alone."

"I had Toby with me, but I'm not sure how much help he was."

"He certainly did a number on the dog treats."

Julia laughed and looked over at the Froyo dispenser before looking back up at Aaron, who was still holding her hand. Julia squeezed back, not wanting to let it go. Now was the time to be brave, she realized. It wasn't every day that a handsome stranger moved to town, rescued her dog, and held her hand. She could spend her whole life watching the world move on without her, walking down the aisle as yet another bridesmaid in yet another friend's wedding, or she could take charge of her own destiny.

"Julia," said Aaron. "I was wondering—"

"Would you and Jack like to go to the gym with me tomorrow?" she blurted out. "There's a saltwater pool that's eighty-five degrees. Jack might have fun in the water. You can use my guest pass."

A huge smile broke out across Aaron's face. "We'd love that."

CHAPTER FOURTEEN

Aaron was preparing for a night out with the boys. Or, in his case, a night out with Jack and Frank. The diaper bag was packed, there was plenty of cash in his wallet, and he wore his lucky T-shirt from Stanford. It said **FEAR THE TREE**, and Aaron had won it during a relay race in his freshman dorm. Jack looked spiffy, too, wearing a onesie with an embroidered necktie.

That morning when they had left Sweet Bliss, Aaron had been so elated about Julia asking him out that he had called up Martha as soon as he'd arrived home and told her that she had the night off.

"Night off from what?" she asked.

"Night off from everything." Aaron looked up the movie schedule on his computer while they talked. "There's a six p.m. showing of *Rebecca* at the Main Street theater. Do you like Hitchcock?"

"I loved *The Birds*, but is *Rebecca* scary? I can't handle any more stress."

"That's why you need the night off. Call up a few friends. Go out to dinner. See a movie. Jack and I will . . ." Aaron paused. He was about to say *watch Frank*, but that seemed demeaning. "Have a great time with Frank," he said instead. "We'll pick up burgers at the drive-through and then get the car washed. We won't leave the car until we get home, but it'll still be fun."

"Sounds thrilling."

"Yeah, I guess I should rethink the car wash part. My idea of fun has really taken a hit lately. Jack loves watching the foaming soap smear across his window."

"No," said Martha quickly. "I think a car wash is a great idea. Frank would enjoy that too. Anything that gets him out of the house makes him happy. But evenings are when he gets the most confused. I'm not sure this is a good idea."

Aaron wasn't sure, either, but he figured it was worth a try. "You becoming burned out is risky too," he said. "Caring for Frank all by yourself can't be easy, and I want to help. I'll activate the safety locks in my Tesla if that makes you feel better."

"You mean the *child* locks?"

Shoot. Aaron had been trying to avoid infantilizing Frank, but Martha went right there. "Yes," he said. "The child-safety locks."

"That would make me feel a lot better," she said, to his relief. "But are you sure about this?"

"Positive. I'd like for Jack to get the chance to know his grandpa." *While he still can,* Aaron thought.

"Well, okay," said Martha. "And really, it could go either way. Frank still has lots of days where his mind is fairly clear. Today's been fine so far, so hopefully you picked a winner."

"I'm glad to hear that."

"I'm not sure about the movie, but it would be nice to go out with some friends from church. I wonder if it's too late to get reservations at the Western Cedar?"

"I don't know." Aaron wedged the phone under his ear while he typed into the computer. "Let me check." He pulled up the website. "Nope, it's not too late. Do you want me to make you a reservation?"

"That would be great. Put down four people, and I'll call up the gals."

Now it was 4:45 p.m., and Frank and Martha would be there any minute. Aaron had already packed the diaper bag with supplies, including the new baby bottles he was trying out for Jack's gassiness. "Are you ready to have fun with Grandpa?" Aaron asked as he bounced Jack up and down on his knee. Jack gurgled with glee, and a bit of drool spilled down his cheek. "Me too," said Aaron. "We better do a sniff test, just in case." He lifted Jack up and smelled his diaper. Still fresh, thankfully. When he heard Martha's Impala pull into the driveway, he put Jack into the carrier and grabbed his keys.

Aaron locked the front door behind him and walked down the steps to the driveway right as Frank and Martha were getting out of their car. Frank wore slacks and a long-sleeve shirt, but Martha was sparkly. She had on a polyester pantsuit with jewels sewn around the collar that glittered in the evening sun.

"Guess what?" Martha opened the back door of her vehicle. "Look what Frank found in the basement."

"What?" Aaron asked, full of curiosity.

Frank looked down at the pavement, a huge smile on his face. "It was nothing," he said. "As soon as I remembered it, I knew it would be perfect for the baby." He shrugged before lifting his head and gazing at Jack.

Aaron set Jack's carrier on the ground and was touched when Frank crouched down to be eye to eye with Jack.

"Hey there, little fella." Frank puffed up his cheeks like a fish, and Jack laughed. "Are you my little halibut?"

"Frank even installed it himself," said Martha. "That thing isn't moving—let me tell you."

"Huh?" Aaron had zero idea what Martha was talking about until he poked his head into the back seat of her Chevy. That was when he saw the car seat. Jared's car seat, by the look of it. The contraption was so old that it had a three-point harness. "Wow," he said, his jaw dropping. "Wow."

A million thoughts raced through his head, starting with *death trap* and ending with *Who keeps a car seat for twenty-nine years?* But he knew he couldn't say anything without ruining Frank's big moment. The only thing he could do was vow to himself that Martha would never drive Jack anywhere, ever.

"It's in such great condition too." Martha patted her curls. "Not to brag, but that car seat has only been in one accident, because I'm such an excellent driver."

"It was a fender bender," said Frank. "She was dropping Jessica off at swim team and rear-ended . . ." Frank scratched his head. "Who's that woman who teaches yoga? The hippie?"

Martha frowned. "Laura Jonas, and I *cannot* believe you remember that. Honestly, I have one teensy-weensy accident, and you lord it over me for the rest of my life."

"It's called marriage." Frank stood up and pinched Martha on the butt.

Martha giggled girlishly. "It's called something, all right." She smiled at Aaron. "I think the three of you are going to have a fun night."

They did have a good night, too. Frank was lucid and full of humor. He didn't raise an eyebrow when Aaron ordered himself a lettuce-wrapped burger from Wendy's. The car wash was fun, and Jack laughed when the rain protectant sprayed across the dashboard and made rainbows. Everything was going great until the ride home, when Jack puked all over the leather upholstery. His gassiness had struck again.

"Uh-oh," said Frank as he sprang into action. He reached into the back seat and unzipped the diaper bag. "You've got a rag in here, right?"

Aaron nodded as the foul odor permeated the car. "There should be some burp cloths."

Frank mopped up the mess. "It looks like a failure-to-burp situation—that's all."

Aaron looked back at Jack and was relieved to see that Jack was smiling now that the gas was out of his tummy. "Dang it, I really hoped those new bottles would help. I wonder if it's his formula." The mothers at Sweet Bliss had told him that some babies had difficulty digesting the formula Jack was currently on.

"It might be worth asking the pediatrician." Frank turned back around in his seat and folded the soiled rags. "Better to be safe than sorry."

"I agree," said Aaron, sensing an opportunity. "Have you made an appointment with *your* doctor to talk about your memory issues?"

Frank furrowed his eyebrows and grunted. "Did Martha put you up to this?"

"No. But I want Jack to have as much time with his grandpa as possible—don't you?"

"I can't argue with that." Frank sighed. "But what if the doctor says I have Alzheimer's?"

"I don't know." Aaron desperately wished he had answers. "But at least you can make a plan."

Aaron and Frank were both glad when they arrived home and climbed out of the car. Frank helped Aaron clean up the back seat and then went into the living room to watch television while Aaron bathed Jack. By the time Aaron put Jack to bed, Frank was dozing in the living room. He slept soundly until Martha came to pick him up.

"Thank you for this," Martha said when she'd hugged Aaron good night.

"Don't mention it," Aaron replied, feeling like he'd ended up with the good side of the bargain.

The next morning, Aaron laid down towels across the back seat of the Tesla, everywhere the car seat didn't touch, in case Jack barfed again. On the drive over to Julia's, he rolled down the windows to air the car out. Hopefully Julia wouldn't notice the smell on their way to swimming.

"I want to make one thing clear," Aaron said, looking at Jack through a complicated system of suction-cupped mirrors that helped him view the rear-facing car seat. "I hate triathlons. Biking hurts my butt, and swimming bothers my ears. Running is where it's at. You hear?"

Jack giggled and grabbed his toes. He wore a one-piece lounge outfit with a smiling alligator on the front. All his swimming gear—trunks, swim diapers, regular diapers, diaper rash cream, wipes, sunscreen, hats, floaties, a change of clothes, baby shampoo, an emergency bottle, and burp cloths—were packed in the overstuffed diaper bag. Aaron was sure he'd forgotten something, but he couldn't remember what. He also didn't know if he needed sunscreen. Was the pool inside or out? He would have texted Julia to find out, but he didn't have her number, a fact that made him feel like an idiot. But the sunscreen issue was a big deal because he didn't want Jack to be burned, but he also didn't want to load the baby up with chemicals. Aaron felt the back of his neck tense up. Swimming with a baby was a lot harder than he'd anticipated.

Still, he couldn't believe the giddiness he'd felt ever since that moment yesterday morning when Julia had asked him out, right before he was about to invite her to dinner on Friday. He knew it was too soon after the trauma of January to think about dating anyone. Between grief and sleep deprivation, Aaron was on a roller coaster of emotions.

But, for some reason, Aaron was eager to talk to Julia, one on one, and discover everything about her. Julia was unique. He wanted to know more about her. Except for Froyo yesterday, every moment they'd been together so far had been filled with one sort of stress or another. Toby swimming off to sea, Jack's diaper disaster, Frank wandering away, Julia being injured, or that polo-shirt-wearing, carb-pushing property developer making her breakfast. A swim date sounded perfect.

He parked by the curb between the Reynoldses' house and hers, admiring how pink roses cascaded over her white picket fence. There was a car parked in her driveway, which unnerved him. It was a silver Cadillac with bucket seats. Had Aaron gotten the date wrong? He looked back at Jack and panicked. Maybe she had meant next

Wednesday instead of today. Icy sweat prickled out all over his back, underneath the light-blue T-shirt he wore. The last thing he wanted was to walk up to Julia's door and have her turn him away. This was exactly why he didn't want to start dating yet. It was too stressful. Aaron wasn't sure he could handle it.

Jack chortled from the back seat. The sun beat all around, and the car began to heat up, even though the windows were still rolled down. "Okay, buddy," said Aaron. "It's now or never." He got out of the car and opened the back door, unclicking the car seat from its base. "Let's go see if Julia is ready to go or if your uncle . . . I mean daddy . . . I mean whatever . . . is a huge idiot." This day was going nowhere fast. Aaron couldn't even speak to Jack without stumbling over his words. He clenched his jaw and vowed to do better.

Julia stepped out onto the porch right as Aaron began to walk up the path. She wore shorts that showed off her toned legs and sparkly purple flip-flops. The top of her swimsuit peeked out of the faded University of Washington sweatshirt she wore. Her blonde hair swung in a high ponytail, and lipstick made her mouth look rosy, although the rest of her face was clean, without one hint of makeup. "Aaron," she said, smiling brightly. "You're here. I meant to run out to the car as soon as you drove up so you wouldn't have to unsettle Jack, but I had to put Toby in his crate first." She swung a gym bag over one shoulder and locked her front door. Toby barked in the distance, somewhere in the house.

"We just got here." Aaron looked at the silver Cadillac. "Do you have company?"

Julia pocketed her keys. "Nope. That's the property appraiser that the mortgage broker sent out, which is why Toby is in his crate." She sighed. "It's a long story." She peered into the infant carrier and smiled at Jack. "Hey there, cutie. Are you ready to swim?"

Jack giggled and whacked the rattle that swung from the car seat handle.

"He's excited to see you," said Aaron. "And so am I."

Julia's cheeks flushed the same color as her lips. "I'm excited to see you guys too."

"Here, let me get your bag for you."

"Thanks, but aren't you loaded down already?"

"This is nothing." Aaron used his free hand to lift the gym bag off Julia's shoulder. He opened the passenger-side door for her and then got Jack and her bag situated on the clean towels covering the back seat. The Tesla still had a faint aroma of puke about it, but he hoped Julia wouldn't notice.

"Oh no," said Julia after Aaron climbed into the driver's seat.

"What?"

She wrinkled her forehead. "The other night when I had my concussion and you drove me to urgent care . . . did I throw up in your car?"

Aaron laughed. "Nope. You did a number on that rug by your front door, but it was all out of your system by the time we drove to the doctor's office. I apologize for the smell." He pointed his thumb to the back seat. "My wingman can't hold his liquor."

Julia laughed. "That's a relief. But I'm sorry you had to see me throw up, wherever it happened."

Aaron started the car and pulled into traffic. Since Ninth Avenue was at the top of town, it was busy, especially this time of day. "The Cascade Athletic Club is down near the water, right?"

Julia nodded. "Yup. Across the street from the yacht club."

"Two clubs right next to each other?"

"The yacht club's for boating, and the CAC is a gym. Two different business models. But I think you'll like it. The pool's as warm as bathwater, which makes it good for older adults and babies. Has Jack ever been swimming before?"

Aaron shook his head. "First time in a swimsuit. Hey, I forgot to ask. Is the pool outside or inside?"

"Inside," Julia said in a definitive voice. "Otherwise nobody could use it for half the year because it would be too cold." She looked at him sideways and smirked. "Your California is showing."

"I'm originally from New Jersey, you know." Aaron reached into the door compartment for his sunglasses. The sunshine had burned through the marine layer, and the day was heating up even more. "Do you own a boat?"

Julia shook her head. "Not anymore. My father owned one, but my mother sold it after he died."

"When did he pass away?"

"When I was ten." She folded her hands in her lap.

"What was he like?"

Julia took a deep breath and held it. Aaron wondered if he'd said something wrong. Maybe he shouldn't have pried. But then she exhaled. "My father did everything with me," she said in a quiet voice. "He took me fishing, taught me how to crab, helped me with my homework, came to all my school events, and even came with me to sell Girl Scout cookies."

"He sounds like a great guy," said Aaron. "And the complete opposite of my dad," he added before he could help it.

"Really? But you're such a wonderful parent to Jack that I figured you'd learned from the best."

Aaron shook his head. "Nope. The only type of parenting my dad knew how to do was open his wallet."

"Well, at least Jack has an excellent grandfather on Jared's side. Frank was a good father," said Julia. "*Is* a good father," she corrected herself.

"Jack and I hung out with Frank last night while Martha went to dinner with friends. It was fun."

"That's great. I'm glad you're in their lives."

"Yeah. The only awkward part was when they showed up at my house with Jared's old car seat installed in Martha's Chevy. It must have been thirty years old." He felt guilty snitching on them, but he had to tell someone.

"What?" Julia covered her mouth with her hand and suppressed a laugh. "Oh my goodness, that's awful." She pulled her hand down, but it was too late; she laughed.

"I know, right? What am I going to do? I can't let Martha drive Jack around in a car seat that old. It doesn't even have a five-point harness."

"I'm Facebook friends with Jessica. Maybe I could message her," Julia offered.

Aaron sighed. "I don't know . . ."

"Or how about I casually mention to Martha that car seats have an expiration date when I see her car parked in the driveway? 'Oh, hey, by the way. I noticed that Jack's car seat looks out of date. Did you know that . . . blah-blah-blah?'" Julia looked at Aaron. "What do you think?"

"That could work." Aaron felt like she'd lifted a load from his shoulders. "Thank you." He clicked on his blinker and turned into the Cascade Athletic Club's parking lot. Luckily, he was able to find a place in the shade.

Aaron plotted his next move as he rolled up the windows. Not with Julia, unfortunately, but in trying to figure out how best to carry Jack and all his various paraphernalia into the gym. Would a stroller fit in the locker room? No, that seemed inconvenient. Probably the infant seat wouldn't fit either. Besides, it could get wet. That meant he either needed to suit up in the front-pack carrier or hold Jack in his arms.

"Are you okay?" Julia touched his elbow.

"What? No, sorry." Aaron shook his head quickly to recenter himself. "I was trying to figure out if I needed a stroller—that's all."

"Oh." Julia undid her seat belt. "I don't think so. I've never seen a stroller in the women's locker room before. But I did bring you a padlock for the men's room." She reached into her pocket and pulled out a lock. "The code is eighteen zero zero. That's the temperature that frozen yogurt freezes at. Eighteen degrees Fahrenheit."

"Thanks. I knew I forgot something." Aaron plucked the lock out of her hand, and their fingers touched. He thought about squeezing her hand again like he had yesterday at the Froyo shop, but the car was already starting to warm up, and he didn't want Jack to fuss. Plus, he was a coward. He didn't know if he could handle rejection. There had already been so much destruction in his life that year that his bruised heart couldn't handle the possibility of more. Aaron pushed a button, and the hatchback automatically lifted. He exited the car and collected the diaper bag before wrestling Jack out of his car seat.

Julia carried her own bag since Aaron's hands were full. She led him down the sidewalk to the entrance and held the door open for them. Right before they entered the gym, Jack ripped off Aaron's sunglasses and threw them on the ground. The plastic splintered on the hard floor.

Aaron sighed. "There goes another pair," he said, shaking his head. "Good thing I buy cheap ones."

"Oh no!" Julia let the door swing closed, and she bent down to pick up the debris.

As she bent over, Aaron's eyes studied her backside longer than was necessary, but not nearly long enough. She could be the cover model of a rock-climbing magazine, with the camera angled right below her butt. He blushed when he realized he was ogling her and hoped she hadn't noticed.

The air conditioner was turned up so high that walking into the club was like entering a refrigerator. The two-story lobby had floor-to-ceiling murals of the Cascade Mountains. Aaron stared at them in awe for a moment, wondering what each peak was called. He'd like to climb them in person someday. Couches and coffee tables created cozy seating areas, and a smoothie bar occupied the far corner of the room. Gym goers of various ages and ability levels walked through the lobby carrying tennis rackets and yoga mats. A group of older ladies sat on one of the couches drinking cappuccinos in tall glass mugs.

"Hi, Laura, here's my guest pass," said Julia, handing the woman at the counter her keys along with a small piece of paper. Laura's long gray hair was braided into a bun, and she wore a navy-blue shirt with the Cascade Athletic Club logo on the front. "Aaron, this is Laura Jonas, co-owner of the club. Laura, this is Aaron Baxter."

"Laura Jonas, as in the person Martha rear-ended?" The words tumbled out of Aaron's mouth before he could stop them.

Laura laughed, making the crystal earrings that dangled from her ears quiver. "The one and only. But that was a long time ago, unless Martha's rear-ended me more recently and I don't know about it." She scanned a tag on Julia's key ring and handed it back.

"No, sorry." Aaron held up the baby. "This is Martha's grandson Jack." It was so much easier introducing Jack that way.

"What a cutie!" Laura pumped hand sanitizer on her hands before she wiggled Jack's bare toes.

"Can we please have six towels?" Julia asked.

"Six towels?" Aaron asked at the exact moment he remembered he'd forgotten to bring some. "Why do we need six?"

"One for the pool. One for the shower," said Laura.

"Exactly." Julia put her keys back into her bag. "But actually, can we have eight instead? With the baby, we might need extras."

"No problem. I remember those days when my daughter, Marlo, was a baby." Laura slid a piece of paper across the counter and handed Aaron a pen. "You just need to sign the waiver first." She turned around to collect the towels.

Aaron juggled Jack from his right hip to his left and tried to prevent the diaper bag from sliding off his arm.

"Here," said Julia, holding out her hands. "I'll hold Jack while you fill out the paperwork."

"Thanks." He handed the baby over and picked up the pen. Most of the form was easy to complete. He jotted down his name, address, date of birth, and insurance company, and then ticked off the box about his health history. Except for a shoulder injury from a vicious tenth-grade soccer match that sometimes still bugged him, Aaron was in excellent condition. At first when he got to the line for including an emergency contact person, he didn't know what to write. But then he realized that even though he hadn't asked her, Martha would absolutely want him to write down her name, so he scribbled down her number. "All set," he said as he capped the pen. He passed the paper to Laura and reached for Jack.

"Oh no you don't." Julia spun out of his reach. "At least let me hold Jack until we get to the locker room. Come on; I'll show you where they are. The men's room is upstairs, and the pool is over here to the right."

What should have been a short trip ended up taking a century because so many people stopped to gush over Jack. Julia couldn't walk five feet without running into someone she knew.

"Julia!" A middle-aged man with shoulder-length hair rested his yoga mat on his shoulders and stopped to greet them. "Who's this cutie-patootie?"

"Hi, Matt." Julia swayed from side to side, and the baby giggled. "This is Jack." She turned to look at Aaron. "And this is Aaron, and we're going swimming." She spoke in a singsong voice that completely captured Jack's attention. The baby couldn't take his eyes off her.

"Matt Guevara," said the man, holding out his hand. "Are you new to Harper Landing? I haven't seen you around."

"Duh." Julia stopped swaying. "I'm so sorry. I should have properly introduced you. Aaron, Matt owns the Gnome's Backyard, which is the best gardening store in all Snohomish County. Matt, Aaron just moved here a little over a month ago."

"That's right." Aaron shook Matt's hand. "Good to meet you."

"If you're not saying where you moved here from, then I'm guessing California," Matt said with mock disapproval.

Aaron grimaced. "Guilty as charged."

Matt slapped him on the back. "We won't hold it against you—will we, Julia?"

Julia shook her head. "No, but I suggest you start telling people you're from New Jersey. Washingtonians get rather peeved about Californians moving up here and disrupting our real estate market."

After Matt, they ran into two old ladies who had been friends of Julia's mother; Paige's husband, Bob; a woman who'd won the Sweet Bliss auction basket at the Orca Tree Preschool; and finally a total stranger who seemed to be the only person in the whole place who didn't know Julia but who stopped to fawn over the baby based on Jack's natural attractiveness. "How do you go anywhere with this kid?" Julia asked at the entrance to the locker rooms. Her sweatshirt slid off her shoulder for a second before she tugged it back into place, and Aaron got a glimpse of her long neck and silky-smooth skin. "Jack's so cute that everyone wants to say hi."

"It's not usually this bad," said Aaron as he took the baby back. "The problem is, you seem to be a local celebrity."

"Not true! Half the time people don't even notice me." She tickled the baby's knees, and he giggled. "It's Jack, silly. He's a heartbreaker."

He's not the only one, thought Aaron as he gazed into Julia's warm-brown eyes. That roller coaster of emotions he rode zipped up and down. Aaron was falling for her fast. The grief still lingered, along with the overwhelming sadness at losing his sister and best friend. But there was something else headed his direction, too, and it was getting so close he could almost taste it: joy. Standing there next to Julia, holding Jack in his arms, and listening to them both laugh, Aaron felt happy for the first time in months.

CHAPTER FIFTEEN

The water was warm and inviting, but Julia didn't want to get her face wet. She stretched her arm out to the side and kept her head above the surface as she glided across the pool in an old-fashioned sidestroke. Julia was a better swimmer than this, but ten summers of forced swim-team participation had done nothing but make her loathe putting her face in the water. She hated the burning sensation of it accidentally going up her nose and the way her ears became waterlogged for several hours after she got out of the pool. But right now, that was the least of her worries. Julia wondered where Aaron and Jack were. It had been twenty minutes since they'd gone into the men's locker room, and they still hadn't emerged.

Maybe this was a bad idea, Julia thought to herself. Maybe Aaron had only said yes because she'd put him on the spot. As soon as she started with the self-doubt, her other worries kept piling up. How would she come up with a million dollars if she couldn't mortgage her house? Everything depended on that property appraiser. What was he discovering? It was true that she had moisture ants. She sprayed every year, but they kept coming back. There was a part of her banister that needed to be replaced because Toby had chewed it. Probably the appraiser would knock points off for that. And how was Toby surviving, locked up in his crate? Normally Julia let him loose in the house since there was a doggy door to the backyard, but she couldn't do that with a stranger poking around with his clipboard and calculator.

Julia pushed off from the edge of the pool and swam another lap. She looked at the wall clock and watched the second hand tick. Now it had been twenty-four minutes since she'd last seen Aaron. He'd bailed on her. That was the only explanation. Why had she acted so ridiculous when she had held Jack in the lobby? She'd loved watching him laugh every time she'd said the word *wow*. He'd giggled even harder when she'd hopped from one foot to the next. Aaron must have thought she was a crazy person who pranced around gyms saying, "Wow! Wow! Wow!" Julia's stomach clenched into knots. She should never have taken the risk to invite him swimming. How could she have been so stupid?

But then the door to the lobby swung open, and Aaron walked in wearing navy-blue swimming trunks, holding Jack against his bare chest. The knots in Julia's stomach morphed into butterflies. Jack looked adorable in pale-green shorts with a shark on the seat, his squishy soft skin the color of milk. He wasn't a chubby baby, but there was a doughiness about him, in sharp contrast to Aaron's rock-hard pecs. Julia sucked in her abs on instinct and prayed that the spandex in her bathing suit held true. She tightened up her triceps before waving at him from the water. The last thing she wanted to show off was arm jiggle.

Aaron smiled back and lifted Jack's hand to help him wave. As soon as Jack saw Julia, he burst into a grin. But when the two of them climbed down the steps into the pool, Jack's expression changed from glee to concern. He opened his eyes up wide, slapped the top of the water with his hand, and watched the droplets splash. Then he looked up at Aaron to see how he'd react.

"It's okay," said Aaron in a soothing tone. "This is a pool. It's like a giant bathtub."

Julia swam over to join them. "Does he like baths?"

"Loves them," said Aaron. "But he hates to get in baths, and he hates to get out."

"That makes no sense whatsoever."

Aaron shrugged. "You're telling me. Sorry it took us so long. It was a lot harder getting both of us changed than I thought. I couldn't set him down on the benches in front of the locker because I was afraid he'd roll off onto the tile floor. Luckily, Matt came in and held Jack for me while I put on my trunks."

"Oh gosh. I'm sorry. I didn't think about how hard it would be."

"It's not your fault." Aaron descended the rest of the steps and sank in the water up to Jack's shoulders. "Everything's more challenging with a baby—grocery shopping, going to the mailbox, sleeping . . ." He frowned for a second before kissing Jack's cheek. "But that's okay. Jack's worth it. I just wish I'd remembered to bring my phone with me, because I wanted to get a picture of Jack's first time in the pool."

"I have my phone in my locker. I'll go get it." Julia climbed up the steps of the pool and tried not to feel self-conscious that her bathing suit–clad body was on full display. She squeezed water out of her pony-tail. "I'll be right back." She slipped on her flip-flops, wrapped up in the towel, and dashed to the locker room. The air was cold compared to the warmth of the water, and goose bumps erupted down her skin. She ran into a friend from high school in the locker room but didn't stop to chat. Instead, she raced back to the pool to take pictures.

"That was fast," said Aaron when she returned.

Julia crouched down to her knees and put her phone in portrait mode. "Smile," she said before snapping a picture. "Wait, Jack wasn't looking at the camera." She moved her face away from the phone and tried to catch his attention. "Ja-ck," she called in a singsong voice. "Jack, Jack, Jack." The baby turned to look at her, and Julia clicked the phone. "That's one picture," she said. "But he's so serious in it."

"Let me see if I can get him to smile." Aaron tickled underneath the baby's chin and even tried swishing him around in a circle. Jack remained stoic in the face of all Aaron's efforts.

"Wow," said Julia. "Wow, wow, wow." Jack turned his head in her direction and giggled. "Wow," she said again, snapping the picture. "Wowey, wow, wow, wow." The baby chuckled and splashed the water.

"I don't know what you're saying in baby language, but it's obviously working," said Aaron with a grin.

"What's your number?" Julia poised her thumbs over her phone. "I'll text them to you." Aaron rattled it off, and Julia hit send. Then she deposited her phone next to her belongings and hopped back in the pool. Once she was safely back in the water, she realized what she'd done. First, she'd asked him out. Then, she'd gotten his number. Who was she, and what had she become? "You're plain," Waverley used to tell her. "Good-looking boys don't like homely girls." Julia caught a glimpse of her reflection in the window and noticed that all her lipstick had washed off. Her face was red and puffy from the chlorine, and her ponytail sagged. Julia turned away from the window and treaded water so that every part of her up to her neck was covered.

"Did you always dream of owning a frozen yogurt shop?" Aaron asked.

Julia pushed the dark thoughts out of her mind and focused on the present. "Yes," she said. "I mean, kind of. My dad owned Sweet Bliss back when it was an ice cream shop, and it was one of the saddest days of my life when it closed. When I was a teenager, I dreamed about reopening it someday, but after going to college and studying abroad, I decided that a frozen yogurt shop might be a better business model for our community. I thought about gelato, but then I changed my mind."

"Why? Gelato sounds like a good idea too."

"It is." Julia nodded. "I love gelato. But frozen yogurt sounds healthier, and Harper Landing is an active community. We have families who pack their weekends with soccer games and baby boomers who go to the gym every day. I decided frozen yogurt had the better chance to make money because consumers were less likely to view it as a treat reserved for special occasions." She changed the direction her arms were paddling. "I mean, in Italy people eat gelato all the time because they only have a small scoop. But this is America. One small scoop is hard to do. I have customers who come in a few times a week and load up on the nonfat, sugar-free blend and then pile on the berries. Since it's low calorie and full of calcium, it's not that bad for them."

"Except for the artificial sweeteners," said Aaron.

Julia shrugged. "That's their choice. Most of my flavors are made with natural ingredients. What about you? How did you and Jared build up Big Foot Paleo?" It felt raw, mentioning Jared, but Julia wanted to know. Plus, she hoped to steer the conversation away from Sweet Bliss. Her business was her baby, and Aaron's comments about the artificial sweeteners stung. Besides, who was he to talk? She thought that any diet that focused on eliminating entire food groups was ridiculous, but she wouldn't say so to Aaron, not when it was so important to him. That would be rude.

"Jared and I met freshman year, two doors down from each other in the same dorm. During the spring quarter, we both began training for a triathlon."

"I didn't know you did triathlons."

"I don't." Aaron grimaced. "I discovered that by mid-May and switched to running my first marathon instead. But Jared kept at the triathlon training, and we were both frustrated by the fueling component of it. The dorm food was decent, but we didn't have any portable snacks. Plus, I kept getting sick." Aaron frowned and knit his eyebrows together. "Actually, I'd been sick my whole life but didn't realize why until Jared suggested that I might be dairy intolerant. It turns out that it's not only dairy that bothers me, but other inflammatory foods, too, like sugar and corn."

"And you didn't realize that until college?"

Aaron shook his head. "Nope. When I was growing up, we had a new nanny every six months. They never lasted too long at my house before they quit or my mom fired them. In high school, I was too clueless to realize that what I ate was making me sick. But then in college, Jared read a book about the paleo diet and suggested we give it a try. After three days, I was ninety percent better. After a month, I was a whole new person. But eating paleo in the dorms was hard. That's how we started baking batches of grain-free granola in the communal kitchen and bringing them to practice with us. The people we trained with, who were all rich techies in Silicon Valley, started buying from us, and before we knew what had happened, we were paleo granola dealers."

"Did you have a business license?" Julia asked. "Or a food-handling card?"

Aaron chuckled. "Nope. We weren't using a commercial kitchen, either, so luckily we weren't caught. But one of our customers was a venture capitalist, and he helped guide us. We both officially dropped out in the middle of our sophomore year. Even with the venture capitalist's money, it was a gamble. My parents refused to help, because they were furious with me for dropping out of college, but my sister, Sara, sent us money from time to time to bail us out."

"Jared was always a big risk taker." Julia stopped treading water for a moment, remembering. "Once when I was ten, he climbed the cedar tree in my front yard to get a balloon that was tangled in the branches."

"That sounds like Jared." Aaron shifted the baby from one side of his body to the other.

Julia looked away so that he wouldn't see the tears forming in her eyes. It had been a long time since she'd thought about that balloon, or all the balloons they'd released at Harper Landing Cemetery at her father's graveside service. It had been fate, or poor luck, that one of the balloons had drifted away and ended up tangled in the branches next to her bedroom window a few days later. Julia didn't want to be reminded of her father's funeral every time she looked out her window. She begged her mother to retrieve it, but Waverley yelled at her. "What do you want me to do, climb up a ladder?"

Jared didn't use a ladder. He free-climbed up thirty feet without any harness, even though he was only in fifth grade. When he reached the balloon, he yanked it out of the needles so hard that he almost lost his balance. It fluttered to the ground a few seconds later, but Jared held firm to the trunk. When he finally reached the ground again, Julia burst into tears. She'd thrown her arms around him and promised to be his friend forever.

"Can I hold Jack while you swim some laps?" Julia asked, her voice a little shaky.

"That would be awesome," said Aaron. "Thanks."

Jack felt weightless in the water, and his bare skin stuck to her shoulders like he was an extension of herself. He grinned and grabbed her ponytail, putting the end in his mouth. "Hey," she said, gently pulling it out. "Hair's not for eating." Jack grabbed her cheeks instead and smooshed them together. "Wow," said Julia, making him laugh. He slapped her cheeks to make her repeat it. "Wow, wow, wow." She wanted to kiss his cheeks like she'd seen Aaron do but didn't know if that would be appropriate. Instead, she snuggled him for a moment before she zoomed him around in circles. "Superbaby!" she called as she guided him around the pool. She concentrated so much on Jack that she didn't see who'd entered the swim lane next to her.

"Well, look who's here," said a grouchy voice. "The slumlord of Harper Landing."

Julia looked up and saw Walt Lancaster's wiry white hair billowing out the side of his head and his paunchy belly hanging over sagging swimming trunks. She brought Jack into the crook of her arm and held him close. "I'm not a slumlord, Walt."

"Tell that to Dave Parson." Walt pointed up at the ceiling. "He has a leak the size of Elliott Bay in his roof."

"New roofs are going up this August." Julia stood up straight and wrapped her other arm around Jack.

"Another one of your friends?" asked Aaron as he swam up to them.

"No," Walt barked. "A better term would be *victim*. The Harpers have been victimizing me for thirty-eight years."

Julia felt her cheeks go hot. "It's not my fault my mother jilted you at the altar," she said before she could stop herself. "Any woman in her right mind would choose my father over you."

"Exactly," echoed a voice from the side of the pool. It was Matt, wearing his yoga gear but holding a sneaker. "Get over yourself, Walt. Everyone knows Julia's properties go for below-market rent. She's practically running a charity organization."

"Rents are going up soon to adjust for inflation," said Julia, feeling mortified. First Walt bullied her, and now Matt defended her—by exposing her lack of business acumen.

"Why should we pay more money when your buildings are falling apart?" Walt asked.

"I just told you I'm reroofing all my properties this August," said Julia.

Walt pointed his finger directly at her. "If your mother were alive, she would be ashamed of you."

"Yeah? So?" Julia ignored the tears that made her blink. "My mother was always ashamed of me, so that's nothing new." Jack latched onto her ponytail again and pulled. Julia grabbed his tiny fist in her hand to remove the hair, and feeling the baby squeeze her fingers gave her courage.

"You can't raise rents just because you feel like it," said Walt. "Tenants have rights, you know."

"Which my lawyers will carefully honor." Julia kissed Jack's hand. "You can talk to them if you have any questions." She spun around in the water and almost collided with Aaron, who was standing directly behind her. "Ready to go?" she asked in a higher-pitched voice than normal. It felt like her throat was closing a little bit.

Aaron folded his arms across his chest and glared at Walt. "Yes. I'm done swimming."

Matt turned his scathing glare away from Walt, and his expression softened. "Do you guys need a towel for the baby?"

"That would be great." Julia rushed as fast as she could to the steps at the edge of the pool. "There's one hanging on that hook over there."

Matt retrieved the fluffy bath towel. He held it open while she climbed out of the pool, then took Jack from her and wrapped the baby up like he was a dahlia bulb being safely guarded for winter. Julia threw her towel around her shoulders and crammed her toes into her flip-flops. She picked up her phone and tried not to look at Walt, but when she did, she was surprised to see him looking angrily, not at her, but at Aaron, who was still in the pool and speaking with Walt.

"Are we clear?" Aaron asked him.

"Mind your own business," Walt said with a snarl.

"She *is* my business. And where I come from, it's not okay to accost people in the pool."

"That's not how things are done in Harper Landing either," Matt added, holding Jack. "And you know that, Walt. What you did today violates the code of ethics for the Harper Landing Chamber of Commerce members. We're supposed to support our fellow business owners, not tear each other down."

There was a crowd gathering as other swimmers who'd entered the pool area stopped to watch the scene. Julia gasped for air after she realized she was holding her breath. She couldn't understand what her mother had ever seen in Walt. What had they discussed during their weekly lunches in Lynnwood? What a disappointment she was as a daughter? Julia let out the gulp of air. *Yes,* she thought to herself. That was exactly what they'd talked about.

"Come on, Julia," said Aaron. "Let's go." He fist-bumped Matt before taking the baby. "Thanks, man. I owe you one."

"How about I hold on to Jack while you get dressed?" Julia offered.

"Really?" Aaron asked. "But you're sopping wet." He looked over her shoulder at Walt. "Plus there's that guy to deal with."

"I'll hold on to Jack," said Matt. "I don't have to be at the Gnome's Backyard until eleven."

"Thanks, but I should probably take him in the shower with me to remove the chlorine." Aaron walked a few steps away. "I'll meet you in the lobby as soon as I can," he told Julia.

"You mean like in three hours?" she replied. It felt good to joke again, like the stress of her confrontation with Walt was already melting away.

"Something like that," Aaron said with a grin. "Will you wait for me?"

"Of course," she teased. "You're my ride home."

CHAPTER SIXTEEN

The way Jack fussed told Aaron that nap time was imminent. It might even be too late to feed the baby a bottle before he went down. Unfortunately, the stroller was in the car. If Jack were horizontal right now, he'd be out cold, bottle or no bottle. Instead, he squirmed in Aaron's arms on the walk out of the locker room. When they reached the lobby, Julia was sitting on one of the overstuffed couches sipping a smoothie. She patted the seat next to her. "I bought you one, too, with coconut water, kale, chard, and peaches. That's paleo, right?"

Aaron nodded and dropped the diaper bag at his feet. "You did good. Would you mind hanging out here a bit while I feed Jack?" She nodded, and he sat down next to her. "Jack doesn't like cold bottles, but he'll take one if he's hungry enough." The baby beat him on the chest and began to wail.

"Uh-oh. It looks like swimming worked up his appetite." Julia swooped Jack out of Aaron's arms and tried to calm him. Jack arched his back and cried louder. People around them stared at the commotion.

Aaron ripped open the diaper bag and located the bottle in fifteen seconds that felt like fifteen years. He uncapped the nipple and popped it into Jack's mouth midwail. The baby latched on, appeased, and greedily sucked. Now that the crying had stopped, Aaron felt tension melt off his shoulders like water. He watched as Julia cradled Jack in her arms and fed him the bottle.

"Do you want to go outside?" she asked. "There's a shady bench where you can watch the boats come in and out of the marina."

"That sounds great." Aaron wasn't particularly eager to have all Harper Landing spy on them. Being inside Cascade Athletic Club with Julia was like swimming in a fishbowl. "Let me grab the bags." He zipped up the diaper bag and collected Julia's gym things as well. Then he followed her outside and down a path toward the water. They sat down on a metal bench underneath a cottonwood tree. The air smelled like brine and rope. Sailboats rocked in the harbor next to motorboats and the occasional yacht. They sat for a few moments in silence before either of them spoke.

"So now you know why there's a property appraiser at my house," said Julia. "I'm mortgaging my house to pay for putting new roofs on all my rentals. My mother let a lot of maintenance projects slide when she was in charge." She said it matter of factly, without judgment.

"Was this Will's idea?" Aaron asked. The thought of the property developer making Julia breakfast yesterday morning made him snarl.

"No, Will wants me to sell him some of my land for a fat profit. No, all my land, actually, but I didn't tell my accountant that. George says that I should take out a loan instead and then raise the rents to market rate to rebuild my funds."

"I'm no real estate expert, but that sounds like wise advice to me." Aaron leaned back on the bench and threw his arm around the edge, hoping that Julia would lean back too.

"I agree," she said, resting against his arm. "And that's what I'm going to tell Will at dinner on Friday. Thanks, but no thanks."

"Dinner on Friday?" *Damn it!* He'd waited too long to ask her out. Would Paige be able to babysit on Saturday instead? Aaron wasn't sure. "Can't you tell Will no thanks over the phone?"

"I could, but I want to pick his brain some more about what he envisions for the downtown core."

"The downtown core." Aaron snorted. "Right. It didn't look like Will was interested in the downtown core when he was making your french toast Monday morning."

Julia chuckled. "Don't be ridiculous. It was a business meeting that I'd totally forgotten about because of my concussion. Will was only being nice."

"There's nice, and then there's walking-around-in-your-apron nice."

"Complex carbohydrates can be very complex." Julia handed him the empty bottle. "Do you have a burp cloth? I should probably hand Jack back to you because my tailbone's bothering me." She shifted her weight to one side, which caused her to lean closer against him.

"I've got one somewhere." He dug into the diaper bag until he found a soft blue cloth.

After Julia handed him the baby, she put her gym bag under her like a seat cushion. Aaron burped Jack by leaning the baby over his forearm and slapping him gently on the back. The baby let out an enormous belch that was way too big for his tiny body, and they laughed. Then he let out another one, which sparked Aaron's worry about the gassiness issue. That was it—Aaron was calling Dr. Agarwal as soon as they got home to ask her opinion about switching formulas. But once the gas was out of his system, Jack's eyes fluttered closed, and when Aaron settled him back on his hand to try for a third burp, Jack fell fast asleep.

"You're good at that," said Julia.

"Now, maybe, but you should have seen what a mess I was when Jack was a newborn." Aaron watched the steady rise and fall of Jack's breathing. "I had no idea what I was doing."

"Most people have nine months to prepare."

Aaron nodded. "Not me. The first time I put a diaper on, I did it backward." He chuckled, trying to keep things light. The truth was that the first few weeks of Jack's life had brought Aaron to his breaking point. Grief, sleep deprivation, and his own incompetence had made him feel like he was drowning. It wasn't until he'd read his first book on infant care, while feeding Jack bottles, that he'd felt like he could swim.

"Being a father seems to come naturally to you," said Julia. "You make that look easy."

Aaron shifted uncomfortably, feeling undeserving of the title. "But I'm not a father; I'm an uncle."

Julia put her hand on his arm. "You sure look like a father to me. But uncle, then. Uncle taking on a paternal role."

Aaron stared into the distance and watched a blue heron soar down from the sky and land on the water. "I don't know what I am." He sprawled Jack out on his lap, resting him safely between both legs, and made extra sure that the shade from the willow tree covered the baby's face.

"You're someone who loves Jack and takes excellent care of him. That's obvious to anyone who sees."

"I do the best I can, but my sister, Sara, would have been better."

"Jared would have been a good father too," said Julia. "Maybe even as wonderful as you—who knows?" She pulled a lock of blonde hair behind her ear and smiled softly.

Julia looked so sweet and innocent that he wanted to confess right then and there what he'd done. He wanted to explain how he'd put his foot down when Jared had suggested moving the offices to Modesto to be closer to the factory. He wanted to spell out to her, in clear terms that would make her understand that it was his fault, why Jared and Sara had been on the road that rainy January night, commuting to Palo Alto. They had sold the company in December but had still been finalizing the transition plan in January. He wanted to describe what it had been like to stand vigil next to Sara's motionless body while the machines had kept her alive long enough for the doctors to save Jack. If only Aaron hadn't been so stubborn. "If only," he whispered.

"If only what?" Julia asked, raising her eyebrows.

"Nothing." He stared down at the sleeping baby.

Julia's shoulders slumped, and she removed her hand from his arm. "What are you going to do now that you sold your company? Does General Mills need you to stay on and manage things?"

"No. They needed me to tie up loose ends at the beginning of the year. We took care of that quickly."

"What happened to your employees?"

"The workers stayed on," explained Aaron. "But the executive management team—which was really just Jared, Sara, and me—was replaced by people from their headquarters in Minneapolis."

"So as soon as you sold, you were out of a job?"

Aaron nodded. "Basically. Sara was happy about it because she'd been doing our PR and marketing. She was excited to become a full-time stay-at-home mom as soon as Jack was born."

Julia reached for Aaron's hand and squeezed it. "And Jared?"

"He wanted to move home to Harper Landing. I'm not sure if he knew that Frank was slipping or not. If he did, he never mentioned it to me. But he did want to raise his family near grandparents, and Sara's and my folks were certainly not an option."

"So that's why you uprooted your whole life, then, to move to a place you'd never been before?"

Aaron nodded. "Pretty much."

"That was extremely unselfish of you. I don't know if I could have done it. But then, I've lived in the same house my entire life, except for two semesters in Florence."

"*Unselfish* is the last word I'd use to describe myself." Aaron clenched and unclenched his jaw.

"Do you think your sister would have liked it here in Harper Landing?" Julia tapped her foot on the pavement a few times as if anxious about how he would answer the question.

"She would have fit right in at that mommy-and-baby group at the library." Aaron shrugged. "Better than me, at least."

"Yeah, but do you think she would like the rest of Harper Landing?" Julia asked. "The trees and the beach and the cute little shops downtown . . . and crappy things, too, like how it can be freezing cold, even in the middle of June, and that it rains one hundred and fifty-eight days a year."

"One hundred and fifty-eight days a year?" Aaron repeated. Sure, it had rained a lot since he'd moved there, but he'd hoped that was because of the season.

Julia wrinkled her nose. "Yeah. We get a lot of rain. But the good news is that it normally doesn't rain all day—only part of it. So if you time things right, you can still go for a walk or work in your garden and not get drenched."

"I'm sure I'll get used to it," said Aaron. "I bought a rain cover for my jogging stroller."

"That'll keep *Jack* dry at least."

"What about you?" he asked her. "Could you ever live someplace besides Harper Landing? Permanently, I mean?"

Julia nodded. "I think I could. Italy taught me that. It would be hard leaving a town where I have such deep roots, but I don't have any family keeping me here. Sometimes I think about how exciting it would be to move to a big city where nobody knows me." Her eyes scanned the horizon and watched a sailboat pull into the marina. "If I took Will up on his offer and sold everything, I could do exactly that. Move on and start someplace fresh." She turned to look at him. "Like you did, Aaron."

"But why would you want to?" Aaron stretched out his legs as far as he could without disturbing Jack. "Everyone here seems to love you—with the notable exception of that Walt guy—and Sweet Bliss is booming."

"Because I've always dreamed of traveling. Studying abroad in Italy was great, but I want to see the rest of Europe too. And Asia and South America." Julia pointed to a yacht docked in the harbor.

"Onward—that's where I would go. If I were brave enough, I'd hop on that boat right now and set sail for Australia." She let out a deep sigh and pointed her toes into the ground. "But I can't. I have too many responsibilities here in Harper Landing. There are my business and rental properties; plus I couldn't leave Toby."

"I've always wanted to travel too," said Aaron, remembering the tiny stone in her purse etched with that word: *onward.* "In fact, before everything happened, my goal was to run a marathon on every continent but Antarctica. But you know, I was going to see the sights while I was there too. It wouldn't all have been running."

"That sounds amazing," said Julia. "Except for the part about running," she added with a grin. "But why can't you still do that? Babies are portable. All you'd need to do would be to hire a nanny to come with you."

"Absolutely not," said Aaron, sharper than he'd intended. "Sara wouldn't have wanted that. We spent our whole childhood raised by nannies. That's not what she had planned for Jack."

"It's good that you're honoring her wishes, but you've got to honor your own path too."

"Jack *is* my path now. There are plenty of marathons I can train for here in Washington with a jogging stroller."

"And your rain cover," Julia said, with a hint of a smirk.

"And the rain cover."

"Well, if you were previously plotting to go to six different continents, then I take it you're already an experienced traveler."

"Not as experienced as I'd like to be," Aaron admitted. "Sometimes, my mom would take Sara and me with her when she traveled for work, but usually that meant staying in fancy hotels in big cities and ordering room service with our nannies."

"That sounds horrible. Sign me up."

Aaron chuckled. "Okay, it wasn't all bad. Especially the warm chocolate croissants in Paris. But later, when we were teenagers, we went on summer trips with school and did the normal tourist things: museums, theaters, landmarks, pyramids—"

"Pyramids? What type of school trip goes to Egypt? The only place my high school went was to Olympia to rally for saving the orcas."

Aaron rubbed the back of his neck and winced, not because he was developing a knot in his muscles but because he knew how strange his high school experience would sound to Julia. "I went to boarding school in Andover," he explained. "So did Sara. We were there starting in ninth grade."

"Wait a second." Julia formed her hands into a T, like she was calling for a time-out. "You mean that you moved away from home when you were fourteen?"

Aaron nodded. "I haven't been back since."

"Wow." Julia leaned back into the bench. "No wonder being a stay-at-home mom was such a priority to your sister. It sounds like she wanted the exact opposite for Jack than what you had growing up."

"That's right." Aaron watched the steady rise and fall of Jack's chest and felt centered. "This was what Sara wanted. Right here. She wanted to be with Jack, to take care of him, raise him, and really know him."

"And that's what you want too?" Julia asked.

"Yes. From the moment I first held him in my arms, that's exactly what I wanted."

"Then that proves my point from earlier," said Julia in a quiet voice. "You're a natural father, and Jack's lucky to have you."

"But—"

"No *buts*."

"I don't even know what to have him call me." Tension crept up Aaron's back. This was one of his biggest anxieties. "All the baby books say to talk to infants as much as possible so that their language development will be on track, but I don't even know how to refer to myself."

Julia paused for a moment, her eyes darting back and forth as she considered it. "Do you want Jack to call you Daddy?"

"No," Aaron admitted. "That feels wrong. But I also don't want him to grow up fatherless."

"He's not fatherless; he has you."

"But I'm not Jack's father, and I want to honor Jared."

"So have him call you Uncle Aaron, then, and when he grows up, if he wants to call you Dad, let him." Julia reached out and gently squeezed Jack's foot without waking him up.

"That seems like good advice." Aaron let out a breath of air he didn't know he'd been holding. "Thank you."

"I don't know if it's good advice or not." Julia tilted her head to the side. "But that's what I would do." She shifted in her seat. "Hey, I'm sorry, because I'd love to sit with you here for Jack's entire nap, but my bruised tailbone won't let me." She gingerly rose to her feet. "Swimming felt good, but that's probably the only exercise I'll be up to for a while."

"Of course. I'm so sorry. Sitting on a metal bench is the last thing that would be good for your injury."

"Why are you apologizing?" Julia picked up her gym bag. "The bench was my idea."

Aaron scooped up Jack into a cradle hold so he'd continue to sleep and slipped the diaper bag over his shoulder. "I don't know," he admitted. "I feel the need to apologize for everything these days." He hated himself as soon as he said it, because it made him seem weak, and Aaron wasn't weak. But it was also the truth. Guilt weighed on his shoulders like a boulder.

Julia took a step closer and stared up into his eyes. "You don't need to apologize for anything. You've faced major life changes in the past few months." She pressed her lips together in a hard line and looked out at the water. "So have I."

Sadness rolled across her face like a veil that Aaron longed to lift away. He imagined cupping her face with his hands and crushing their lips together. He wondered if her lips were as pillowy soft as they looked.

But his arms were full of Jack. "Would you go out to dinner with me Saturday night?" he blurted out. "Assuming I can find a babysitter."

Julia smiled and looked back up at him. "Really? I'd love to."

Aaron stood up straighter. "Great. We can work out the details later. Right now, I should get you back home so you can rest." As they walked back to the car, Aaron vowed to himself that the next time he stood next to Julia like that, he would wrap his arms around her curvy waist and kiss her.

CHAPTER SEVENTEEN

Numbers flashed across the calculator screen. It was Friday afternoon, and Julia was in her office at Sweet Bliss reviewing the offer from the mortgage broker. She hadn't shared the information with George yet, but she planned to, because she was eager to get his opinion. "Banks take away houses," she heard Waverley say as she read the jaw-dropping amount she would owe the bank each month if she went through with the mortgage. Could she really make a monthly payment of almost $10,000? Plus, there was the mortgage insurance on what the broker called her *jumbo loan*. The word *jumbo* alone would have made Waverley balk.

This would be different if she could access her trust fund a couple of years early—twenty-two months early, to be exact—but after conferring with the lawyer this morning, she knew that wasn't possible. Harrison had set the fund up in such a way that Julia's assets would be protected until she was "a fully mature adult," according to the will. For some reason that Julia couldn't figure out, Waverley's will also had transferred her half of Harrison's estate directly into the trust. Julia added up all her rental income one more time. She owned eighteen properties, but one of them was her house, and the other was Sweet Bliss. That left sixteen rent payments a month, which she'd only recently begun collecting since the probate period on Waverley's will had taken so long to resolve.

Rent brought in $22,000 with each flip of the calendar. After property taxes, insurance, and supplementing her meager maintenance fund, she was left with $11,300 a month of profit, $10,000 of which would have to go to the mortgage payment. If just one tenant failed to pay their rent on time, she'd be screwed.

She knew what her mother would have done in this situation. Waverley would have sold off assets before she'd risk the loan. Julia imagined what delicious revenge it would be to sell off the Sugar Factory out from under Walt, but she was loath to get rid of any of her properties. She wished she knew what her father's advice would have been in this situation. She turned around in her desk chair and stared up at his picture on the bulletin board. There he was at the opening of the original Sweet Bliss. That had been a risk, Julia realized. Her father couldn't have been content to be a landlord, living off rental income for the rest of his life. Instead, he'd rolled the dice and opened an ice cream shop. He'd taken a vision and made it a reality.

A knock on her office door pulled Julia out of her musing. "Julia?" called a voice from outside. "It's four p.m., and you told me to remind you to leave on time tonight."

Julia hopped out of her chair and opened the door for Tara. "Thanks," she said. "I definitely needed the time check. How are things going out there?"

Tara tightened her apron strings over her generous hips. Her hair was dyed ruby red this month, and she wore large gold earrings that brushed her shoulders. "It's chaos. A baseball camp just let out, and there are a dozen boys out there abusing the free samples."

"Are you sure you don't need me to stay? I can throw on an apron and—"

"Go," Tara smiled. "Jordan and I have it covered. She's restocking the bowls right now. Have fun on your date with Will."

"It's not a date." Julia's cheeks bloomed red. "It's a business meeting."

"Oh yeah? I thought you said Will was taking you to the Parisian Café."

"He is, and I wish he weren't, especially since—"

"Especially since what?"

"Nothing," Julia said. She'd been about to say that it was especially awkward to eat dinner at the Parisian Café since that was the property she was considering selling, but Tara didn't need to know that. There was no point in her Sweet Bliss employee learning about her financial troubles. Word traveled fast in a small town like Harper Landing, and Julia didn't want there to be any more gossip about her than there already was.

"Will's not picking you up here, is he?" Tara asked.

"No. Why?"

Tara raised her eyebrows and cringed. "You're wearing jeans and a T-shirt."

"I've got my blazer hanging over my chair. Once I throw that on, I'll be fine."

"I know you love that blazer, but that's definitely not what you should wear on a date to the Parisian Café."

"It's not a date; I already told you." *Tomorrow is a date,* she thought to herself, feeling a zing of excitement when she remembered Aaron asking her out.

"Honey, you're talking to a woman who's been divorced for three years. I know a date when I see one. Go home, take your hair out of that ponytail, and put on the dress you usually wear for the Fourth of July."

"My Fourth of July dress? But that's so short!"

"Exactly. Plus it's sleeveless and shows off your arms." Tara lifted up her arm and jiggled the skin hanging below. "If I had your triceps, I'd brag about them all the time."

"I don't want to show off my arms to Will." Julia picked up her purse off her desk and grabbed her blazer while she was at it.

"Why not? He's handsome, rich, tall, pleasant to talk to. Every time he stops by the shop, I find the two of you laughing. Go out and have a good time tonight. Show a little leg."

"You've totally got the wrong impression. Will's only interested in my real estate. If you haven't noticed, he's at least ten years older than me."

"So? Weren't your parents ten years apart?"

"Fifteen," Julia admitted. "But that was different."

"How was it different?"

"They were in love."

Tara pulled her chunky red glasses down to the tip of her nose and stared at Julia across the rims. "Who says Will's not in love with you?"

"You're being ridiculous again, and I'm asking you to stop." Julia marched through the door of her office and into the kitchen.

Tara followed her. "It's not ridiculous to think that a handsome, successful man like Will would be interested in you."

Julia eyeballed the machines to make sure everything was churning properly and paused right before she left through the side door. Her emotions were a tangled mess, and one of those feelings was guilt. She remembered her conversation with Paige from last weekend, when Paige had told her she suffered from low self-esteem. Was that true? To Julia, it *did* seem ridiculous to imagine that a man like Will would be interested in her for more than a real estate deal, but maybe Tara was correct. "I'm sorry I snapped at you," she said. "You're right about the blazer. It's not the best choice for a French restaurant, so I'll leave it at home."

"Good choice."

"But I'm certainly not wearing my Fourth of July dress."

"At least take down your ponytail!" Tara called after her as Julia strode out the door.

Ten minutes later Julia was home and surveying her closet with Toby's help. The Labrador sat next to her, nudging her thigh with his snout so that she would pet him. Julia's fingers massaged his soft fur, and she considered her wardrobe options. The truth was, they were limited. There was the red cotton sundress she wore on the Fourth of July, which she'd already ruled out for tonight. She'd rather save it for her date with Aaron tomorrow. Her other option was the white silk-modal wrap dress that she'd bought in Florence for a date with Mario that had turned out to be one of the worst days of her life. When she'd shown up at his house to surprise him with a picnic basket, she'd found him making out on the couch with his next-door neighbor. Heartbroken, Julia had never worn the dress again, but she'd also not gotten rid of it because it was so expensive.

Julia unzipped the dress from the hanger and stared at the Italian label sewn into the seam. She wasn't sure she could even fit into the dress anymore. Italian clothes always ran small, and she'd purchased it six years ago. As her fingers brushed against the fine fabric, she had to admit that it was the perfect dress for a night like this. It was long enough that it reached just above her knees and was a classic design that worked for every occasion.

Toby whimpered, annoyed that Julia was no longer petting him, and he hopped up on her bed and curled up on his place at the bottom. "What do you think?" she asked him a few minutes later as she spun around in the dress for her dog's approval. "I can't believe it still fits." When she looked in the mirror, she felt like a less-glamorous version of Marilyn Monroe. She brushed her hair out into soft waves that fell down her shoulders and added a pair of gold sandals she'd worn as a bridesmaid last year.

Toby's ears perked up, and he barked. He leaped off the bed and ran to her bedroom door while Julia was pinning on the pearl earrings she'd inherited from her mother. "What is it?" she asked a second before she heard a door slam in the driveway. Will was here five minutes early. Julia grabbed the first coat she saw in her closet, a cropped jean jacket. Luckily, it looked great with the wrap dress and sandals. She dragged

Toby into his crate and gave him a squeaky toy to pacify him and then hurried downstairs to answer the front door.

Will wore pressed chino slacks and a brown silk shirt that glistened in the bright sunlight. Since it was the end of June, the sun wouldn't set until nine o'clock, which was still a few hours away. He whistled when he saw Julia, making her blush. "Look at those legs," he said, giving her an appraising stare.

Julia desperately wanted her blazer. This dress had been a huge mistake. She hadn't meant to give Will the wrong idea. "Is that how you speak to all your business associates?" she asked, surprised at her own moxie to speak up for herself.

"Only the pretty ones." Will winked. He held out his arm to escort her to his Jaguar.

"I need my purse. I'll be right back." Julia shut the door and walked into her kitchen, where her purse and phone lay on the counter. Beads of sweat popped up on the back of her neck, and she wiped them away with a napkin. What had she gotten herself into? A sense of unease tiptoed across her body, but she told her nervous system to calm down. Will must have thought she was flirting just now. She needed to be clearer in the future. That was all. Julia buttoned up her jean jacket to the collar and headed back to the door. When she stepped out on the porch, she avoided Will by locking the door and skedaddling down the driveway before he could offer his elbow again. "Let's get going," she said in a brisk tone. "We have a lot of business to cover tonight."

"Yes ma'am." Will clicked his key fob, and the Jaguar beeped.

When Julia climbed inside, she smelled the rich scent of leather. The odometer showed three hundred miles. "It might be easier to walk," she said. "The Parisian Café is only half a mile away, and parking on a Friday night can be rough."

"Yes, but then you'd have to walk up Main Street to come home. That's an awfully steep hill."

"I don't mind. I do it all the time."

"In those shoes?" His eyes drifted down her bare legs.

Julia crossed her ankles and rested her purse on her knee. "Hope you're good at parallel parking," she said primly. She wasn't used to having her body ogled like that, and the way Will did it made her uncomfortable. Thank goodness she hadn't worn her red dress, which was shorter.

"Oh, I'm good at everything." Will rolled down the window and rested his elbow out the side of the car as they drove down Main Street. "What I love about Harper Landing is that it's so quaint."

"I wouldn't say *quaint*," said Julia. "*Charming* is more like it."

"It's not Bellevue; that's for sure," Will said dismissively.

"Nor would we want it to be. Bellevue has lost its soul. Sure, it has Microsoft money flooding every street corner, but the city has grown so huge so fast that what was once the downtown core has been obliterated by high-rises and condos." Julia looked closely as they drove by Sweet Bliss. It pleased her to see the shop packed with customers. The Nuthatch Bakery and the Smoothie Hut were crowded too. Sure the roofs were patched and the facades were fading, but Main Street locations were valuable, and she needed to protect them.

"Think what all that Microsoft money has done for the citizens of Bellevue." Will spun the steering wheel as they rolled around the fountain at the intersection of Fifth and Main. He tapped the brakes just in time to avoid hitting an older couple strolling through the crosswalk. "Bellevue has excellent schools, beautiful parks, and a booming local economy."

"Harper Landing is booming too." Julia pointed to the busy restaurants that lined the street. "At least as much as we want it to."

"As much as Harper Landing wants it to, or as much as *you* want it to?" Will asked.

Julia didn't know what to say. "I don't speak for all of Harper Landing," she admitted. "But the city council has honored the building-height limits for a reason. We value small-town charm."

"I value small-town charm too," said Will as they approached the Parisian Café. As Julia had predicted, every parking space was full. "But most of the buildings on Main Street are ancient, including yours." He pointed at the cedar siding and shake-shingled roof of the restaurant. "Imagine how great this place would be if we tore it down, dug out an underground parking lot, and rebuilt in a neoclassic style that fit the theme of the restaurant. It would still be two stories to honor the building-height code, but there could be condos on top with wrought iron balconies and killer views."

"There's a parking space over there." Julia pointed to a Subaru backing out of a spot. She thought of how horrendously ugly faux-French architecture would be in the heart of Harper Landing but kept her opinion to herself. Tonight was for gleaning information from Will, not critiquing his ideas. "What would you do to the homes next door?" she asked, referring to the 1900s craftsman-style houses she owned on Second Avenue.

Will slid the Jaguar right up to the curb. "I'd replace those too. Nobody wants detached garages and chopped-up rooms. Who uses basement workshops anymore?"

"My dad did," said Julia. "It's where he repaired his crab pots."

"Those houses were built for fishermen and loggers," said Will, ignoring her comment about Harrison. "I develop properties for software engineers and computer scientists."

"New doesn't necessarily mean better." Julia unclicked her seat belt and stepped out of the car. "And the houses on Second were originally owned by shingle-mill workers, not fishermen or loggers. Harper Landing was a shingle-mill town."

"That explains the sagging roofs." Will looked up at the roofline of the Parisian Café. "Some of those shingles look original."

"They're not original." Julia opened the door to the restaurant herself. "My grandfather replaced the roofs before I was born. That vintage of shake shingles can last for fifty years because the wood was from old-growth cedar."

Will raised his eyebrows. "I wouldn't want to face your property-maintenance bill on these old relics."

Julia shuddered. For once, she agreed with him. Her worried expression transformed to a smile, however, when she saw the hostess. It was Lily Parson, the teenage daughter of restaurant owner Dave Parson.

Lily collected two menus from the front desk. "Bonsoir," she said in a squeaky voice. "Bienvenue au Parisian Café." Her long hair was dyed blue-black and tapered down at her waist in wispy edges that looked like feathers. Her eyeliner was thick and dramatic but unevenly applied, giving her features a lopsided look.

"Bonsoir à toi aussi, jeune fille." Will leaned an elbow on her podium and flashed a toothy grin. "Je voudrais ta meilleure table."

"What?" Lily opened her eyes up with fright. She'd obviously not understood a word Will had said.

Julia mainly spoke English and Italian, but she knew enough French to get by after visiting the Alps. She was about to come to Lily's rescue and say that Will had asked for the best table when Will spoke first.

"Tu ne parles pas français?"

"Huh?" Lily's hands shook so hard that she dropped the menus. "Excuse me. I'm so sorry," she said as she bent down to pick them up.

Julia helped collect them. "No problem," she said. "He was just asking if you spoke French; that's all."

"Oh." Lily's face turned beet red. "Yes. I mean no. I mean, kind of. I'm taking third-year French at the high school." She held the menus in front of her like they were armor. "Let me show you to your table."

Will rolled his eyes. "So far, I'm not impressed with this place," he stage-whispered.

Now Julia's cheeks were the ones burning. She'd never been a huge fan of Dave's cooking, but she knew there were throngs of retirees who adored this restaurant and booked a reservation every time they had something to celebrate.

"Why is it called the Parisian Café?" Will continued. "It should be *Café Parisien*."

Julia knew that Will was right, but her tolerance for his criticism of her hometown was reaching its breaking point. She followed him into the dining room and hoped that Lily hadn't overheard his insult.

Once they were seated in the dimly lit room, Julia put her napkin on her lap and tried to relax. She was here to explore her options; that was all. So far, Will's ideas for redeveloping her property weren't appealing, but that didn't mean she wasn't learning something. Digging down to create underground parking, for example, was a worthwhile idea if it could be done without destroying the historical integrity of her buildings. Julia took a sip of water and vowed to listen carefully.

"When I ran restaurants, I never let guests sit for longer than four minutes without a waiter attending to them." Will looked around the room for any sign of their server.

"I know you mentioned being a short-order cook, but I didn't know you ran multiple restaurants." Julia put down her menu since she always ordered the same thing when she came here: duck à l'orange.

"I'm the living embodiment of the American dream." Will rapped the signet ring he wore on the table. "I started working at Red Robin when I was sixteen, worked my way up to manager, and then opened my own franchise when I was twenty-four."

"Wow," Julia interrupted. "That's impressive that you could take on a franchise at such a young age. Where did you get the capital for that?"

"My father-in-law gave me a small loan of a million dollars." Will shrugged. "He knew I was good for it."

Julia felt like a minor earthquake had rocked the table. "I didn't know you were married," she said.

"*Was* married," Will clarified. "I should have said *former* father-in-law."

Julia had loads of questions about Will's alleged rags-to-riches story—starting with *Did he really pull himself up by his bootstraps if he married into money?*—but she didn't want to appear too curious about his love life. She decided to start with a neutral question instead. "What was it like being a franchise owner?"

"Great at first. I knew all parts of the business at that point, and I made loads of money. I paid my father-in-law back after three years, got divorced, opened up three more franchises, and then cashed them all out when I turned thirty-two and began investing in real estate instead." His eyes scanned the cozy room. "Land's where the real profit is, especially in the Pacific Northwest. If home values keep going the way they're going, we'll be the next Bay Area before you know it. Cute little starter homes will go for two million."

Julia felt chills when Will said that. *Banks take away houses.* The past that her mother had lived in fear of—foreclosure, evictions, and shelters—was about to become a lot of people's future. "And you think rebuilding Main Street with second-story condos is the answer?" Julia asked.

"Absolutely." Will nodded. "Trust me; I know what I'm talking about."

CHAPTER EIGHTEEN

Aaron had never left Jack alone with anyone besides Martha before, and he was trying not to have a heart attack. It was Saturday night, and he was giving instructions to the teenage babysitter Paige had helped him arrange. Paige was unavailable that evening, but she'd lined up a junior named Alyssa from Harper Landing High School, whom Paige assured Aaron was top of her class, CPR certified, and vice president of the National Honor Society. Alyssa could have walked on water for all Aaron cared; he still didn't completely trust her. He would have been more comfortable with Martha watching Jack, but she'd already had Grandma Day that morning.

"This list on the refrigerator here has all the emergency numbers on it," he told Alyssa. "My number, the pediatrician's number, poison control, and Jack's grandparents' number here in town." Aaron kept a firm hold of Jack and felt a panicky shudder race down his spine at the thought of passing the baby over to Alyssa. She looked normal with her short brown hair, jeans, and hoodie, but you could never be certain. What if behind those blue eyes and freckled nose was a serial killer in disguise? Or, worse, what if she began vaping in front of Jack as soon as Aaron left the house?

"Don't worry, Mr. Baxter." Alyssa smiled. "Everything will be fine. When should I give Jack his next bottle?"

Aaron took a deep breath and tried to calm down. "I have one prepared right here, so you can give it to him as I leave. I thought that would help with the separation." He walked over to the kitchen sink, where a glass bottle was warming under the running hot water. "This is a new type of formula the pediatrician recommended when I took Jack in for a checkup yesterday. I've been feeding it to Jack since last night, and he seems to like it. But if it gives you any trouble, there's his normal type in the cabinet right here." Aaron opened the cupboard devoted to all things bottle related. "Just don't heat the bottle in the microwave."

"No way." Alyssa shook her head. "I've gone through Red Cross babysitters' training. I know what I'm doing." She reached for Jack, and for a moment, Aaron refused to let go. But the clock on the oven told him he needed to pick Julia up in five minutes, so he finally relinquished his hold. "Jack and I are going to have a fabulous time, Mr. Baxter," said Alyssa. "You go off and enjoy your evening."

"Okay." Aaron's breaths were shallow, and he knew if he didn't get a grip, he might start to hyperventilate. "I'm going to walk out the door," he said, with his feet rooted to the ground.

"A quick break." Alyssa held Jack in one arm and picked up the bottle with her free hand. "That's what I find is best when parents leave."

"Like ripping a bandage off," said Aaron, who didn't budge. But then he noticed the clock tick off one more minute. If he didn't leave right now, he'd be late. "I'll be home in three hours," he said as he stuffed his billfold in his back pocket. "Maybe two. Call me if you need anything."

"We'll be fine," Alyssa promised.

Aaron chewed his thumbnail the whole drive over to Julia's house, which was something he hadn't done since he was three, and his nanny at the time had washed his mouth out with soap every time she'd caught him. As soon as he parked in Julia's driveway, he checked his phone to make sure there were no messages from Alyssa. Then he triple-checked to make sure he had the sound turned on for notifications, in case she tried to reach him. But once he stepped out of the Tesla and walked up to Julia's front porch, his anxiety took on a new layer of excitement. When Julia opened the front door wearing a short red dress and jean jacket, the knot in Aaron's stomach disappeared, and all he felt was a yearning to hold her in his arms.

"You look beautiful," said Aaron as he stared into her brown eyes. He held out his palm for her hand, and when she placed it in his, he brought it up to his lips and kissed it.

Julia smiled, and the longing he felt to embrace her grew stronger. He was about to do just that when Toby wiggled his way past her, jumped in the air, and tried to lick Aaron's face. "Down, Toby," said Julia, grabbing him by the collar. "Sit."

"Toby, sit!" Aaron commanded, lifting his finger in the hand signal Greta had used with their Portuguese water dogs. "Sit, and then I'll pet you." Toby's butt dropped to the floor, and he wagged his tail across the floorboards. "Good dog." Aaron rewarded him by scratching the Labrador behind his ears.

"Sorry about that," said Julia. "I was going to work on training him again, but then with my concussion, it went on the back burner." Julia brought Toby back into the house and locked the front door. "All set." She put her keys in her purse and reached for Aaron's hand. "Where are we going?"

The name of the restaurant was on his lips, but as soon as he felt Julia's hand in his, he succumbed to the urge to pull her forward. His heart was already pounding a million beats a minute, and pure adrenaline coursed through his system as he slid his arm around her back and held her close. Their mouths were inches apart, and Aaron longed to close the gap between them. He squeezed Julia's hand before releasing it and fully embracing her. When she rested her palm on his shoulder and then slipped her fingers behind his neck, he took it as an invitation to kiss her.

Their lips crushed together, and Aaron forgot everything but the way she tasted of minty toothpaste and smelled like chocolate and lavender. She overwhelmed his senses on every level, and he felt drunk in her presence. Her chest pressing against his was soft and warm. Every nerve in his body fired as he itched to be closer. Julia melted into his arms like their frames had been made for each other. He wanted to bind his arms around her and never let go. She was holding him in place, keeping him steady, making him remember what it felt like to be a man again and not just a father, or uncle, or whatever he was, because Aaron still wasn't sure. All he knew was that when Julia was with him, all things felt right, and now, in this moment, they were more than right; they were extraordinary.

Aaron leaned his head to the side and deepened the kiss, exploring her mouth and touching her tongue with his. When a tiny moan of pleasure escaped her, his pulse went wild with excitement. His hands roamed her back, desperate for a tighter grip. He couldn't believe that a woman as beautiful as Julia was in his arms right now, her heart pressed against his, leaning on him for balance, raking her fingers through his hair. His senses had never been this overwhelmed by a woman's touch. Aaron felt jittery, and he relied on Julia to steady him just as much as she seemed to need him. A tangle of kisses tied them together.

"Wow," said Aaron when they finally pulled apart. "That was pretty incredible, considering you haven't accepted my Facebook friend request yet."

Julia laughed and rested her head on his shoulder. "Sorry about that. I haven't been spending much time online this week because of the accident." She nestled closer, and Aaron was mesmerized by the way her shoulders rose and fell as her rapid breathing slowly settled into a normal rhythm. He inhaled the sweet fragrance of her hair and closed his eyes, completely at peace. For a moment, the only sounds to be heard were the passing cars driving along Ninth Avenue and the cooing of doves in the distance.

Aaron could have stayed like that forever, but then his phone buzzed, and he lurched back, panicked that it could be Alyssa. "Sorry," he said, pulling the phone out of his pocket. "This might be the babysitter."

"Of course. Is everything okay?"

Aaron looked at the screen and breathed out a sigh of relief. "It's just a notice from the grocery store that my items will be ready to pick up on Monday." He held Julia's hand and led her to the Tesla, then opened the passenger door for her.

"That sounds convenient," she said when they were inside buckling their seat belts. "I've never tried that service before."

"It's a lifesaver with Jack." Aaron started the car. "Especially since he goes through formula so fast."

"I can imagine. So where are we going to dinner? Anything but the Parisian Café is fine with me."

"What's wrong with the Parisian Café?" Aaron asked. "Not that we're going there, because we're not."

"I don't think there'd be anything there for you to eat. Everything has butter or gluten in it. Plus, apparently it's not as authentic as everyone in Harper Landing thinks it is. The chicken cordon bleu is from Costco, but with a fancy sauce added to it."

Aaron chuckled. "How did you discover that?"

"Um . . . a friend who knows a lot about cooking told me. Anyhow, where are we going?"

"Down to Seattle." Aaron mentally reviewed the directions that he'd memorized that afternoon. "There's a restaurant called Pure Food and Wine that gets great reviews."

"I read about it in the newspaper but have never been. How fun." Julia settled back in her seat and crossed her legs.

"I almost forgot," said Aaron, reaching into the back seat for a small package. "I brought you a present." He handed her the padded envelope and held his breath while she opened it. As he watched her tear open the seal, he began to have doubts. Why hadn't he brought her flowers instead? This was stupid. He couldn't have gone wrong with roses, but instead, he'd decided to be creative. Now Julia was seconds away from unwrapping what he'd meant to be a romantic gesture but what she'd probably think was crazy. Maybe she wouldn't even know what it was.

"This is so mysterious," said Julia as she felt the envelope. "It feels like there's a test tube from chemistry class in here."

An icy sweat broke out on the back of Aaron's neck, and he felt more unsure of himself than ever. "It's not a test tube," he said. "At least I don't think so." *Shoot!* What if his supplier had mixed up the order?

Julia ripped off the top of the envelope and gently shook the contents into her lap. A clear tube fell out, with what looked like half a dozen nine-inch worms inside. As soon as she saw the cylinder, her eyes lit up with delight. "Tahitian vanilla beans!" she exclaimed. "These are hard to find." Julia unplugged the cap, and the rich scent of vanilla filled the Tesla. She closed her eyes and breathed in the aroma. "Mmm . . . I love them. What a special treat. Where did you find them?" She opened her eyes again and held the tube over so that Aaron could smell too.

He took a whiff and was pleased to see that his natural foods vendor had delivered a premium quality product. Madagascar vanilla would have been cheaper, but he knew from Julia's incoherent ramblings when she'd had her concussion that she preferred Tahitian. "One of my Big Foot Paleo suppliers had a contact with an importer. Oh, I almost forgot." Aaron fished in the back seat for a reusable grocery sack and pulled out a bottle of bourbon. "This goes with it. That way you can make—"

"My own vanilla extract and never have to worry about running out again," said Julia, finishing his sentence for him. "I love it! Thank you so much!" She threw her arms around him and hugged him.

All the tension Aaron had felt as he'd watched her open the present melted away. He closed his eyes and savored the moment, which was entirely perfect until his stomach rumbled.

"Uh-oh." Julia giggled. "It sounds like someone's hungry." She pulled away and adjusted her seat belt.

"Guilty." Aaron grinned. "I'm also excited to eat something that someone besides me cooked. I haven't been out to a restaurant in months," Aaron admitted. "Not since the memorial service." He started the car and pulled out of the driveway.

"Eating out with Jack must be tricky."

"At least he's portable," said Aaron as he merged into traffic. "At the memorial service, he—" Aaron was about to say that newborn Jack had slept in his infant carrier the entire time, but when his phone began ringing, he didn't get the chance. He clicked on the media console to transfer the call to the dash. "I need to get this," he said. "It might be—"

"The sitter," Julia finished for him. "I understand."

"Mr. Baxter?" Alyssa's voice squeaked over the speakers. "Jack's throwing up." The baby wailed in the background.

"He's what?" Aaron looked in the rearview mirror and clicked on his left-turn blinker, preparing to make a U-turn.

"Puking!" Alyssa cried. "All over the place. I can't get him to stop."

"Can he breathe?" Julia asked. "Does he have a rash?"

"Yes, he can breathe. No, he doesn't have a rash," said Alyssa. It was hard to hear her over the crying baby. "But he keeps puking and puking."

"I'll be right there." Aaron yanked on the wheel and turned the car around. "We're five minutes away, tops. Stay on the phone with me, you hear?"

"I can't stay on the phone. I've got to help Jack." The sound of Jack retching filled the speaker. "Eeew!" Alyssa squealed. "It got on my iPhone!"

"Should we call 911?" Julia unzipped her purse. "I think we should call 911. What if it's anaphylaxis?"

"Yes," said Aaron. "No. I mean, maybe. He's crying, right? That means he can breathe. Alyssa," he said loudly. "You didn't give Jack peanut butter, did you?"

There wasn't any answer. Aaron could hear Jack crying over the phone, and he heard water running, but that was it.

"Do you have peanut butter in your house?" Julia asked. "I thought legumes weren't paleo approved."

"No, I don't have peanut butter. I usually eat almond butter or cashew butter instead." Aaron gripped his forehead. "What am I doing talking about tree nuts when Jack is in danger?"

"*Could* be in danger." Julia gripped the dashboard. "We don't know for sure. Maybe he has a tummy bug, and that's it."

Aaron sped through the quiet residential streets at a breakneck pace, doubling the speed limit and barely pausing for stop signs. When he reached his driveway, he careened to a halt so hard that he and Julia both jerked back in their seats. "Sorry," he apologized as he threw open the door.

"No problem." Julia grabbed her purse and jumped out of the car, then raced up the steps with him to the front door. She followed him inside.

Aaron charged across the threshold and up the stairs to the kitchen, where he heard Jack bawling. Alyssa held the baby in her arms, sitting in the middle of the linoleum floor, covered with vomit. It looked like a bottle of half-digested formula had exploded. Every cupboard and appliance had been hit.

"Mr. Baxter," Alyssa said, tears streaming down her face. "Sorry, but I didn't know what to do."

Aaron whisked Jack out of her arms and tried to console him, but the baby kept retching up bile. His little eyes were squeezed shut tight, and his face was as bright as a cherry tomato, but at least Jack's wailing proved that his lungs were working just fine.

"You poor girl." Julia helped lift Alyssa to her feet. "You did the right thing by calling. What happened exactly?"

"I don't know." Alyssa wiped her phone on her jeans. "All I did was give Jack the bottle you made him. It seemed to go down fine, but then when I burped him, he barfed everything up."

"The new formula!" Aaron exclaimed, feeling like an idiot. He ran to the cabinet where the new container was kept and looked at the ingredients. "Soy," he muttered. "Why didn't I notice that before? Jack's never had soy before."

"Where do you live?" Julia asked Alyssa. "Do you need a ride home?" She put a wad of cash in the girl's hand.

"Thanks. I don't need a ride." Alyssa pocketed the money. "I can walk home. It's still light outside."

"Great. So sorry this happened," said Julia as she led Alyssa away. "It was a good learning experience for everyone."

Aaron was filling up a new bottle with water when he heard the door close. *Did Julia leave too?* He wondered how Julia would get home but didn't know what he could do about it. Maybe she used Uber. His biggest concern was Jack being dehydrated right now. Was water the answer, or should he make him a bottle of his normal formula? Aaron wasn't sure. As soon as he could get Jack settled, he would call the pediatrician's after-hours line. But Julia popped back in the kitchen a minute later and surprised him.

"I thought you had gone home too," he said, trying to get Jack to take the bottle of water.

"What? Of course not. Why are you giving Jack water?"

"Because he might be dehydrated."

Julia bit her lower lip. "Look," she said. "I drink tap water every day and think that the Harper Landing Water Department is trustworthy, but I'm not sure it's good enough for Jack to drink. Are you sure babies should drink water?"

Aaron tried to remember what the baby book had said. But he was so frazzled he couldn't remember. "I have no idea." He set the bottle down on the counter.

It was just as well, because Jack wasn't taking the bottle anyway. His cries had softened, and his head was flopping over to one side like he was awake but listless. Every minute or so, he'd retch, but nothing would come up. Julia walked closer to Aaron and Jack and stared into the baby's face. "Aaron," she said in a soft and steady voice. "I don't want to alarm you, but I think we should bring Jack to the children's hospital. You go put him in the car; I'll grab some things for him."

"The hospital. Right," said Aaron, like that was the most natural thing in the world to say. "Okay. Let's do it. I'll get the diaper bag. Where is the diaper bag?" His voice rose into a shout as hysteria took hold.

Julia's voice became even softer. "I'll get the diaper bag," she practically whispered, with her hand on his shoulder. "You put him in the car and make sure you have your insurance card. Okay?"

"It's in my wallet. In my pocket. Right here." Aaron hugged Jack, who still wasn't sleeping but wasn't active either. "Should we call 911?"

Julia put two fingers on Jack's neck, checking his pulse. "No, I don't think so. But let's call the pediatrician once we're in the car and have them tell the hospital we're coming." She pointed her finger away from the kitchen and toward the front door. "Go. I'll be there by the time you start the car."

"Okay." Aaron did as he was told. He cradled the most important person in the whole world to him in his arms and tried not to predict the future or think on the past. He focused on the simple instructions Julia had given him and walked out of the kitchen, being careful not to skid on the slippery floor. He walked down the stairs, out the door, and directly to the car, not even bothering to lock up the house. Jack was easy to put in the infant seat since he didn't squirm. He seemed like a rag doll with blinking eyes. Just as Aaron clicked the last buckle on the car seat, Julia was there, handing him the diaper bag.

"You sit next to him," she said. "I'll drive while you call the doctor."

Aaron had never sat in the back seat of his own car before, and there wasn't nearly enough room for his long legs. But his own discomfort was the last thing on his mind. He dialed Dr. Agarwal's office as Julia drove them away from Harper Landing, talked to the answering service as they reached the freeway, and waited for what seemed like an eternity for the physician on call to call him back. That doctor confirmed that they were headed to the right place, and Aaron felt comforted when he saw the sign for the children's hospital up ahead. Especially since Jack was vomiting again.

CHAPTER NINETEEN

Fluorescent lights and beeping monitors put Julia's nerves on edge. She stood up straight behind the leatherette chair and gave the emergency room doctor her full attention. Aaron sat in front of her, cradling Jack in his arms. The baby was in a clean diaper now and a tiny outfit the hospital had given him to wear that looked like a kimono. Jack also had a security band on his wrist that matched the one Aaron wore so that the baby couldn't be stolen from the hospital. Julia rested her hands on Aaron's shoulders and tried to stay calm. The past twenty minutes they'd been at the hospital had flown by fast, but they still didn't have answers.

"The short answer is no," said the doctor. "We don't know what caused Jack's vomiting, but that's what the blood tests are for. We'll order imaging if needed." The doctor had dark circles under her eyes and looked like she hadn't slept in a while, but she wore a clean jacket and seemed to be taking Jack's condition seriously.

"The new formula," said Aaron. "It had soy in it, and Jack's never had soy before."

"That's information we will definitely keep in mind. Soy intolerance sounds likely." The doctor checked the tablet in front of her and tapped on it twice. "I've ordered an IV to build up hydration and to administer the ondansetron. That's a medicine that blocks the chemicals in the body that trigger nausea. It will help Jack keep fluids down. As soon as he's off the IV, we'll switch him to a formula called Alimentum, which should be easy for him to digest."

"If it's not a reaction to the formula, what else might it be?" Julia asked. "Norovirus or something?"

"That's possible." The doctor nodded. "But so are many other scenarios. There's a condition called pyloric stenosis that infants sometimes have where a muscle blocks food from entering the small intestine. Surgery corrects it, but usually that's diagnosed in the first month."

"Oh no." Aaron squeezed his eyes shut.

"But it could also be something like acid reflux," the doctor said. "Try not to worry. The nurse will be here soon with the IV." She gave them a weak smile and then walked away.

"Right. That's it, then. Jack probably needs surgery," said Aaron, a note of panic in his tone.

"That's not what I heard at all." Julia walked around the chair and sat on the edge of the empty hospital bed. "The doctor said there are lots of possible things that could have caused the vomiting, and the muscle-intestine problem is just one possible scenario. In the meantime, Jack's in the best possible place to receive the care he needs." Julia leaned down and gazed at Jack, who was dozing restlessly in Aaron's arms.

"I'm glad we came. Thank you for bringing us here."

"I'm glad we're here too." Julia looked up at Aaron. "But now you need to change, too, or you'll get Jack's kimono dirty." Rising, she zipped open the diaper bag and took out a long-sleeve button-down shirt she'd found at the front of his closet. It was the first thing she'd seen when she'd raced into his bedroom to grab him clean clothes. Julia set the shirt down on the bed. "I'll hold Jack while you put this on."

"You mean I don't have to wear a puke-covered shirt all night?" Aaron grinned fleetingly before handing Jack over.

Feeling Jack's still body in her arms made Julia's heart lurch, especially since the baby was paler than usual. If she weren't so worried about Jack's health, she would have enjoyed watching Aaron peel his T-shirt off and slowly button up the dress shirt.

"Seriously, thank you, Julia," said Aaron as he balled up his contaminated shirt and zipped it up in a special compartment at the bottom of the diaper bag. "If you weren't here with me right now, I'd be a total mess." He reached to take Jack back.

Julia clucked her tongue. "Go wash your hands first with hot water and lots of soap."

"Soap. Right." Aaron stood up and walked to the handwashing station at the corner of the room. "You know . . . wait. I'll go find a restroom, if that's okay. Since you're here with him."

"You're not feeling nauseated yourself, are you?" Julia looked at him closely but didn't see any signs that he was turning green.

"No." Aaron shook his head. "I need to pee; that's all."

"Good. Hopefully that means it's not norovirus."

Aaron nodded. "I'll be right back." He walked out the door.

"Well, kiddo, it's you and me." Julia held Jack close and swayed side to side, shifting her weight from one foot to the other. "We're going to make sure you get all better—I promise." She felt her heart squeeze with worry as she held the sleeping baby. Jack was so helpless and weak in that moment that all she wanted to do was protect him. Julia desperately wished she knew how. The truth was that being in a hospital terrified her, especially after watching her mother die in one last year. Even the smell of the lemon-scented disinfectant they used made her eyes burn. This was the last place she wanted Jack to be. "You'll get to go home soon," she whispered to Jack. "Okay?" Tears rolled down her cheeks, and she quickly wiped them away.

A nurse in pink scrubs knocked on the door and came in, dragging an IV cart behind her. "Hey there, Mama, I'm here to give baby some fluids."

"Oh, I'm not the baby's mother," said Julia. "But his daddy will be right back." As soon as she said it, she felt guilty because she knew

Aaron struggled with the term. But it seemed easier than saying *uncle* and *guardian*.

"Well, it appears baby is in good hands." The nurse nodded. She was heavyset with a kind smile and gray hair twisted into dreadlocks. The nurse read the chart she held. "Can you please verify baby's name for me?"

"Jack Franklin Reynolds," Julia said, remembering his full name from having just helped Aaron fill out the intake form. She supplied Jack's birthday too.

"Very good." The nurse pointed to the clear plastic bassinet in the corner. It looked more like a tub than a crib. "Please put baby in the bassinet so he can be still while I set up the IV."

"Okay." Julia swallowed hard. She didn't want to let Jack go but knew she had to. The plastic crib had a soft pad on the bottom covered with a clean white sheet. Julia laid Jack down with exquisite care, thankful that she was able to remove her arms without his waking up.

"What did I miss?" Aaron asked as he rushed back into the room.

"Nothing yet," said Julia. "The nurse is about to put in the IV." As soon as she saw the woman pull out the needle, it felt like all the blood drained from her head. She wanted to be strong for Jack, but she wasn't sure she could watch the procedure.

"What teeny-tiny veins," said the nurse. "Let's do this in your head tonight."

That was it. Julia needed to sit down. She sank into a chair and held on to the armrest with all her might.

"Uh-oh," said the nurse, looking across Julia's shoulder. "We've got a fainter on our hands."

"I'm fine—" Julia started to say, right as she heard the sound of Aaron crashing onto the bed and sliding off onto the floor.

Sure enough, Aaron Baxter, multiple-marathon runner and paleo-living devotee, had passed out cold. Julia scrambled down next to him and slapped his cheeks a few times to get him to come to.

"I need to care for baby," said the nurse with a chuckle. "Why don't you take Daddy out into the lobby as soon as he can walk?" She put her hands on her hips. "Better yet, go upstairs to the cafeteria and grab a bite to eat. I promise you baby will be safe. By the time you come back, the IV will be in, he'll be wearing a cute cap, and you'll hardly notice the tubing."

"Okay," said Julia in a tone that she hoped exuded positivity. "We'll do that." She hooked her hands underneath Aaron's armpits and lugged him to his feet.

"Is it over yet?" he asked.

"Not quite," she said, pushing him out of the room. "The nurse said you need to eat something before you can come back."

"But Jack—"

"Will be fine while we're gone. Come on; the quicker we eat a sandwich or something, the sooner we can come back."

"Okay." Aaron nodded. He wobbled on his feet in the bright light of the hallway.

"Do you need to put your head between your knees?"

"No." Aaron swallowed and gripped her arm. "I'll be fine. Needles get to me, is all. You must think I'm a real idiot."

"I do not."

"A coward, then."

"Nothing could be further from the truth." She hugged him tightly. "I hate needles too," she whispered. "That's why I could never become a doctor." She pulled away and linked her hand through the crook of his arm. "Or a diabetic. Thank goodness for that."

"Yes." Aaron stumbled forward and then anxiously looked back in the room. "I should be there. Sara would be there."

"We don't know that. The nurse might have sent your sister away too. It'll be easier for her if we're not in the way. Let's move." She steered him forward.

They walked through the maze of corridors in the emergency room until they found the elevator up to the cafeteria. Julia's worry over Jack was difficult to deal with already, but being at the children's hospital added an extra layer of pathos. When the elevator opened on the third floor to let in new riders, a couple entered who had tears streaming down their faces. Julia looked discreetly away, and as she did, she noticed the words PEDIATRIC CANCER UNIT in big letters on the wall behind them. Aaron must have seen, too, because he squeezed her hand so tightly for a second she thought her circulation would stop.

The elevator let them off on the seventh floor, and Julia and Aaron followed the arrows to the cafeteria, which was closing in fifteen minutes. "Looks like we made it just in time," Julia said as she picked up a tray. "That was lucky." Aaron nodded and scanned the offerings. The hot-food section was closed, but there was still food available in the salad bar and refrigerator section. Julia selected a prepackaged chef's salad and a carton of low-fat milk. When she got to the register, she added chocolate-covered almonds because she wanted the pick-me-up. Aaron arrived a few seconds later with a custom plate from the salad bar that included greens, vegetables, and shredded chicken.

"This isn't how I wanted to buy you dinner," he said as he opened his wallet and handed the cashier his credit card.

"Saturday nights at medical facilities seem to be our thing." Julia collected two plasticware packs from the bucket next to them and grabbed a wad of napkins. She slathered her hands with sanitizer. "At least I'll be able to remember tonight." She smiled for a moment before becoming serious again.

The truth was, hospitals creeped her out. They brought back bad memories of accompanying Waverley to appointments for her cancer treatments. "This is your father's fault," Waverley would grumble. "Him and those expensive death sticks." Julia had never known what to say, because her mother had been right. It *was* Harrison's fault that Waverley succumbed to lung cancer. But even though her father wasn't perfect, she still loved him. Every time Waverley blamed Harrison for her cancer, Julia felt like she was forced to choose between her parents, and for Julia, there was no choice. Harrison had filled her childhood with unconditional love and laughter. Waverley had given her nothing but angst and self-doubt. Julia pushed away the dark thoughts and focused on Aaron. "I'll go find us a table," she said.

A minute later, she found a spot by a window that looked out into the atrium. The tropical plants and ornamental glasses created a calming atmosphere. Julia opened her carton of milk and took a swig directly from the box. She was hungrier than she would have liked to admit. Her Fourth of July dress was a wee bit tight, so she hadn't snacked since lunch.

"I don't know if I can eat anything." Aaron set his tray down next to her. "My stomach is in knots."

"Try to get something in your system." Julia handed him a plastic-ware pack. "Eat at least three bites." It was the same thing she used to say to her mother when she was ill.

Julia felt a quick flash of pain as she thought about Waverley. "At least I'm thin," her mother had murmured from her hospital bed. "Tell me again how much weight I've lost."

Aaron nodded and unrolled the napkin binding the plasticware in place. "I just froze up back there. At the house. In the room. Even when they were doing the intake form with the insurance stuff." He rested his elbow on the table and propped up his forehead. "Julia, if you weren't there giving me instructions, I don't know what would have happened."

"You would have been fine." She rubbed his back in small circles. "Maybe you would have taken a different path to get here is all, like in an ambulance. Who knows? That might have been the right thing to do all along, and I'm the one who led you astray."

Aaron squeezed his eyes shut. "I'm horrible at this."

"Handling an emergency? Many people are, and that's normal. The only reason I have practice is because of my mother's lung cancer. I have lots of experience rushing to emergency rooms and dealing with crises because of that. When she was finally approved for hospice care, it was a blessing."

Aaron opened his eyes and gave her a questioning look. "How could hospice care be a blessing?"

Julia took her hand off Aaron's back and placed it on the napkin covering her lap. "Because before hospice, every time my mother's blood pressure dropped or she was in respiratory distress, the paramedics would rush her to the hospital, and they would hook her up to life support machines and bring her back—just barely. It was torture for her. My mother was a proud woman, and that's not how she wanted to be seen. But once hospice was involved, she could rest peacefully at home." Julia took a deep breath and sighed. "Because of hospice, she was finally able to have a natural death."

"I'm sorry, Julia. I didn't know."

"Don't be sorry. I loved my mother, but in a lot of ways, my life is easier without her."

"Really?"

Guilt overwhelmed her, and Julia couldn't believe what she had said. They were the same words George had spoken to her when discussing her cash flow problem. But that was about finances; this was about life. Was Julia's world really easier without Waverley in it? Julia shuddered. She felt guilty even posing the question. It was being in the hospital, she decided. One whiff of that citrusy antiseptic they used, and all the memories came flooding back. "Never mind." She crumpled her napkin. "Forget I said anything."

But for Julia, there was no forgetting. "You can't do anything right," she heard Waverley say as she waved her wooden spoon. "It's a good thing your father isn't alive to see how stupid you are."

Julia speared a bite of cheddar cheese and lettuce with her fork but no longer felt hungry. "Maybe we should go back now," she said as she set down her cutlery.

"We should." Aaron pointed at her salad. "But first, you need to eat three bites."

CHAPTER TWENTY

True to her word, the nurse had covered Jack's IV tubing with tape in such a way that it didn't look too bad. Aaron sat on the bed, watching him sleep in the plastic bassinet. The fluids were returning the baby's color to normal, and he slept peacefully, with his palms open on either side of his cheeks. It was almost midnight, but Aaron was wide awake. The blood test results were supposed to arrive any minute, and there was still the imaging order to fulfill. Hopefully, an ultrasound would rule out pyloric stenosis once and for all. Aaron wanted to believe the soy-based formula had caused all this, because a diet change would be easiest. But he also felt tremendous guilt. If that were the case, it would be his fault that Jack was in distress, because he was the one who'd asked for Jack's formula to be changed after he'd blindly followed the advice from the moms group. Sure, Dr. Agarwal had thought it was a good idea, too, but why hadn't he asked her more questions? Yes, the new formula had more DHA. Yes, Dr. Agarwal had thought it would be easier for Jack to digest after his carsickness with Frank the other night. But it had also put the baby in the emergency room.

"If Sara were alive, this never would have happened," Aaron said quietly.

"You don't know that." Julia picked up his hand.

"I do know it. She wanted to breastfeed."

"Wanting to and being able to are two different things," said Julia. "Fed is best. That's what they say at the infant-toddler group. There was one baby a couple of years ago who was exclusively breastfed but who developed a rash all over his body because it turned out that he was allergic to pretty much everything. The mom went on a chicken-and-rice diet to help the rash clear up."

"Yikes. But it was the moms group who told me to try the new formula."

"I'm not a parent, but it doesn't seem to be an exact science, right? Things happen, and parents deal with them. You're doing a great job, Aaron, and I know that if Jared were here right now, he'd agree." She rested her head on his shoulder.

Aaron sniffed and leaned his head on top of hers. "You're probably exhausted. Let me call you an Uber or something so you can go home."

Julia lifted her head. "Do you want me to go home?" she asked. "I don't want to intrude."

"No." Aaron put his arm around her back. "And you're not intruding. I want you here, but I also don't want to take advantage."

"You're not taking advantage." She snuggled in closer. "I wouldn't be able to sleep a wink without knowing the test results. Besides, someone needs to be here to make sure you take care of yourself."

"That sounds like something Sara would say. She was always looking out for me, even when we were little."

"She must have been an amazing person."

"She was."

"And it sounds like she loved you very much."

"She did." Aaron's heart shattered into a million pieces. Julia was so kind and understanding and honest. She deserved to know the truth. "It's my fault Sara and Jared died," he said.

"What?" Julia jerked back, which made Aaron's arm fall away.

"It's true." Aaron's shoulders slumped, and he looked down at his shoes. "It's my fault they were on the road that night. If it weren't for me, they would still be alive." He explained to her, as clearly as possible, how he was to blame for Big Foot Paleo's business office remaining in Palo Alto when it would have made more sense to move it closer to the factory in Modesto. "Now you know the truth," he said. "Jared and Sara would be alive today if I wasn't so stubborn."

"How can you say that?" Julia twisted toward him. "You can't know that for certain. Car crashes happen all the time, even in Harper Landing. Why, only last year there was a crash right on Main Street when a car was hit by a coal train crossing the tracks. Paige was hit crossing the street on her way home from her bookshop by a drunk driver last year and broke her leg. She was in a cast for six months. Car crashes are horrible, but let me tell you something, Aaron—drivers are responsible for accidents, not people one hundred miles away."

"But—"

"There is no *but*." She pointed at Jack. "If it weren't for you, Jack would be an orphan right now, not the other way around. You're the hero in his life story, not the villain."

When Julia said that, it was like a dam broke. All the pent-up turmoil and shame of the last five months of drama burst forth at the same time. Aaron's heartbeat pounded hard, and beads of sweat broke out across his forehead. His body quaked, rocking back and forth as he struggled to manage his emotions. Was Julia telling the truth? Was he Jack's savior instead of his tormentor? Life would be a lot easier from now on if only Aaron could believe that to be true, and he saw no reason for Julia to lie to him. She was honest and trustworthy to her core. With her sitting beside him, his world became not only bearable but capable of joy.

He wanted to kiss her, right there in the emergency room, but it wasn't the right place, not with Jack hooked up to an IV tube. Besides, he didn't want Julia to taste the tears on his cheeks that he knew were falling. In the glowing light of the monitors, maybe she couldn't see him cry. If she could, it didn't matter. He wasn't ashamed of how he felt. He wore his heartbreak like the well-earned scars that the last five months had inflicted upon him. But he had survived. Jack and Aaron were both here, moving forward, fighting for a happy life together. The doctors would tell him what was wrong, and Jack would get better. They would go home and keep living one day at a time, turning pages on the calendar until years had passed and all they knew was happiness. The rocky start of Jack's first few months would become a distant memory.

"Julia," he said slowly. "I'm sorry Toby didn't come when you called, but I'm incredibly grateful that he swam off after that harbor seal two weeks ago. Otherwise, we might never have met."

"Oh, we would have met," she said, hanging her head. "This is Harper Landing. You meet everyone who lives here eventually. But you probably wouldn't have noticed me."

"How could I not notice you?"

"I've had twenty-eight years of my beauty-queen mother steering attention her way. But there's nothing wrong with being average, so long as—"

"You're *not* average," Aaron said, interrupting her. "You're exceptional." He gently held her hand in both of his own. "The first time I saw you, I thought you were the most beautiful woman I had ever seen, and the more I get to know you, I realize that you're equally beautiful on the inside. I love how you drop everything to help your neighbor, or even a perfect stranger like me."

"You helped *me* rescue Toby, even though you didn't know me at the time. That's helping a stranger."

"I didn't help *you*; I helped your dog," he admitted. "I would have done the same for any canine." Julia chuckled, and Aaron continued. "You stay calm in a crisis. You're generous to your whole community." He let his eyes roam over her curvy figure. "And in case you haven't noticed, you look gorgeous no matter what you're wearing, whether it be shorts and flip-flops or this smokin'-hot red dress."

"Oh please. It's the sundress I wear to the Fourth of July parade," Julia said with a smile. "That's a family-friendly activity."

Aaron slid his arm around her back and pulled her in close for a side hug. "Trust me when I say that nobody's watching the parade when you walk by in that dress."

"That's not true. You haven't been to the parade before, so you don't know how awesome it is. There's free candy." She leaned forward to check on Jack, who was still sleeping peacefully. "Next Thursday, you'll be able to see for yourself. I'll have a chair in front of Sweet Bliss with your name on it." She looked back at him. "Right next to mine if you want it to be."

"I do." Aaron nodded. "More than anything. Well, more than anything except for Jack getting better." He stared at Jack's vital signs on the monitors and concentrated on the baby's steady heart rate.

"It's a date, then," Julia whispered. "Only this time, we'll bring Jack with us because I don't want to ever leave him with a stranger again."

"My thoughts exactly." This time, Aaron did kiss Julia. His lips brushed tenderly against hers, and he savored the sensation of closeness. He closed his eyes and felt peace wash over him like a wave. Julia's palm cupped his cheek, and her fingertips wiped away his tears. When they hugged, he felt stronger—more capable—and ready for anything that lay ahead.

The doctor came in twenty minutes later with the blood work panel and to check on Jack. The nurse was there, too, and she turned up the lights to be able to verify that Jack was wetting his diapers. Everyone was grateful to discover that Jack's diaper was utterly soaked. That was a good sign. He was still asleep, since the ondansetron had knocked him out, but all his vital signs were good.

"I'm not ready to rule out pyloric stenosis yet," said the doctor, "which is why I've put in the order for imaging, but based on the blood results, it does seem like Jack is extremely allergic to soy. His immuno-globulin antibodies were off the charts."

"How long will the imaging take?" Aaron asked. "When can we go home?"

"I put in the order an hour ago," said the doctor with a deep sigh. "But I know they're backed up. It's been a long night." She clicked on her tablet and looked. "It appears that Jack is next in line. Once that's done—if the results are clear—Jack needs to have three more wet diapers before I send you guys home. He's not technically admitted to the hospital, but he shouldn't leave yet either."

"I can bring a reclining chair in here for you," offered the nurse as she bagged up Jack's dirty diaper. "In case you both want to stay the night."

"That would be great," said Julia. "Thank you."

Aaron didn't know how he'd gotten so lucky that Julia was willing to stay by his side, but he was grateful.

Twelve hours later, they left the hospital with a fully hydrated Jack, who had a clean bill of health other than a medically diagnosed soy allergy. Aaron felt surprisingly well rested, considering the turmoil. He and Julia had taken shifts sleeping in three-hour increments the night before so that one of them was always awake to monitor Jack. But Aaron definitely was looking forward to a hot shower and a hard workout. He also needed to touch base with Martha and Frank. He'd called Martha last night from the ER, and Julia had spoken to her, too, asking her to feed Toby. It was clear that Martha wouldn't rest easily until she held Jack in her arms and saw that the baby was okay. Aaron had even texted his parents, Darren and Lorraine, to let them know what was happening with their only grandson. Neither of them had responded personally, but Aaron did receive an automated message saying they were both out of the country and that he could contact their respective secretaries.

Once Jack was loaded into the Tesla, and Aaron and Julia were driving away from the hospital, he felt lighter. Jack fell asleep almost immediately, even without his pacifier, and once they hit the freeway, Julia fell asleep too. Aaron kept the radio turned off and enjoyed the silence. One thing that impressed him about Washington was how many trees grew along the road. As he drove north to Harper Landing, he could see the Cascade Mountains to his right and the Olympics to the left. Mount Rainier was right behind him, like a giant looming over his path. The Pacific Northwest sunshine was blinding, even though the thermostat only registered sixty-four degrees. Closer to the water, the marine layer smothered Harper Landing like a thick blanket. Aaron removed his sunglasses and drove the last mile to Julia's house, marveling at the drop in temperature.

"We're home," he said as he parked the car in her driveway. "I mean, we're here."

Julia fluttered her eyelids open and yawned. "Sorry. I must have drifted off."

"Julia," Aaron said as he turned off the car. "I don't know how to begin to thank you."

Julia glanced at the suction-cupped baby mirror like she was double-checking that Jack was still asleep. "How about a kiss?" she asked with a mischievous look in her eyes.

"With pleasure." Aaron couldn't believe that after such a horrible night, the most beautiful woman in the world was sitting next to him asking for a kiss. He unclicked his seat belt so fast that the buckle flung against the side of the door. "Oh crap," he muttered, looking back to see if it had woken up Jack.

Julia giggled. "Careful there."

Aaron's face broke out into a smile as he leaned one hand on the center console and used the other to caress her cheek, pulling her mouth gently toward his. Julia's lips were silky soft, and when he pressed his against hers, he eagerly parted his mouth and reached out to her with his tongue. Julia moaned as Aaron deepened the kiss. He tilted his head to the side and laced his fingers through her golden hair, breathing in the scent of cocoa and lavender that she still carried with her, even after the ordeal from the night before. He was distantly aware of the world around him. Starlings chirped outside, cars whizzed down Ninth Avenue, and the Tesla warmed up from the anemic Pacific Northwest sun. But the deliciousness of Julia's mouth crushed against his, and her palm gliding across his chest and urging him forward, was what Aaron noticed most. That was why he didn't hear the sharp rapping at his window until the knocking became so loud that Julia jerked back and quickly looked away, her cheeks flushing the color of cherries.

Aaron looked to see who had interrupted them and was annoyed to find Martha standing there wearing a floral-patterned tracksuit and red lipstick. "You're home!" she said loud enough for him to hear inside the car. "We just got back from church. This is perfect timing." She took a step to the right and prepared to open the back door.

Aaron hesitated for a moment before pressing the button to pop out the door handles. He didn't want Martha to wake Jack up. But he also understood her need to check on the baby and see with her own eyes that he was okay. Besides, it was growing hot in the car. He needed to get some air in here or else turn the car back on and drive home. Aaron wasn't ready to do that yet, not after his goodbye with Julia had been so abruptly interrupted. Maybe he could score one more kiss.

"He's sleeping," Martha said, louder than necessary, as soon as she opened the door. "And I don't want to interrupt his nap. I only want to kiss him." She sat on the back seat and leaned into the car seat.

"Wait!" said Julia. "No kisses. He just got back from the emergency room. I don't want either of you to accidentally give each other germs."

"I don't have germs," said Martha. "I feel perfectly fine, and I don't mind the risk."

"You just got back from church," Julia said in a sterner tone than normal. "Who knows what you picked up when you shook hands with people? Jack's been in the hospital."

Martha sighed and leaned back in her seat. "You're right." She wiggled Jack's foot. "He's sleeping so peacefully now that you'd never know he was sick last night." Martha raised her eyebrows and cringed. "Heather told me all about it."

"Who's Heather?" Aaron asked, disturbed that total strangers were talking about his baby's health.

"Alyssa's mom," explained Martha. "She goes to my church. It was definitely a babysitting experience for the books."

"You mean Heather who owns the Ferry's Closet?" Julia glanced at Aaron. "That's ferry with an *e*, not an *a-i*. This is Harper Landing, after all. Ferry traffic is huge here."

"Yup," Martha nodded. "That's the one."

"I don't understand why Jack's private business would be a conversation topic in church," said Aaron, a tiny muscle in his jawline twitching.

"Of course it was a topic." Martha adjusted the zipper on her tracksuit. "He was on the prayer list, right after Frank."

"Of course he was." Aaron closed his eyes and shook his head.

"This isn't Silicon Valley," said Julia. "I wouldn't be surprised if there was a meal train set up for you by the time you drive home."

Aaron opened his eyes up wide. "I do *not* need a meal train."

"Think of all the casseroles you could get." Julia chuckled. "All that pasta, and cheese, and condensed mushroom soup."

"Stop," said Aaron, trying not to laugh, because he didn't want to offend Martha.

"I have a great recipe for tuna casserole," Martha offered.

"Thanks, Martha," said Aaron. "But—"

"No really. Jared gave it to me. It's paleo. Instead of cream-of-mushroom soup, you use coconut cream, and instead of pasta, you use sweet potato noodles. I thought it was delicious, but Frank wasn't a fan."

"Huh," said Aaron. "Maybe I *would* like that recipe."

"I'll take it, Martha." Julia picked up her purse and kissed Aaron lightly on the cheek. "I'll make it for dinner and drop it off at your house tomorrow night. Sound good?"

"Sounds great." Aaron smiled. "Jack and I will probably go home and crash until then."

"I guess that's my cue to leave too." Martha blew air-kisses all around Jack's car seat. "Germs, scherms," she muttered. "I mean, really."

CHAPTER
TWENTY-ONE

The $300 she had withdrawn from the ATM was almost gone. Julia wasn't usually a big shopper, but today she was making an exception. It was Monday morning, and she was visiting every property on Main Street that she owned to deliver the news in person. All the buildings would be getting new roofs in August, and over the next two years, she would gradually raise rents to proper market value. Buying a smoothie, teacup, hat, or box of stationery along the way seemed like a gesture of goodwill on Julia's behalf that she was happy to make. Most of the shop owners took the news well, except for Dave Parson, who said, "It's about time," when she visited the Parisian Café. Dave typically wasn't so rude, but Julia figured his feelings were still hurt after the other night when Will had sent his chicken cordon bleu back to the kitchen not once, but twice, and had made a scene over how it couldn't possibly have been prepared on-site. Dave had finally stormed into the dining room and cussed Will out, waving a baguette in the air like a sword. Julia had been shocked, because Dave was usually meek and mild mannered. Apparently, Dave took his chicken cordon bleu's reputation seriously.

Now Julia was at the Ferry's Closet, where Heather was helping her select a new outfit to wear this Thursday on the Fourth of July. By the time Julia had gotten home from the hospital yesterday, she'd been ready to burn her old dress after having worn it for so long. Eighteen hours in a strapless bra was seventeen and a half hours too many. Julia knew that the Ferry's Closet would be the perfect place to find a replacement dress because Heather's boutique always stocked cute items that couldn't be found in standard stores. Plus, she chose fabrics that were forgiving enough for any waistline. Julia worked hard to maintain her weight, but her curves were sometimes tricky to dress without a little help from spandex.

"I hope Alyssa wasn't too traumatized by this weekend," said Julia as she looked at the display mannequins.

"How do you know about her babysitting job gone wrong?" Heather asked. She wore slim gray shorts, high-heeled sandals, and a lacy blue shirt with a wide silver belt.

"I was with Aaron when she called him."

"Ooh." Heather raised her eyebrows. "That sounds promising. I mean, not about little Jack being sick but—"

"I know what you meant." Julia twirled a strand of hair around her finger. "Thankfully Jack's okay now. It turned out to be a soy allergy."

"That's good to hear." Heather selected a hanger with a sparkly yellow dress. "So do you need an outfit for a follow-up date?" She passed Julia the hanger.

"Kind of." Julia examined the dress and put it back. "I need something for the Fourth of July, and I have to be able to sit down in it, even on concrete if necessary." Julia looked at the rack of options. "If I bend over to pick up candy, I don't want to accidentally flash anyone."

"I hear you." Heather's curly brown hair was slicked back in a low ponytail. The high-heeled sandals she wore added an extra three inches to her petite frame, but she was still shorter than Julia. Heather searched through the rack and selected a blue sundress with a V-cut neckline. "This one is silk and completely breathable. Which is good, since they're predicting Thursday will be hot."

"Silk?" Julia scrunched up her face and shook her head. "It's gorgeous, but I forgot to mention the outfit also has to be machine washable, because of Jack."

"Oh. Duh." Heather jammed the dress back on the rack. She sorted through the clothing and pulled out several hangers. "Okay, I know you said a sundress, but this outfit could be perfect. It's like what you normally wear, so I know you'll feel comfortable in it, but the style is elevated a notch."

"What are you saying about my normal style?"

"Your normal style is fine." Heather patted her on the back. "But this is a bit more festive. You know," she said, nodding her head, "for the Fourth of July."

Julia frowned and looked at the hangers Heather held up. "Those shorts seem awfully short to me."

"They're cutoffs, and you have the legs to pull them off." Heather picked up a pair of high-heeled sandals off the rack behind her that matched the ones she was wearing. "These would look great with them."

"I don't know." Julia wrinkled her forehead. "The Fourth of July usually involves a lot of walking." But she took the sandals anyway. "I guess it wouldn't hurt to try it all on."

"That's the spirit. Let's get a dressing room started for you."

Half an hour later, Julia was paying cash for three new outfits and adding a large bag from the Ferry's Closet to her other purchases from that morning. She squared her shoulders, knowing it was time to deliver the news about the rent increase. "Heather," she began. "I need to tell you something as your landlord. I wanted you to hear it from me before the official letters go out."

Heather slammed the register shut with a loud click. "What is it?" she asked, freezing in place.

"You're getting a brand-new roof in August, for starters."

"Oh." Heather smiled with relief. "That's great news."

"It's not all great news, unfortunately." Julia explained about the rent increase. "It'll be gradual," she said. "In the next sixty days, we will bring the rent up to keep up with inflation, and over the next two years, with each annual renewal, we'll bring the leases up to current market values."

Heather sighed and rested her palms on the counter. "I knew that was coming eventually," she said. "Matt told me that his rent for the Gnome's Backyard is almost double what I'm paying."

"That's probably right." Julia nodded. "I don't own that building."

"So why haven't you raised the rents before now?"

"That was my mother's decision, and I'm sure she had her reasons. But I need to raise the rents in order to adequately maintain all my buildings so they can last another hundred years. It's not just the roofs that need to be replaced; I intend to make a whole batch of upgrades that will increase safety, reduce heating costs, and make things better for my tenants."

"Well, now that you mention it," said Heather, opening a drawer under the counter. "I have a list of things that need to be fixed. I didn't want to give it to you before since I knew you were undercharging us."

Julia took the piece of notebook paper and scanned the items. "Leaking window seals, a rattling boiler, a piece of carpet that's worn down to the floorboard . . . yes. All this needs to be taken care of." She pointed up to the ceiling. "I will be refreshing things top to bottom, I promise. But it will be a process that will take some time."

"I think that sounds more than fair." Heather picked up a pencil. "Oh! One more thing." She took back the list and scribbled on the paper. "The front door sticks."

"Of course it does." Julia's shoulders sagged as she picked up her bags. When she twisted the doorknob to leave, the door wouldn't budge.

"Give it a little jerk to the right," said Heather. "That should do the trick."

Julia wrestled the sticky door open and went out into the bright sunshine. She wished she had her car with her so she wouldn't have to lug home her multiple purchases. The climb up Main Street was steep, and Ninth Avenue seemed a long way away. At least she had now spoken to every tenant except for one—Walt Lancaster. Technically, Julia had already talked to Walt about the upcoming rent increase when he had accosted her in the pool last week. She lifted her chin and marched past the Sugar Factory without bothering to stop in and chat. After the way he had talked to her at the pool, why should she bother buying anything from him? But she'd barely passed the shop before Walt bolted out the front door and confronted her, right there on the Main Street sidewalk, in front of Starbucks.

"What's the deal?" Walt asked, his bushy white hair blowing in the light breeze. "Why did you buy something at every storefront you own except mine?"

"I did not," Julia said, her arms feeling heavy from all her new goods. "I didn't buy something at *every* store."

"Every store but mine, it would seem." Walt crossed his arms in front of his chest. "What's the matter—don't you like candy? Or are you waiting for the free stuff the floats will pass out in the parade this Thursday, thanks to you and your idiot friends at the chamber?"

"Whoa," said Julia, dropping her bags on the sidewalk. "Don't talk about my friends that way. They're your colleagues too."

"I'll talk about them any way I want," Walt said with a sneer. "It's called the right to free speech. Maybe you've heard of it?"

The small crowd gathered in front of Starbucks drinking coffee stared at them. Julia saw Melanie and her son, Timmy, eating cake pops. George walked up the sidewalk with his wife, Shelly, rolling next to him in her wheelchair with their Jack Russell terrier on her lap. Shelly's red hair was freshly dyed.

"Good day, Walt," said Julia. "Watch for a letter from my lawyers about the rent increase coming up."

"You can't raise my rent!" Walt snapped, his face turning puffy. "Your mother promised that it would never change."

"Well, my mother's not in charge anymore, and I'm the one who sets the rent."

"Shows you what you know. You think you're so smart with your University of Washington degree. Lording it over everyone just like your father."

"I would never." Julia's hands clenched into fists and unclenched. Her breaths grew shorter as adrenaline raced through her system.

"I'm not paying one dime of rent more, and that's final." Walt spat on the ground right next to Julia's bag from the Ferry's Closet. "Waverley and I had an agreement."

"Maybe so," Julia said in a quiet voice. "But that's in the past now. As soon as your lease is up, I'm terminating your tenancy."

"You can't do that!"

"I can, and I will."

"You can't evict me!" Walt sputtered. "I have rights."

"I'm not evicting you . . . yet. But I will file a notice to terminate your tenancy as soon as my lawyer says I'm allowed to do so. Good luck finding a new location for the Sugar Factory." Julia picked up her bags and stomped away, straight up the sidewalk toward Sweet Bliss and home.

"Your mother was right about you!" Walt called after her. "You've got a fat ass."

"Oh no he didn't," said Melanie. She handed her cake pop to Timmy and began filming the scene with her phone.

Julia's eyes burned. She didn't need Walt hurling insults at her to remember her mother's words. "You're homely and fat like your father," Waverley used to say. She must have heard those words a thousand times and believed them a thousand more. But not today. Julia dropped her bags again and spun around.

"I've got a fine ass," said Julia, putting one hand on her hip. "Not that it's any business of yours. Body-shaming is wrong, especially coming from the owner of a candy store."

"You tell 'em, Julia," hollered George. Midas yapped at Walt.

Walt screwed up his face. "Body-shaming is wrong," he said in a singsong imitation of Julia. "Cry me a river, fat ass."

"Shut up, Walt." Julia pointed, directing all her wrath toward him. But as soon as the words came out of her mouth, she realized she was talking to Waverley too. Only a bitter, coldhearted wreck of a human being would belittle her own daughter. She needed to stop letting Waverley's misery poison her life. Paige was right. She did have low self-esteem, and it was because of her mother. But that stopped now.

"You think you're so special just because your last name is Harper." Walt pranced a few times like he was an angry elf. "Well, guess what? Nobody cares."

"*I* care." Julia's heart pounded madly in her chest. "This town means something to me, and I'm proud my ancestors founded it."

"As you should be!" Melanie shouted, still filming.

Julia jabbed her thumb up the street toward Sweet Bliss. "I don't only sell frozen yogurt; I sell a dream. The Seattle Freeze creeping into Harper Landing needs to stop."

"I agree," said George as Midas barked.

Pent-up emotion that had been stored inside Julia's heart poured out in a rush. "I believe that Harper Landing is still a place where neighbors come to each other's rescue. Where dogs can swim at the beach. Where a frickin' fire truck and a bunch of preschoolers can roll down Main Street on the Fourth of July, and everyone will cheer." She took a sharp breath to steady herself. "And if you can't have the common decency to at least be kind, then you don't deserve to be here."

"That's right!" Shelly called.

George and Shelly began clapping. Other people joined in, some of whom Julia recognized and some of whom might have been ferry passengers from Port Inez. Julia heard a wolf whistle—there was Matt, wearing his garden gnome hat and standing off to the side. Paige was there, too, arriving at the last second and yelling, "What did I miss?" Officer Dillan was right behind them.

"Don't worry," said Melanie. "It's already on Harper Landing Moms." She put down her phone.

"I saw the commotion, and I came running," said Paige, breathing hard. "I thought someone might have put soap bubbles in the fountain again."

"Can we do that?" Timmy asked his mom.

"No," said Officer Dillan. "Not without permission."

"The chamber of commerce's next president, ladies and gentlemen," Matt called out in his booming voice and pointed at Julia. "Right here."

"Unbelievable!" Walt stomped his feet and stormed off back to his store.

"So I guess this means you're not selling to Will Gladstone?" George asked as Midas sniffed her hand.

"Sell to Will Gladstone?" Shelly asked. "You weren't seriously considering that, were you?"

"Nope." Julia shook her head. "Not really." She reached down to pet Midas before standing upright again. "I'm guilty of stringing Will on a bit in order to discover how he thought Main Street could be improved, but that's it. Our historic buildings need to be preserved, not torn down. I'd rather cut off my arm than sell one of my buildings to a greedy property developer like him."

"Hear! Hear!" said an elderly lady drinking a latte. Julia vaguely recognized the woman as someone from Martha's church.

"Thank you, everyone, for your support just now." Julia collected her shopping bags yet again and waved to the Starbucks crowd.

"Where are you headed?" Paige asked.

"Home," said Julia with a smile. "And then to the grocery store. I've got a tuna casserole to bake."

CHAPTER
TWENTY-TWO

It was inconceivable how such a tiny human being could make such a big mess. Aaron wore Jack in the baby wrap because that was the only way he was able to get anything done. Between dealing with the barfy kitchen, doing the laundry, and straightening up before the housekeepers could come this morning, it seemed like Aaron had spent all day tidying up after Jack. Now the cleaners had gone, and the house was cinnamon fresh, but there were still bottles to be washed and sanitized because Aaron didn't trust the crew to meet his standards of cleanliness for that. Jack chewed on the fabric carrier until there was so much drool that Aaron's right armpit was wet, but at least the baby was content.

"Okay," said Aaron as he checked the oven clock. "Julia will be here in half an hour. Now that these bottles are washed, how about we change your diaper?" Aaron didn't smell anything unpleasant, but that didn't mean Jack hadn't left him a surprise. "I could use a fresh shirt too. This one's wet with drool." Aaron put the last bottle on the drying rack and hung up the dish towel. He was about to walk to the back bedroom when the doorbell rang. "Is that Julia?" he asked, his pulse elevating. Aaron squeezed Jack's tiny hand. "Maybe she's early."

When the doorbell rang again and then kept buzzing over and over on repeat, Aaron realized it couldn't be Julia. There was only one person in his life who rang the doorbell like that, and she was supposed to be in a different time zone right now. Aaron climbed down the steps to the entryway landing, his heart full of dread. "Hi, Mom," he said as he opened the front door.

Lorraine Baxter was sixty-two years old but didn't look a day over fifty thanks to quarterly laser peels and a gifted plastic surgeon. The only parts of her ageless body that betrayed her birth year were her hands, which was why she purposely wore blouses with too-long sleeves and flouncy cuffs that reached her knuckles. Today she was in a leather skirt and silk blouse. Her caramel-colored hair had so much hair spray holding it in place that it could have doubled as a football helmet. An enormous designer purse rested on her shoulder. The first words out of her mouth when she saw Aaron were, "*This* is where you live?"

Aaron's mouth gaped; he didn't know what to say. He hadn't seen his mother since the memorial service. Lorraine barged right past him into the house, the spikes of her shoes grinding into the wood floor. She reached for Jack. "There's that sweet face," she said. "I want my grandson."

That was when Aaron remembered how to talk again. "What are you doing here? I thought you were in Thailand or someplace. That's what your auto text said." He stepped backward so his mother couldn't reach Jack, who was secured in the front-facing carrier.

"What do you mean, 'What are you doing here?'" Lorraine frowned—or would have if there had been less Botox in her forehead. "I chartered a jet as soon as I received your text that Jack was in the hospital."

"That was two days ago."

"It took me four flights to get here from Fiji." She kissed Jack on both cheeks. "Your father sends his love, by the way. But he's the keynote speaker at a conference and couldn't leave."

"Litigation lawyers have conferences in Fiji?" Aaron asked. He figured his father was on a black sand beach right now drinking Hurricanes.

"Only the rich ones." Lorraine grabbed the buckle of the baby wrap and tried to loosen it.

"Hey, watch it." Aaron twisted out of her reach. "Be careful, or Jack could fall." He walked up the stairs to the living area. "Go wash your hands first, and then you can hold Jack. You might have brought germs with you from the airport."

"Darling," said Lorraine as she gripped the wrought iron railing and climbed up the stairs behind him. "It's not like I was flying commercial." But she went into the kitchen and turned on the faucet. "This kitchen is minuscule. It might as well be in a dollhouse." She dried her hands on the dish towel and then brought the cloth up to her nose. "Goodness gracious, this towel reeks of mildew. When's the last time the maid changed it?"

"What? I just used that to wash bottles." Aaron picked up the towel to smell what Lorraine was talking about. She was right; there *was* a faint smell of mold, like the cloth was a couple of days old. "Dang it. Now I need to rewash the bottles." He undid the clasp of the baby wrap and handed Jack over. "Here, you can hold Jack while I do that."

"While you wash the bottles?" Lorraine held Jack out at arm's length and stared at her grandson. "Doesn't the daytime nanny do that?" Jack stared back and gnawed on his fist, which was slimy with saliva.

"There is no daytime nanny." Aaron squirted soap into the dish tub and turned the faucet to hot. "When's the last time you held a baby? He's not going to bite."

"I know that," Lorraine snapped. "But he's drooling, and this blouse is dry-clean only. Haven't you got a cloth to give me?"

"You mean a burp rag?" Aaron shook his wet hands over the sink and leaned down to open a drawer. "The burp cloths are in the nursery, but here's a clean towel." He arranged it across Lorraine's shoulder.

"Much better." She hugged Jack against her and left the kitchen, kicking off her stilettos when she reached the carpet and walking over to the couch with bare feet. Aaron followed her. Before Lorraine sat down, she surveyed the room. Besides the sofa, recliner, wobbly coffee table, and big-screen TV, there wasn't much to see except the giant cardboard cutout of a Sasquatch in the corner. "I see that horrid gag gift from Jared is still with you."

Aaron glanced over at the original Big Foot Paleo marketing campaign and smiled. "It wouldn't be home without him." He sat down on the recliner.

"I suppose now that the buyout has gone through, it could be considered a vintage relic." Lorraine rolled her eyes. "If you had asked for my advice, I would—"

"You weren't speaking to me at the time, if you'll remember."

"Because you dropped out of Stanford!"

"Which you didn't want me to attend anyway, so why did you care?"

She sighed. "Five generations of Baxters have been Princeton Tigers, and you wanted to abandon that to be what, a tree?"

Jack's face scrunched up, and he began to fuss, quietly at first, but then he launched into full-blown wails after Lorraine started to comfort him.

"There, there," she said sternly. "Settle down. Mama Lorraine is here."

"Mama Lorraine?" Aaron hopped up from the recliner and walked over to the couch, swooping up Jack before his mom could frighten the baby any further. "What's wrong with him calling you Grandma?"

"Do I look like a grandmother to you?" Lorraine pouted, and her unnaturally plump lips seemed in danger of bursting at the seams. "Now, tell me how Jack's doing. He looks perfectly fine to me, but your text sounded like he was on death's door."

Now that the baby was back in the safety of Aaron's embrace, he stopped crying. Jack snuggled up to Aaron's shoulder and looked sideways at Lorraine, tracking her as if he was afraid she would nab him again. Aaron sat down in the recliner and rocked back and forth, rubbing Jack's back in steady circles. He didn't want Jack to fall asleep this soon before bed, but he didn't want the baby to be frightened either. "Jack's better now," said Aaron. He explained about the soy allergy and how the ultrasound had ruled out pyloric stenosis. "It looks like you flew out here for nothing. Didn't you get the text I sent you yesterday? I tried to keep you and Dad up to date on all this."

"No." Lorraine reached into her purse and pulled out a phone. "I most certainly did not." She stared at the screen. "Nope, nothing."

"That's weird." Aaron took his phone out of his back pocket and checked his messages. "Oh," he said, feeling guilty. "It says the text to you and Dad is still in draft mode. It must not have gone through. Sorry about that."

"Well, *I'm* not sorry." Lorraine stood up and smoothed her skirt. "This gives me an opportunity to see your campsite."

"Campsite?"

"Campsite . . . squatter's habitation . . . hovel . . ." Lorraine held up her hands. "I don't know what you want to call this dump, but it's good I came here and saw with my own two eyes how you're living. Thank goodness I left my things at the Fairmont in Seattle and took a cab here. Obviously, Jack cannot continue in this environment."

"What are you talking about?" Aaron rose to his feet, which caused Jack to wake up a bit. He'd been on the verge of drifting off to sleep from the rocking. "This is a four-bedroom house in a nice neighborhood. Harper Landing has some of the best schools in the Seattle area."

Lorraine winced. "You can't honestly mean to tell me you are thinking of sending this poor child to public school?" She walked over to the front window and stared out at the street. "Those people have an RV in their driveway. In their *driveway*, Aaron. Does someone live in it?"

"Of course not. They use it for camping. This is summer, Mom. People go on family vacations around here."

"Do not use that tone with me, young man. We went on plenty of family vacations, and you know it. Just not in a"—she lifted up her fingers and made air quotes—"recreational vehicle."

"Once I give you a tour of the whole house, you'll feel better," Aaron offered, wishing it could be true. "I haven't done much decorating besides replacing the carpet, but I did buy Jack a nice crib and changing table. It converts to a dresser when he's older. You'll love it."

Unfortunately, showing Lorraine around the split-level home didn't help, because she had a criticism about everything, starting with the way the new carpet reeked of off-gassing and going all the way to how the forced-air central heating system would dry out Jack's skin. But when they got to the master bedroom and Lorraine saw the bassinet next to Aaron's bed, she became furious.

"This is not how I raised you!" She pointed at the bassinet and then at him. "What is the nighttime nanny doing in your bed? Doesn't she have her own room?"

"Mom, there is no nighttime nanny." Aaron lifted Jack in the air and did a sniff test. He couldn't put off changing the baby any longer. "I told you there aren't any nannies."

"Well, that's a relief." Lorraine dropped her hand to her side. "No, wait a second. That doesn't make sense. If there aren't any nannies, then how are you coping?"

"The best I can." Aaron walked out of his room and crossed the hall to the nursery. He laid Jack down on the changing table and unsnapped the baby's pants. How soon would be too soon to drive his mother back to the Fairmont?

"Sara wouldn't have wanted this," Lorraine said from the doorway.

"No, she wouldn't have." Aaron undid Jack's diaper. He had a brand-new one waiting in the wings, just in case. He only needed to be peed on in the face one time to learn *that* lesson. "Sara would have wanted to be here herself."

"That's not what I meant." Lorraine walked down the hallway to the restroom and came back a moment later, wiping her eyes with a tissue. "She wouldn't have wanted you to put your life on hold and give up everything important to you."

Aaron didn't say anything at first, because the conversation hurt too much. The truth was, this was exactly what Sara would have wanted—and not wanted at the same time. She wouldn't have liked the fact that Aaron's world had turned upside down, but she absolutely would have wanted Jack to have a stay-at-home parent loving him more than anyone who was on a payroll could. "Sara would want what's best for Jack," Aaron said in a low voice. "Right now, that means me."

"Oh, darling," said Lorraine as she crept up behind him. "It doesn't have to be you. Let's bring Jack back to Rumson, and I'll have the service send a whole team out. You can't possibly be with Jack twenty-four hours a day, but once I hire a daytime nanny and a night nanny and the weekend nanny, then Jack will be properly cared for."

"No," said Aaron in a firm voice. "That's not what Sara or Jared would want, and their will was clear. I'm Jack's guardian. You and Dad weren't even on the backup list."

Lorraine shrank back. "You don't need to be cruel," she said. "I'm sure that was an oversight."

Aaron snapped Jack's pants back into place. "It wasn't an oversight." He picked up the baby and held him in both arms. "Sara and Jared wanted Jack to have a normal life, and that's what I intend to give him." He nuzzled his head next to Jack's. "Now maybe I'll be able to have a normal life too."

"What's that supposed to mean?" Lorraine asked in an accusing tone of voice. But before the conversation could continue, the doorbell rang.

"Julia," Aaron whispered, his mood suddenly feeling lighter. He smiled at Jack, and the baby grinned back. "Let's go answer it."

"Who's Julia?" Lorraine asked, following them to the landing. "Do I know her?"

"Not yet," said Aaron. "I guess you're going to meet her." He wished he had been able to change his drool-stained shirt, but it was too late for that now. Besides, he knew Julia wouldn't mind. She didn't care about fancy clothes. But how would she feel about his mother? If only Aaron had been able to warn her that Lorraine was here. When he opened the front door, he felt like he was leading Julia into a trap.

Julia stood on the doorstep wearing short shorts, a green T-shirt, and a long sweater that rested at her knees. She held a casserole dish in front of her wrapped with tinfoil, and there was a reusable grocery bag dangling from her elbow. Her hair was pulled back into a loose ponytail, and she wore a huge smile on her face. "Hi, Aaron. Hi, Jack. Are you hungry for dinner?"

The truth was, Aaron was hungry for Julia. Just the sight of her calmed down his nervous system to the point where he might be able to make it through Lorraine's visit without exploding. Julia's smile filled him with warmth. It was a relief to see her standing there and know that she was on his side—and Jack's side too. But as eager as Aaron was to fling the door open even farther and welcome Julia inside, he also wanted to protect her. She didn't know what she was walking into.

"My mom surprised me with a visit," he said through a forced smile. "She arrived half an hour ago."

"Your mother?" Julia's face froze. "Oh," she said, stumbling back. "I'll go, then."

"Don't you dare." Aaron grabbed her by the elbow and pulled her inside. "Dinner smells delicious." He kissed her on her cheek and closed his eyes, breathing in her scent.

"I don't know about that." Julia paused at the bottom of the stairs. "I've never made it before, and it might be awful and—" She turned around to go. "I should leave."

"Please don't go," he whispered in her ear. "I'm begging you."

CHAPTER
TWENTY-THREE

The idea of meeting Aaron's mother seemed like more than Julia could deal with, especially after today's stressful confrontation with Walt on Main Street. But when Aaron asked her to stay in such a pleading tone, her heart begged her to be courageous. Julia needed to step up, not only for Aaron but also for herself. She wanted to stop living in fear of other people's judgment. She had done nothing wrong. There was no reason for her to fear Aaron's mother. It wasn't Waverley standing up there waiting to meet her; it was a stranger. Besides, this tuna casserole she'd made smelled terrific, even if it did have sweet potato noodles in it. Julia squared her shoulders, turned around, and climbed up the stairs to the kitchen.

"Mrs. Baxter," she called out as she set the casserole on the stove. "So nice to meet you." There was no one there, but Julia was trying to be proactive.

Lorraine walked into the kitchen wearing her high heels. "That's *Ms.* Baxter." Her lipstick was freshly made up. "We don't live in the dark ages."

"Oh." Julia's cheeks turned pink. "Right. Of course." She desperately wished that she had shined her shoes that morning. With any luck, the woman wouldn't see the scuffs on her leather sneakers.

"But I'm *so* pleased to meet you," Lorraine said with a smile. She held out her hand, palm down, like she was expecting Julia to kiss it.

Julia took the offered hand in her own and turned it ever so slightly into a normal handshake. "My name's Julia Harper. I'm Jared's neighbor. *Was* Jared's neighbor," she added. "Have you eaten dinner yet?"

"Not one bite. The food they served on my flight was completely inedible." Lorraine shuddered. "Chartered flight standards have really deteriorated over the years."

"I'll get the plates." Aaron scooted behind Julia and opened a cabinet. "Mom, would you like to open a bottle of wine?"

"Do you have anything worth drinking?" Lorraine asked.

"I brought a bottle of sparkling cider." Julia took it out of the shopping bag along with the bowl of tossed salad.

"Sparkling cider? I'm not six," Lorraine said with a laugh. "I assure you I've been twenty-one for a while."

"Longer than you'd ever admit." Aaron reached into the refrigerator. "I've got a Chateau Ste. Michelle chardonnay that I think you'll like." He handed the bottle to his mother.

"I've never heard of it." Lorraine squinted at the label.

"It's a Pacific Northwest winery that's popular here," said Julia. "Their wines have won several awards."

"Well." Lorraine shrugged. "If this is all you have."

Aaron rolled his eyes. "It'll be fine, Mom."

"Okay, then," said Julia, her voice accidentally squeaking. "I'll set the table." She took the plates from Aaron and walked over to the kitchen table, moving a stack of mail out of the way and onto the kitchen counter. *So far, so good,* she thought. This wasn't how she'd envisioned the evening going, but hopefully the casserole was still warm. When Julia had taken it out of the oven twenty minutes ago, it had been hot and bubbling. The scent of coconut, sweet potatoes, and tuna had mixed into a fragrant aroma that had made Julia's mouth water. Julia went back to the cabinets and opened the first drawer she came to, looking for silverware. She happened upon a utensil drawer full of serving pieces and a wooden spoon.

Chills prickled down her spine when she saw that spoon. Inanimate objects shouldn't make grown women quake, but Julia's knees wobbled a bit before she got hold of herself and reached past it for a slotted spoon. "You ruin everything," she heard her mother scream at her. "First my figure and now my life!" Julia felt the whack of hundreds of punishments on the tender spot where her tailbone was bruised. Now here she was, trapped in a tiny kitchen with another mother who didn't like her. "You can't do anything right," she heard Waverley say. Why had Julia not thought to bring an expensive bottle of wine? Lorraine was probably right. Adults didn't drink sparkling cider.

"You know," Julia said, backing away from the still-open utensil drawer, "I think I'll go home. I don't want to interrupt your time together." She laid the slotted spoon next to the casserole and picked up her grocery bag. "I can pick up my dishes later."

"What are you talking about?" Aaron asked, a note of panic in his voice. "You can't go. I've been looking forward to this."

"Julia, darling, please stay." Lorraine sat down at the head of the table. "I find you fascinating."

Aaron thrust Jack into Julia's arms. "Here, hold the baby while I pour wine." Aaron retrieved the bottle of chardonnay from his mother and ripped off the foil covering the cork. "Or would you rather have the cider?"

"Wine is fine with me," said Julia. Jack's warm, squishy body in her arms had grounded her. She breathed in the sweet scent of him and felt instantly better. The baby laughed and grabbed her hair, trying to pull the golden strands into his mouth. "No you don't," said Julia as she disentangled herself. Then, she couldn't help it. "Wow," she whispered.

"Wow, wow, wow." Jack burst out laughing, and his giggles were music to her ears. She shifted her weight from one foot to the other and swayed back and forth. "Wow," she said again, this time a bit louder. Jack squealed in delight.

"Dinner is served," Aaron announced from the table. The casserole and salad were in the middle, and Jack's bouncy chair was at the opposite end, on top of the table, where he could see them.

"Is this safe?" Julia asked as she nestled Jack into the fabric and clicked the straps. "What if he bounces off the table?"

"I do it all the time," said Aaron.

"Bounce off the table?" Lorraine said with a sly grin. She sniffed her chardonnay before taking a sip.

"You're a regular comedian, Mom." Aaron held out the chair for her to sit down and then held out a chair for Julia too.

Julia couldn't keep her eyes off Jack in that bouncy seat. She would have felt more comfortable if it was on the floor, where Jack wouldn't topple over. But Aaron seemed confident that his choice was safe, and she didn't want to second-guess his decision-making skills. Besides, it wasn't like she had the authority to overrule him. Jack was Aaron's baby, not hers.

"I'm intrigued by this." Lorraine stared at the serving of casserole that she had just scooped onto her plate. "What is it? I smell fish."

"Tuna fish." Julia put her napkin on her lap. "It's a paleo version of tuna noodle casserole."

"Like a blue plate special." Lorraine poked at a morsel of sweet potato with her fork. "How quaint."

"I used to eat tuna casserole in the dining hall at Andover every Friday night," said Aaron, dumping a generous portion onto his plate. "It was my favorite."

"Martha told me that Jared loved it too," said Julia, "and that's why he sent this recipe to her so she could make it the last time he visited."

The words *last time* hung in the air like poison gas. Nobody spoke for a minute. Julia took a small sip of her wine. She needed to be careful and not drink the whole glass, or she wouldn't be safe to drive home. Julia was unused to drinking alcohol. She reached for the salad tongs and served herself, hoping she had done a good enough job tearing the lettuce into bite-size pieces like Waverley had taught her. She doused her salad with the paleo dressing she'd purchased at the store that afternoon and passed the bottle to Lorraine.

"I love salad." Lorraine looked at the mountain of greens on her plate. "It's hard for chefs to screw up unless they overdress it." She looked at the dressing label's nutritional content and squinted as she tried to read the writing.

Julia took her first bite of casserole, praying it would be good. Thankfully, it was still hot, and the tropical flavors of coconut cream and sweet potato blended into perfection, with just the right amount of tang from the tuna fish. She let out a breath she didn't know she'd been holding, relieved that the casserole was a success. At least, to Julia it was delicious. She looked anxiously at Aaron to see if he was enjoying his food too.

Julia needn't have worried. Aaron slapped his palm on the table and closed his eyes with pleasure. "Wow," he exclaimed. "Wow, wow, wow."

Jack chortled in his bouncy seat, and the springs swayed up and down.

"This is outstanding." Aaron reached for Julia's hand and squeezed it. "Thank you so much for cooking us dinner."

"It's not a big deal." Julia smiled and stared at her plate.

"No, it is." Aaron brought her hand to his mouth and kissed it. "Home-cooked meals are a rarity where I come from."

Lorraine bristled. "Anyone can cook," she said stoutly. "It's not that hard."

"Your mother's right." Julia let go of Aaron's hand and picked up her fork. "All you need to be able to do is follow a recipe."

"Something a woman like you would be good at," said Lorraine in a dismissive tone.

"What's that supposed to mean?" Aaron demanded.

"Nothing," Lorraine said brightly. "It was a compliment." She blotted her mouth with a napkin, and her lipstick stained it red.

An awkward silence settled over the table, and it gave Julia a moment to realize that something else wasn't right. In a moment, Julia remembered what it was. "The brownies," she exclaimed. "I forgot the brownies in the car, and now they're probably heating up in the hot sun." She pushed back her chair and rose to her feet.

"Brownies?" Aaron's eyes lit up.

"Made with almond flour and honey," explained Julia. She picked up her keys from where she'd left them on the counter. "I'll be right back." Julia hurried out of the kitchen and down the steps to the front door. When she opened the tailgate of her Subaru, she discovered that the brownies were warming up in the heat, just as she'd feared. There were beads of moisture on the inside of the plastic wrap covering the top of the pan. Julia peeled back a corner of the wrap to let the moisture escape and then walked back up the driveway to the house. But when she reached the threshold, she paused. Aaron's and Lorraine's voices carried, and it sounded like they were having a heated argument.

"No, it's not okay," snapped Aaron. "You've been rude to Julia since the moment she arrived."

"And she's too simple to realize it," Lorraine shot back. "Can't you see how beneath you she is?"

Simple? Julia's stomach clenched into knots. Under normal circumstances she wouldn't have eavesdropped, but she tilted her ear forward and concentrated.

"Julia is an intelligent woman," said Aaron. "You have no right to be rude to my girlfriend."

The knot in Julia's stomach transformed into butterflies. Her jaw relaxed, and she grinned. Girlfriend?

"She's parochial," said Lorraine. "As in 'having a limited viewpoint on life.'"

"That's not true. You don't know her."

"I can see why you were attracted, because Julia's pretty in a provincial Katy Perry sort of way. But she's definitely *not* whom I want for my son."

The smile on Julia's face faded. She *knew* these shorts were cut too high. She should never have let Heather talk her into buying them at the Ferry's Closet.

"Mom, take that back," Aaron said in a steely tone.

"I meant what I said," Lorraine responded. "You're rich, and thanks to that *Wall Street Journal* article, everyone knows it. Between your business success and your trust fund, every fortune hunter from here to Seattle will be after you."

Now Lorraine thought she was a gold digger? Julia couldn't take it anymore. She barged through the front door and stomped up the stairs to defend herself.

"You don't know what you're talking about, Mom, and you're wrong," growled Aaron. He turned around when he heard Julia. The furious expression he wore melted away with one look at Julia's face. "Julia, how much of that did you hear?"

"Enough," Julia said as she dropped the brownie pan onto the kitchen table. "I am not a gold digger."

"Of course not." Aaron clenched his jaw and glared at his mother. "Apologize to Julia at once."

"I never apologize for telling the truth." Lorraine sat up straight and lifted her chin.

"Neither do I." Julia tugged at the hemline of her shorts. She stared into Lorraine's eyes and saw venom. Julia felt adrenaline trickle across her nervous system like dripping water. "It's summer, it's hot out, and I didn't know I'd be meeting anyone's mother this evening. I'm not a tramp." She crossed her arms in front of herself protectively. "I'm also not after Aaron's money. I own half this town. I have my own money, and my own business, and even my own trust fund once I'm old enough to access it."

Lorraine inspected her french-tipped manicure. "How quaint. I'm sure you do fine for a backwater like this. But Aaron's used to the best society. And, sweetie, you wouldn't know high class if you baked it in the bottom of your tuna casserole."

Julia clenched her hands into fists and dropped her arms to her sides. "Just so you know," she said in a calm voice, "Harper Landing is *not* a backwater. We're the oldest incorporated town in Snohomish County. Some of the best people in the whole country choose to live here—engineers, lawyers, politicians, bankers, plumbers, bookstore owners, teachers, and more." Julia rested both hands on the table, leaned forward, and stared directly into Lorraine's eyes. "Do *you* have a town named after *you*? Is there a Baxter, New Jersey, that I should know about?" When Lorraine didn't answer, Julia stood up straight. "I didn't think so." She spun on her heel to go, with one last look at the baby.

"Julia, wait!" Aaron called after her. He caught up to her by the time she reached her car in the driveway. Aaron carried Jack with him, bouncy seat and all. He set the chair down in the front lawn, next to a cluster of blooming orange daylilies. "I'm so sorry about that. My mom should never have spoken to you that way. She didn't mean any of what she said about you. She's just bitter that I won't give her Jack and let her army of nannies raise him. She knows nothing she can say to me will make me change my mind, so she hurt you instead. I'm sorry."

"Army of nannies?" Julia processed Aaron's words while looking down at Jack, who was bouncing happily in the shade. Finally, she bit her lip and met Aaron's eyes again. "That would break Martha's heart."

Aaron nodded. "Mine too. I could never send Jack away like that. I can't tell you how many nights I lay awake in boarding school, racked with homesickness." He threw out his arms, encompassing the whole neighborhood. "And I hated my parents! I didn't even have a home, not like this one. Not like the one I want to create for Jack." Aaron took a step forward and put his hands on her hip bones. "Julia, I—"

Whatever he was about to say was interrupted by the loud ringing of Julia's phone. Weird Al Yankovic's 1983 hit "I Love Rocky Road" blasted from her purse. "That's Tara, my manager at Sweet Bliss." Julia unzipped her bag and took out her phone and ended the call before she picked it up. But when she saw the screen, she did a double-take. "I've got dozens of messages!" Her thumbs scrolled through the notices as quickly as she could. "Oh my gosh, there's an emergency at the shop. Tara said to come right away." Julia texted Tara back, telling her she would be there in ten minutes, and stashed the phone in her pocket. "I'm sorry, Aaron, but I need to go." She kissed him on the cheek. "The last time Tara called me with an SOS was when the freezer failed."

"Okay. I understand," said Aaron, stepping out of her way. "Drive safe. We can talk later."

Julia hopped into her SUV. Right before she closed the door, she looked up at him with a grin. "Did you mean it back there when you called me your girlfriend?"

Aaron sauntered forward and rested his arm on the edge of the door. "That kind of slipped out. I hope you don't mind."

She smiled. "Not in the slightest. But your mom might." Her phone buzzed again, and she ignored it. "We're still on for the Fourth, right?"

"Wouldn't miss it." Aaron leaned down and kissed her, and Julia felt tingles of excitement as their lips parted and their tongues touched. "Drive safe," he said again when he pulled away. "I'll call you later."

"Great. Talk to you then." Julia turned on the car and drove away, pushing the edge of the speed limit but being careful to follow the law. Her mind raced with a million thoughts, starting with *Aaron's mother hates me* and ending with *I've got a boyfriend!* She was so focused on her personal life that she didn't bother deciphering Tara's cryptic messages. When she drove down Main Street and saw a massive crowd overflowing the sidewalk in front of Sweet Bliss, she was stunned.

There wasn't any place to park, which was unusual for a Monday night. While the weekend was typically packed, Harper Landing's nightlife cooled down at the start of the week. Julia overshot Sweet Bliss by four blocks before she finally found a space by the Ferry's Closet. She slung her purse over her shoulder and hoofed it up Main Street as fast as she could. By the time she reached the Sugar Factory, she could hear chanting.

"Kindness matters!"

"Kindness matters!"

It wasn't a mob of people in front of Sweet Bliss; it was a mass of happy customers eating Froyo and waving their spoons in the air. "Kindness matters!"

A line of people snaked down the sidewalk in her direction. "Look," someone called. "There's Julia!" It was the mother from the library parent group with the baby who looked like Winston Churchill. "Ju-li-a!" she began chanting. Within moments, everyone in the crowd joined in. "Ju-li-a! Ju-li-a!"

"Wha-at?" Julia asked, her mouth dropping open. Then she closed it when she realized someone was filming her on their phone.

"Put this on Harper Landing Moms!" a woman shouted. "Get her reaction."

Melanie and Timmy elbowed their way down the sidewalk holding gigantic bowls of frozen yogurt. "Julia!" Melanie cried. "The post from this morning already got three thousand views. We want you to know that Harper Landing Moms has your back. Nobody has the right to belittle you, especially not Walt Lancaster."

"This is because of a Facebook group?" Julia's eyes hurt because they were so wide open that she'd barely blinked.

"Yes," said Winston Churchill's mother. "But it's also because of you, Julia. We believe in Harper Landing too." The baby in front of her laughed, his chubby knees kicking in the front-facing carrier.

Melanie nodded and pulled a spiral of dark-brown curls behind her ear. "We're proud to live in a place where neighbors still come to one another's rescue."

"Julia!" Tara screeched, running down the sidewalk. Her long dangly earrings flew behind her, tangling in her ruby-red hair. "We need your help at the register, pronto!"

Timmy dug his spoon deep into his scoop of pineapple and gobbled up bronze crumbs of brownie. "You're wrong, Mom," he said in his tiny voice. "Chocolate and pineapple *is* yummy."

Julia blinked back tears. "Six free ounces of Froyo for everyone," she called to the crowd, "and if you already bought some, come back for a free topping!"

CHAPTER
TWENTY-FOUR

Aaron was anxious to see Julia. It had been three days since their disastrous dinner with his mom. He'd spent the past seventy-two hours with Lorraine. Aaron still hadn't gotten over his anger about how his mom had treated Julia, but he tried to remember that Lorraine was still grieving the loss of her daughter. He knew that his mom honestly wanted what was best for Jack and Aaron—she just didn't know either of them well enough to know what that was. For this reason, he'd driven her around Western Washington the past couple of days, taking her to scenic vistas and gourmet coffee stands. He tried to convince her what a great place the Pacific Northwest was to live and also give her the opportunity to bond with Jack. Lorraine still wasn't sold on Harper Landing, but she was warming to the idea of Aaron's living in Washington. Right before Aaron had put her on the plane back to Fiji last night, she'd looked at him and said, "Have you considered moving to Mercer Island instead? If it's good enough for Bill Gates, it might be good enough for my grandson."

Now it was Thursday, and Aaron was loaded down like a Sherpa climbing Mount Everest. Jack hung from his chest in the carrier and wore a wide-brimmed bucket hat to protect him from the sun. Julia had been clear with her instructions about the Fourth of July parade: be prepared for anything. Thankfully, he'd been able to park in her driveway, because Harper Landing was so crowded that it appeared people were hiking in from miles away. The police had blocked off Main Street, mobs of people roamed all over the place, and the town looked more like Main Street, U.S.A., at Disneyland than ever before.

"You can always count on the Fourth of July," said Frank as he strolled along beside Aaron and Jack. "For the weather, I mean." He seemed to be having a good day, memory-wise.

"That's right." Martha's arm linked through her husband's, and she kept a firm hold. "It hasn't rained on the Fourth since Jared was in third grade."

"And his Cub Scout float was ruined." Frank chuckled. "All those blue-and-gold streamers turned to mush."

Martha leaned her head on Frank's shoulder. "That's right, dear." She wore a blouse with tiny American flags embroidered into the fabric.

"Jared was in Cub Scouts?" Aaron asked.

Frank nodded. "He was in Boy Scouts for a few years, too, before he got too busy with school."

"That's good to know." Aaron held Jack's tiny hand. "Maybe I'll sign Jack up for a pack someday."

"There's one that meets at our church," said Martha, with an excited look on her face.

As they began walking toward Main Street, Aaron did his best to keep the conversation light. He didn't mention Frank's upcoming doctor's appointment next week, although he knew it was on everyone's mind. "Where did all these chairs come from?" he asked instead. There was a double line of stadium chairs on every sidewalk, making it difficult to walk. The Reynoldses were now in front of him, and they were practically walking single file to avoid running into people camped out on the curb.

"People put them up the night before," Martha explained.

"It used to be that you could stroll down here twenty minutes before the parade started and grab a spot," said Frank. "But then all the Californians moved in and wrecked it."

"Now, Frank," said Martha, giving him a sharp look. "Don't be rude. You forget that Aaron moved here from California."

"Technically, I'm from New Jersey," Aaron said quickly.

"I hope Julia remembered to put chairs out in front of her shop," said Martha as she led Frank down the sidewalk. "Otherwise, we'll have to stand out in the hot sun for hours."

"Hours?" Aaron raised his eyebrows. "How long is this parade, exactly?"

"It's not one parade," Martha said, looking back at him over her shoulder. "It's two. First the children's parade, where they pass out candy, and then the real deal with the floats and the politicians."

"Great," said Aaron. He meant it too. The tension he'd carried all morning—all year, in fact—melted away. Jack was healthy, he'd made peace with Lorraine, and now he was spending the day with Julia in his adopted hometown. His grief for Sara and Jared would never lessen, but each day it was becoming easier to bear.

Aaron bent down and kissed the top of Jack's head, which meant kissing the bucket hat. This was the first holiday they'd celebrated together. Mother's Day had been too sad to mention. Father's Day, he'd ignored. But now it was the Fourth of July, and Jack was here in Harper Landing, in the company of his grandparents, and all around, happy people were wearing red, white, and blue. The happiness in town was contagious. Aaron felt it lift him up and carry him down Main Street, like he was caught in a big wave of joy.

Sweet Bliss, like all the businesses along Main Street, had the Stars and Stripes waving proudly in front. The big window sign said **CLOSED. BUT THE RESTROOM IS AVAILABLE.** A family Aaron didn't know sat in chairs in front of the store with a wicker picnic basket. Two twin boys, who must have been three or four years old, danced in front of their mothers, blowing bubbles. The entire family wore matching shirts with Rosie the Riveter on the front.

Aaron scanned the sidewalk for Julia but didn't see her. Then he spotted four chairs next to the Rosie the Riveter family with rope linking them together and a sign that said RESERVED FOR JULIA HARPER AND GUESTS. In the distance, he heard a marching band practice the opening bars of "Louie Louie." Bubbles blew past him and twirled in the air until they popped next to the waving flag. "Where's Julia?" he asked, his sense of excitement growing.

Martha parked Frank in front of the reserved seating and untied the rope. "I don't know, but I assume these chairs are for us."

"Here, Martha, let me help." One of the mothers hopped to her feet and undid the knot. A red-and-white polka-dot bandana tied up her hair, just like Rosie the Riveter.

"Thanks, Alison. I appreciate it," said Martha. Before Aaron knew what was happening, Martha grabbed him by the elbow and dragged him forward. "Have you and your wife met Aaron Baxter and my grandson Jack?"

"Are you sure we can sit here?" Frank asked, settling down in one of the chairs.

"Julia said they were for you," said Alison. She held out her hand to shake Aaron's. "I've heard so much about you. Martha is in my Bible study at church. This is my wife, Laurie."

"Nice to meet both of you," said Aaron, shaking their hands.

Instead of a bandana, Laurie wore a Mariners cap. "Julia's out in the middle of the street somewhere passing out free popsicles to all of the Scout troops."

"When does the children's parade start?" Martha asked as she sat down next to Frank. "I've lost track of time."

"In about twenty minutes," said Laurie. She took off her cap and used it to fan her face. "It sure is warm today."

"You can always count on the Fourth of July for good weather," said Alison as she passed out apple slices to the boys.

"That's just what Frank was saying," Martha said with a smile. "Isn't it, Frank?"

"Huh?" he asked.

Aaron looked at Frank closely and noticed that his eyes seemed unfocused. Perhaps the heat, or the excitement of the day, was getting to him. Aaron unhooked the backpack and dropped it in one of the two remaining chairs, grateful they were in the shade, and pulled out a thermos. "Here's some cold water," he said, offering the bottle to Frank. "Are you thirsty?"

"Water sounds like a great idea," said Martha. She helped Frank unscrew the cap.

The back of Aaron's shirt was damp with sweat—good thing he'd put the bottles of formula next to the blue ice. "I'm going to look for Julia," he said. "Any idea which direction I should head?"

"I'd suggest the corner of Main and Third, next to the old Red Slipper dance studio," said Alison. "I think that's where the Scout floats were assembling."

"Thanks." He patted Martha's shoulders. "Are you two okay until I get back?"

"We'll be fine," said Martha. "Won't we, Frank?"

"Sure we will." Frank took another swig from the water bottle and then closed his eyes. "I think I'll take a little nap until the parade starts."

"We'll be right here with you," said Laurie as she squirted out sunscreen into her palm. "Alison's a firefighter, you know."

That made Aaron feel better about leaving, and he took off as quickly as he could. Finding Julia was difficult, especially now that even more people were flooding the sidewalks. Aaron held his arms out like a barrier in front of Jack's body so he wouldn't accidentally be smashed. Next year, when Jack was older, maybe Aaron would be able to carry him on his shoulders. Could toddlers do that? Aaron wasn't sure. Possibly Jack would need to be three years old for that trick.

Once he got to the corner of Third and Main, Aaron hung a left and kept walking until the crowds thinned and the floats began. This was the waiting zone for the official parade to start. There were marching bands polishing their instruments, classic convertibles with banners along each side, and a troop of bagpipe players warming up their lungs. Aaron walked by a group dressed up like *Star Wars* characters and a drill team wearing white cowboy boots. He kept going until he finally found a swarm of girls in blue-and-brown and green-and-khaki uniforms patiently waiting in line, as well as boys who were jumping up and down in a separate line of their own.

Julia had on the cutoff shorts she'd worn Monday night and red platform sandals that showed off her killer legs. Her white T-shirt glistened in the sunlight from tiny sequins sewn into the fabric, and her blonde hair was swept to the side in a sparkly red clip that matched her lips. Julia reached into a giant cooler on wheels, then passed out popsicles as fast as she could. Aaron watched her bend over to retrieve the treats and felt his pulse spike. He might have stood there, lost in a trance of admiration, if Jack hadn't squealed and snapped him out of it.

"Need some help?" Aaron asked as he approached Julia.

"That would be fabulous." Julia stood up and kissed him on the cheek before blowing a kiss at Jack. "Wow," she said with a laugh. "Wow, wow, wow."

Jack giggled with delight.

Between the two of them, Aaron and Julia were able to make short work of passing out the rest of the popsicles. Thankfully, there were enough for every Scout, even the ones who showed up out of uniform and claimed they were part of the Scouts too. Aaron closed the cooler and picked up the handle, glad that it rolled, since he carried Jack in front of him. The cooler's wheels rumbled along the asphalt road, but the crowd was so noisy it would have been difficult to carry on a conversation anyway.

They turned the corner onto Main Street and walked up the hill two blocks. Just when they crossed Fifth Avenue, Walt burst out of his candy shop and accosted Julia again right there in the middle of the street. His goofy white hair fluffed out the side of his head like a triangle, and his face burned beet red. "Julia Harper," he screeched as he waved a piece of paper in front of him. "If you think you're going to terminate my lease, you've got another thing coming."

"Oh boy," said Julia, rolling her eyes. "Here we go again."

Aaron reached for her hand and squeezed it. "It's okay," he murmured in her ear. "I'm here. We won't let him ruin our day."

"You'll be hearing from my lawyer, bitch," Walt snarled.

"Whoa!" Aaron exclaimed. All thoughts of ignoring Walt's antics evaporated. "You don't talk to her like that."

"I'll call her whatever I want." Walt ripped up the letter and let the scraps flutter to the ground. People around him stepped back as much as possible, but nobody got out of their hard-earned chairs.

Julia squared her shoulders and spoke in a voice loud enough for everyone to hear. "Like the letter said, if you have any questions, you can contact my lawyer, who will be handling all communications between us from now on."

"If the Sugar Factory is ruined, it will be *your* fault." Walt pointed a gnarled finger right at Julia. "I would own this town if it weren't for you."

"What's that supposed to mean?" Julia asked.

"Ignore him." Aaron stood in front of Julia to shield her from Walt. "Let's go."

"Your mother wanted to marry me!" Walt shouted. "We were in love."

"She dumped you thirty-eight years ago," said Julia. "Get over it."

"No!" he explained, his face turning purple. "I mean three years ago. Waverley wanted to marry me."

"What?" Julia sidestepped around Aaron. "That's a lie."

"It's the truth." Walt puffed up his chest. "But Waverley wanted me to sign a prenup that would cut me out of everything she owned."

Julia's face became as pale as her white shirt. "That was my father's money, and you had no right to ask for it."

"I had every right," Walt said as his nostrils flared. "Waverley and I could have been happy if it weren't for you and Harrison. Why she wanted *you* to have that money, I'll never know." He spat on the ground and marched back into the Sugar Factory before Julia could respond.

"My mother was going to remarry?" Julia asked. She looked up at Aaron with shell-shocked eyes. "But she didn't because of me? How is that possible?"

Anger boiled inside him for how Walt had treated Julia. "Maybe she realized that Walt was an asshole," he said, wrapping her up in a hug with Jack sandwiched between them. "Come on. The parade is about to start. Don't let Walt win."

"You're right." Julia rested her head on Aaron's shoulder. "I can't let Walt ruin today." She stepped back and smiled at the baby. "Not on Jack's very first Fourth of July." She picked up Aaron's hand and led him up Main Street. "Nobody does a parade like Harper Landing. Nobody."

Julia was right. Once they were safely nestled in their stadium chairs and the children's parade began, it was like everyone Aaron had met in town rolled past him on bicycles, wagons, and Rollerblades. The library parent group marched with decorated strollers, streamers outlining the spokes of each wheel and ribbons flying from the handles. Aaron saw people he'd observed at the beach when he'd run past the dog park and also the neighborhood kids from his street, assembled with their soccer and basketball teams. Many of the parade walkers threw candy, and Alison and Laurie's twin boys scooped it up gleefully and brought it to their moms' picnic basket.

Thirty minutes later, the official parade began with a team of Harper Landing police officers on Segways clearing the path. When Officer Dillan scooted past them, she waved, but Aaron's attention was quickly captured by the cavalcade of classic cars following her carrying veterans, both young and old. The crowd rose to its feet, and Laurie took off her Mariners cap. Beside him, Julia had her hand across her heart. Once the solemn procession passed, everyone sat back down, and a high school band marched past playing a John Philip Sousa song that Aaron recognized but couldn't name. Antique fire engines rolled by next, and the firefighters on board hollered Alison's name and threw the boys heaps of taffy.

The sirens woke up Frank. "I love the Fourth of July parade," he said as he nabbed a Tootsie Roll. "This is my favorite day of the year."

"I wish Jessica and the kids could have driven up from Seattle for it," said Martha. "But you know teenagers." She shrugged. "At least they're coming to the barbecue in our backyard." Martha patted Aaron on the back. "Thanks for offering to operate the grill later."

"No problem," said Aaron, who had no interest in letting Frank near lighter fluid. "I'm anxious to try those bison burgers you were telling me about."

"I found them at Sprouts," said Martha. "I don't know how good they'll taste without hamburger buns, but I have those, too, for the rest of us."

The last float in the parade was a giant replica of the Harper Landing–Port Inez ferry that the chamber of commerce had sponsored. Matt Guevara was riding on top, since he was the current president. He pointed at Julia as they slowly rolled past and said, "Next year, Julia. Next year." Julia laughed and waved back.

"Well," said Martha. "I guess that's it."

Frank lumbered to his feet. "Let me help put these chairs away."

"Thanks, Frank." Julia collapsed the first chair in a matter of seconds, but Frank scooped his up intact.

"We can help too," Alison offered.

Aaron swung his backpack on and helped with the rest of the chairs. Jack was out cold after a diaper change and a bottle. It was a good thing they were going home now, because Aaron felt like the baby'd had enough time in the heat, even though their chairs had been in the shade.

"Are we ready?" Martha asked. "Hamburgers sound excellent right about now." She winked at Aaron. "Even if they are bison burgers."

"You guys go ahead," said Julia. "I need to wait for the last people to use the restroom before I can lock up Sweet Bliss."

"I'll wait with you," Aaron offered.

Everyone said their goodbyes, and Aaron and Jack sat at a booth in the air-conditioned shop while Julia bustled around Sweet Bliss, waiting for the last few customers to leave. Then, once Main Street was considerably quieter, Julia locked up the shop, and Aaron took her hand for the short walk home.

"I keep thinking about what Walt said," Julia admitted. "I know I shouldn't let it bother me, but I can't help it."

"He's a miserable old man who projects his misery onto others." Aaron stopped in place and gave Julia a side hug since Jack was sleeping in front of him. He kissed the top of her hair. "I'm sure your mom had lots of good reasons not to marry him, and they had nothing to do with you."

"Maybe." Julia kept walking. "But I'm not so sure. The thing is, my mother was weird about money. I can see that now. She was constantly afraid of losing it or the two of us being thrown out onto the streets."

Aaron wrinkled his forehead and looked at Julia to see if she was joking. "How can that be possible when your family owns so much property?"

"It's how she was," Julia said. "She grew up being evicted from apartment after apartment, and it left a big impression on her."

"Childhood scars leave deep wounds," said Aaron. "Maybe that explains your mom's actions."

"Yeah." Julia nodded. "But she also didn't want to be called a cheapskate or a greedy landlord. It's complicated."

They were at the driveway to Frank and Martha's house now, and Aaron could see the minivan belonging to Jared's sister, Jessica, in the driveway. He knew she was eager to spend time with Jack. She was still a bit jealous that Aaron had been named the primary guardian instead of her. But Jared and Sara had written in their will that they didn't want Jessica to have to start over with another child now that she and her husband were so close to being empty nesters.

"Aaron, before I go in there, I need to check something at my house. It's about my mother. Plus, I want to check on Toby."

"Do you want some company?" he asked. "I could drop Jack off with Jessica and be right over."

"That would be great." Julia stuffed her hands in her pockets. "I'll meet you on the porch. That way, Toby won't freak out twice in a row when people arrive."

"I'm going to help you train him, I promise."

Julia grinned. "Good, because we need all the help we can get."

Aaron hurried into the Reynoldses' house and passed off Jack to an eager Aunt Jessica. Once he was relieved of both baby and backpack, he felt a hundred pounds lighter. Since his shirt was covered in sweat, he changed into a clean shirt from the backpack. Then he hustled over to Julia's house, eager to see her.

"I love Jack," Aaron said as he stepped onto the porch, "but I've been waiting to do this all day." He bound his arms around her and pulled her curvy frame against his chest, smothering her with kisses until they were both breathless. Julia's hands roamed over his back, and Aaron was glad that he'd changed out of his sweaty shirt. She smelled like chocolate and lavender, and her lips tasted like taffy. "You've convinced me, Julia," he said when he steadied her on her feet. "I've fallen in love with the Fourth of July." That wasn't all he'd fallen in love with, but it seemed too soon to say it.

"I knew you would." Julia beamed pure joy. "Harper Landing is irresistible."

"You're irresistible." Aaron dipped her back for another kiss.

Their front-door make-out session was interrupted by the sound of incessant barking. Toby was on the other side of the door, and the Labrador was seriously displeased with both of them. Julia sighed. "We'd better go in and say hi to Toby so he can calm down."

"Good plan." Aaron nodded. He stepped off the doormat to give Julia the space to unlock the door. He also needed space to cool down his raging hormones.

Toby's exuberant greeting was precisely the wet blanket Aaron needed. Once Toby's tongue washed over Aaron's face, he didn't want to kiss Julia again until he could get his hands on soap and water. "Toby," Aaron said as he stood in the entryway. "Sit." The dog dropped to his feet and looked up at Aaron expectantly. "Good boy," Aaron crooned, massaging Toby's fur. "Good sitting." He stood up straight again and smiled at Julia. "Okay, you try that while I visit the bathroom."

Julia's face contorted into a doubtful expression. "I'll try, but he never listens to me."

"Lots of people listen to you, Julia, and your dog should be one of them."

Julia gave it a go. Toby had already stood up and was sniffing Aaron's hand. "Toby," she commanded in a clear and direct voice. "Sit!" Toby looked up at Julia and did as he was told. "Oh my goodness, he did it," she whispered. "My dog actually listened to me."

"You're darn right he did. Now reinforce him with an ear scratch. I'll be back." Aaron hurried off to the bathroom to wash his face. When he came back, Julia and Toby were still practicing their new trick.

"First stop, sitting; next stop, bringing in the newspaper and making me lattes," Julia said with a grin. "I have faith in you, Toby." She stroked his back, and the Labrador wagged his tail.

"What was that you said earlier about wanting to check something of your mom's?" Aaron asked.

"Oh. Right." Julia climbed the stairs. "Come on; you can look with me." When she reached the second floor, she walked down the hallway to the first of the two rooms Aaron had discovered were locked on the night of her concussion when he'd searched for her shoes and socks. Julia took out her key ring. "I want to see if there's anything in my mother's things that confirms what Walt said." She shrugged. "Maybe there won't be anything, but it won't hurt to look. I haven't been in here since after her funeral." Julia unlocked the bedroom door and flicked on the light switch.

"You've got to be kidding me," murmured Aaron as he walked into the room and saw what was inside. Every direction he looked, he saw trophies. Some were as tall as the ceiling. Along the back wall was a shelf of rhinestone crowns. Framed pictures of Waverley Harper hung on the wall, each one draped with a silk sash. It appeared as if Julia's mother had won every beauty contest in the Pacific Northwest.

"I don't know what to do with them." Julia ran her finger along one of the trophies and inspected the dust. "They used to be downstairs in the living room, and I moved them up here as soon as my mother died. But now what?"

Aaron didn't know how to answer. Storage unit? Dumpster fire? The answer was unclear. "You should do whatever you want," he finally said. "This is your home. It doesn't have to be a shrine to your mom or a museum of her accomplishments."

Julia sighed and looked down at her red sandals. "You're probably right. But I know my mother would never forgive me if I got rid of these things. They were her most precious items."

"Then maybe keep one crown and one trophy and take a picture of the rest?" Aaron was ready to leave the room. The entire atmosphere creeped him out, especially the way that Waverley's eyebrows arched up from every picture and watched him with a judgmental expression.

"Okay, well, I knew there was probably nothing about Walt in this room, but I wanted you to see it." Julia walked out of the room and waited for Aaron to exit, too, before she shut the door and locked it. Then she opened the second door. The next room was considerably larger than the first and held a king-size bed and matching dresser. "This was my parents' room," Julia explained. "It's not exactly a master bedroom, because a hundred years ago, when this house was built, they designed things differently. But it does have the best view of the water." She walked to the window and pulled the drapes to the side. A cloud of dust billowed around her, and she sneezed.

"It seems like a shame that the best view is locked up." Aaron walked up to the window and whistled. "You deserve this room if you want it."

Julia's shoulders sagged. "Maybe. I don't know." She went over to the nightstand next to the bed and opened a drawer. "If my mother was serious about Walt, she might have kept something of his as a memento."

"Or written something in her diary," suggested Aaron. "Do you want me to help you look?"

Julia nodded. "Would you? That would really help. Only I don't think my mother kept a diary."

Together they searched every drawer and every pocket in Waverley's wardrobe. After twenty minutes of fruitless searching, Aaron knew two things about Waverley: she'd favored some of the same designer labels that his own mom adored, and she'd kept her clothes forever. Lorraine would have said the clothes in Waverley's closet were so old they qualified as vintage.

When they finally gave up on finding any clues, Julia sat down on the edge of the bed. "I guess that's it, then. I'll never know if Walt was telling the truth or not."

"I think you know the truth." Aaron sat down next to her. Realizing that he was on her deceased parents' marriage bed pushed all romantic notions straight out of his mind and helped him focus. He needed Julia to understand the truth—at least the truth as he saw it. "You said your mom was weird about money, right?"

Julia nodded. "To her dying day. She was afraid that the insurance company would bill her too much for her chemo treatments."

"I don't think Walt would lie about your mother refusing to marry him. That's got to be a humiliating story for him to recount."

"If it's true, then, it means my mother blamed me for her not being able to be happy with Walt."

"No." Aaron shook his head. "You've got that wrong. What it shows is that your mom loved you. She loved you so much that she wanted to protect your assets and secure your future."

"My mother hated me." Tears filled her eyes. "You didn't know her, but if you heard the things she said to me, you'd agree."

"Okay," said Aaron, not wanting to discount what Julia was saying. "Maybe I said it wrong. What I think her turning down Walt shows is that she wanted you to have a sound financial future. She loved the idea of you having money. She wanted to keep you safe, because that was the thing that mattered most to her. Financial security. That was her way of saying *I love you* without actually saying the words."

"I don't know." Julia bowed her head and blinked. "It could also be that she didn't want anyone to think that her daughter was poor, because that would make her look bad."

"That's a hard thing to realize about your own mother." Aaron wrapped his arms around her and pulled her close. "I'm sorry."

"And your mother hates me too." Julia sniffed, and then the tears fell.

"You two got off to a rocky start, and my mom was incredibly rude, but once she gets to know you, she'll love you, I promise."

"That sounds hard to believe."

"It's the truth." Aaron rocked her from side to side as she wept. "My mother wants what's best for me and Jack, and that means you."

"Really?" Julia looked up at him.

"Absolutely." Aaron squeezed her tighter and looked around the room. "You know," he said. "If you sell the furniture, tear off the wallpaper, and give this room a clean slate, it would make the perfect bedroom for Julia Harper, beloved patron of Harper Landing."

Julia laughed and wiped her nose with a tissue she'd pulled from a box on the nightstand. "I could get rid of all the ridiculous trophies while I'm at it," she said, with a twinkle in her eye. "Paint the room blue and put a—" She stopped abruptly and looked away.

"Put a crib in there?" Aaron asked, hoping that was how Julia had meant to finish her sentence. Right then and there, he abandoned his resolve to keep his true feelings hidden.

Julia snapped her head back in his direction and parted her lips. "You are the kindest, most devoted, and most excellent uncle Jack could ever have," she breathed. "You know that, right? You're not Jack's father, but at the same time, you are."

Aaron nodded, a river of emotions running through him. "My sister would want me to be happy," he said. "Jared too. And I realize we've only known each other a few weeks, but I feel like I've known you my whole life. You're my missing link, Julia. You're the woman I've needed since the moment I was born." He picked up both of her hands in his own. "I'm in love with you." He stared into her eyes, begging the universe that she would look back with a small fragment of the deep love he felt. And with one glance, he knew that Julia's heart held more than a fragment of affection for him. She was a goner, just like he was.

"Oh, Aaron," she murmured, throwing her arms around his neck. "I love you too." She crushed his mouth with kisses, and it wasn't until later—much, much later—that Aaron remembered the barbecue.

EPILOGUE

One year later

After three months of backpacking across Europe, the Baxter-Harper family was used to wild adventures, but Aaron and Julia didn't appreciate the way the Uber driver pushed the speed limit in Harper Landing, especially since Jack was in the car.

"Can you please slow down?" Julia asked from the back seat. She hung on tightly to the handle above her door.

"Yeah," said Aaron in a firm voice. "The speed limit's twenty-five. People live here, man."

The driver, a middle-aged man wearing a backward baseball cap, shrugged. "You said you were in a hurry."

"To see the Fourth of July parade," said Julia. "Not the emergency room." She glanced down to make sure Jack was okay. The wild car ride had put him to sleep, which wasn't surprising considering the whole family was jet lagged. Rome, Paris, London, Vienna—they'd seen it all. Jack had taken his first steps in the Swiss Alps and smashed his first birthday cake in Berlin.

"Gotcha," said the driver. "I'll slow down. The traffic's becoming bad now anyway."

"Extra people are here for the parade," said Aaron, looking out the window. "Harper Landing's not normally this congested so far from the shops downtown."

They were still five blocks away from home on Ninth Avenue, and Julia was anxious to see the final results of the remodel. They'd kept track of the contractor's work as best they could while overseas but were eager to see things in person. The trophy room was now Jack's bedroom, and there was a brand-new master suite where Julia's parents' room used to be. Aaron had been looking for a place to invest some of his Big Foot Paleo proceeds, and improving their house seemed like a wise choice. Julia would never forget the way Aaron's eyes had shone when he'd paid off their mortgage as a wedding present.

"Do you think Toby will forgive us for leaving him?" Julia asked. She was grateful to George and Shelly for caring for him while they'd traveled but worried that her Labrador might not have had the best of times with Midas, their Jack Russell terrier. Midas was so feisty that George had to feed the dogs in two separate rooms or else Midas would steal Toby's kibble.

"Why don't you ask him yourself?" Aaron grinned and pointed out the window to where George and Toby were walking up the sidewalk.

"Toby!" Julia waved madly through the window, but her dog didn't see her.

"This is it, right?" The Uber driver peered across the steering wheel to their freshly painted house. Pink roses cascaded over the archway of the white picket fence. "Is it okay if I park in the driveway?"

"Absolutely!" Julia smiled with all her might and continued trying to catch George's and Toby's attention. The dog was too busy sniffing the sidewalk to notice, but George waved back.

"Time to wake up, Jack." Aaron gently wiggled the sleeping toddler's foot. "I see Grandma and Grandpa." Sure enough, Martha and Frank were standing on their porch, waiting. There was a big **WELCOME HOME** flag hanging behind them. Martha kept a firm grip on Frank's hand and used her other to shade her eyes from the sun. Frank's Alzheimer's disease was still in its early stages, thankfully, but they now had an eldercare aide helping out three days a week. Jack stirred and slowly fluttered his eyelids open.

The car rolled to a stop, and the driver turned off the ignition. "Well, folks. You're home."

Aaron looked at Julia, and Julia looked at Aaron. They leaned across Jack's car seat for a quick kiss before they were interrupted by Jack, who reached forward and squished their cheeks together. "Home," he squealed.

Julia and Aaron stared at each other in amazement. It was Jack's first word.

"That's right, buddy," said Aaron. "We're home sweet home."

ACKNOWLEDGMENTS

Thank you to my literary agent, Liza Fleissig of the Liza Royce Agency, who has stuck with me for years and always treated me like a million bucks, even when I brought in pennies. The publishing team at Montlake Romance has been phenomenal. I am blessed that Alison Dasho read my manuscript and took a chance on me. I am extremely grateful to Krista Stroever's wisdom for making it better.

My critique partners—Sharman Badgett-Young, Laura Moe, and Penelope Wright—have met with me in good times and bad. I'll never take meeting in person for granted again. Whether I'm writing as Louise Cypress or Jennifer Bardsley, they always find a way to help me improve my story lines.

Thank you to authors Joshua David Bellin, Alessandra Clarke, Nicole Conway, Jennifer Anne Davis, Jennifer M. Eaton, Tobie Easton, E.M. Fitch, Jennifer Jenkins, Emily R. King, Everly Frost, Melanie McFarlane, Derek Murphy, Shaila Patel, Jenetta Penner, Julie Reece, Jo Schaffer, and Leigh Statham, who have given me their advice and friendship. I am also grateful for my membership in the Sweet Sixteens, the Nine Lives Authors group, the Author Support Network, and An Alliance for Young Adult Authors.

When I'm not writing books, I pen a column called I Brake for Moms for the *Everett Daily Herald*. Thank you to all my I Brake for Moms readers who have stuck with me for almost a decade.

My husband, Doug, did not sign up to marry a romance author when we wed over twenty years ago. But he provides inspiration for romantic heroes every day. All women deserve partners who treat them respectfully, who help out around the house, and who wake up at two o'clock in the morning to give the baby a bottle without being asked.

Finally, thank you to my children, Bryce and Brenna, who are quickly becoming grown-ups right before my eyes. In my heart you'll always be my smiling little babies. I wish I could go back in time, squeeze your tiny feet, and say, "Wow."

ABOUT THE AUTHOR

Photo © 2020 Angie Langford/Verb Photography

Jennifer Bardsley believes in friendship, true love, and the everlasting power of books. A graduate of Stanford University, she lives in Edmonds, Washington, with her husband and two children. Bardsley's column, I Brake for Moms, has appeared in the *Everett Herald* every week since 2012. She also writes young adult paranormal romance under the pen name Louise Cypress. When she's not writing books or camping with her Girl Scout troop, you can find Bardsley walking from her house to the beach every chance she gets.

Sign up for Bardsley's author newsletter, and you'll receive Julia Harper's paleo brownie recipe: http://landing.mailerlite.com/webforms/landing/c8u3i2.